At first, Detective Janice Anderson tried not to pay much attention to the terrifying notes she received. But with the discovery that some stranger had gotten into her house, tampered with her mail and murdered her pet, she knew she was dealing with a lunatic killer. But why her? Why was she the object of some psycho's revenge?

When the killer kidnapped her family Janice knew she had to find them before the killer destroyed them all. She had only days to track down the murderer. Not nearly enough time.

There were more taunting, tormenting notes. In one of them a clue. But the killer was playing a waiting game... waiting for time to run out and for Janice's life to be laid on the line...

ANGEL

OF THE

NIGHT

B.W. Battin

FAWCETT GOLD MEDAL • NEW YORK

A Fawcett Gold Medal Book
Published by Ballantine Books
Copyright © 1983 by B.W. Battin

ISBN 0-449-12380-4

Printed in Canada

First Gold Medal Edition: February 1983

Prologue

She would never go back. Never. Not to the stepfather who wouldn't keep his hands off her, not to the high school in Des Moines, where most of the girls she knew wanted nothing more than to become good little wives and mothers with a reliable hubby to provide for them. Good little girls with the right attitude. Good little girls, many of whom would find out too late that the good provider they'd hoped for was really a good-for-nothing son of a bitch who would slap them around—like her stepfather. And like her mother, they'd find themselves middle-aged, with no skills, with little chance of finding another husband, with nothing to do but stay, put up with it, live life for its precious few happy moments, and try not to let him catch you crying. And try to learn, as her mother had, to look the other way when your husband gropes your teenage daughter. And when he takes her into the bedroom, closes the door, and forces her to submit.

Sally Parker immediately pushed those thoughts aside. Images of that night—her stepfather holding her down, ripping her clothes, his face pushing down on hers, his breath smelling of beer and cigarettes—those recollections were still too sensitive for her to deal with.

The dreaded memories shoved back into her subconscious, Sally took in her surroundings. She was walking along a little-used two-lane highway that wound its way through the woods

1

of northern Minnesota, toward Canada. It was a sunny June morning, and the trees had that early-summer healthy look about them, that delicate shade of green that came from new leaves, as yet untroubled by insects or disease. This far north, summer had barely begun. She took a deep breath; the woods smelled of a cool, damp freshness. It was beautiful here. She was glad she had come this way.

It wasn't a choice route for hitchhiking, but there was no rush to cross over into Ontario, as she had no idea what she would do when she got there. At least all her options were open; she could thumb her way west to Vancouver or east to Toronto, a much shorter trip, deciding what to do next after her arrival. Sure, she was afraid, a little. A seventeen-year-old girl alone in a strange city—not to mention a strange country— could have a tough time. But she would not go back, no matter what happened. And she'd already had a taste of what it would be like.

Last night, her first night as a runaway, she had spread her bedroll under a tree near Interstate 35 and, remarkably, had managed to fall asleep. Then, about 1 A.M., it rained. And continued doing so for the rest of the night. Not only had that put an end to her sleep, but also now the damp bedroll strapped to her back smelled foul and musty.

And then there were some of the people who offered her rides. A tall, slender young woman with long dark hair and a pretty face, she had no trouble getting male drivers to stop for her. But some of them she refused to ride with; they had that peculiar look in their eyes, the same look she'd seen in her stepfather's eyes. What worried her the most was that one of these times she might not notice that look until after she'd gotten into the car.

Again forcing herself to clear her mind of unpleasant thoughts, she concentrated on the trees. Unlike Iowa with its endless miles of farmland, here the whole world seemed to be a continuous forest, the trees so close together they barely had room to grow, stretching off into the distance, forever. Some were white-barked, popples or birch she supposed, and others were what she called needle trees, like pines, although she didn't know whether these were pines or spruce or some other variety. Somewhere, hidden in the branches, a bird was chirping.

Behind her, she heard a car approaching and decided simply to let it go by. It was nice walking in the woods; she was in no hurry to thumb a ride. The driver tapped his horn, a friendly little toot that said *Hi there* and at the same time warned her of his presence; then a blue Chevy passed her and disappeared down the road.

After walking another twenty minutes without seeing any other cars, she decided traffic was too light here to let very many prospects get away, so when she again heard a vehicle approaching from behind her, she reluctantly turned to face the driver and stuck out her thumb. And quickly dropped it. Coming toward her was a light-green bus full of people. As it passed, she saw a blur of faces at the windows and below them black letters that spelled out ELK RIDGE STATE HOSPITAL. Through the back window, two of the passengers stared at her, one of them laughing as if she were the object of a joke. There was something in the eyes of that laughing face that made her uncomfortable, and she involuntarily checked the buttons on her blouse. Then the bus and the faces were gone, out of sight around a bend in the road, and she felt relieved. She could guess the sort of place Elk Ridge State Hospital was.

A few moments later, the silence of the woods was shattered by a crash. Sally froze, listening intently. Now the sounds were the occasional chirp or squawk of a bird and the faint roar of a distant jet, but she was sure of what she had heard. Somewhere, not too far away, something big and heavy had just smashed into something else. Sally started to run. The only thing she knew of that was big and heavy and not too far away was the bus.

Her heart pounding, she raced around the curve, and then she saw it. Still several hundred yards ahead, off the road, the bus lay on its side. Gasping for breath as she neared it, she saw what had happened. It had hit the soft shoulder and been pulled to the right, slamming into a tree and overturning. It lay on its left side, its rear end facing her, its right front wheel still spinning lazily. The rear-end emergency door had popped open, and she saw at least three people, apparently thrown out during the crash, lying on the ground.

Reaching the bus, she collapsed against it, trying to catch her breath. Inside, people were moaning. She smelled gasoline and, looking down, saw a puddle of it near her feet, a small stream running toward the front of the bus. Suddenly, she realized the bus might explode, and she had to try to get the injured passengers away from it.

"Help me," someone called weakly. Turning in the direction the voice had come from, Sally saw a chubby woman of about thirty-five with long blond hair. The woman lay on her back, her eyes fixed on Sally, pleading. Sally hurried over to her.

"I've got to get you away from here," she said. "There's gasoline leaking."

"Please," the woman whispered, "please help me."

"I'll try," Sally replied firmly. "But you have to stand up. I can't carry you. I'm not strong enough." The woman, her eyes still fixed on Sally's, nodded.

With Sally's help, she was able to sit up, but as soon as she had, she groaned and fell back again, her eyes closed.

"Wake up!" Sally cried. "Please! You have to get away from the bus!" But the woman wouldn't respond.

A loud groan came from within the bus. Sally ran to the open emergency door and peered inside. The passengers who had been sitting on the right side of the aisle had been hurled on top of those sitting on the left. Some were draped limply over what, with the bus on its side, had become the bottom row of seats; others had two or three people piled on top of them; no one moved.

"Please," Sally called desperately, "can anyone help me? We've got to get everyone away from here." She was answered by a moan, the source of which she was unable to determine.

She leaned against the bus, trying to decide what to do. She could hear the gasoline dripping from the ruptured tank, but maybe it would all soak into the ground and nothing would happen. It didn't necessarily have to explode. Perhaps she'd be doing the victims more harm than good by trying to move them. She simply didn't know, and she wished someone would come along who did. Feeling helpless and confused, she looked in both directions along the road, seeing no signs of any assistance. The only sounds were the quiet of the woods and the persistent drip of gas.

Uncertain whether it was the right decision, she concluded that the only thing to do was to wait for help and hope the leaking gasoline would trickle harmlessly away or evaporate or whatever gasoline did.

In addition to the now unconscious woman, two other people, both middle-aged men, had been thrown out of the bus, and she hurried over to examine them. They were sprawled in some low weeds within five feet of each other, one face down, the other on his side. Unable to tell whether they were breathing, she considered feeling for a pulse, but other than by holding the victim's wrist, she had no idea how to do it. All she could do, she supposed, was turn the head of the man whose face was buried in the weeds so he could breathe more easily if he was still alive. As she reached down to do so, from the corner of her eye, she saw movement.

But before she could turn to see who was there, something heavy smacked her in the back of the head, and the world went black. She was only vaguely aware that she had fallen across the man whose head she had been about to turn. In the swirling of her thoughts, her mind seemed to focus on the sound of liquid dripping, and she vaguely sensed it was gasoline, but it was miles away, in another world, of no importance.

The same pair of hands that a moment ago had brought a large rock down on Sally Parker's head now held a book of matches. Striking one, the hands held it for a moment, the flame flickering in the gentle breeze, then dropped it into the puddle of gasoline.

The fire instantly raced along the trail of leaked fuel. In seconds, the bus was engulfed in flames, the blaze growing until even the people lying on the ground were hidden behind a roaring wall of orange.

A solitary figure stepped back from the heat of the burning bus, turned, and disappeared into the woods.

One

_____

Janice Anderson groped for the alarm clock beside her bed,
found it, and succeeded in shutting it off at the precise moment
she knocked it off the bed table. It fell on the floor, the carpet
reducing the sound of its impact to a gentle clunk—not to
mention saving the clock from any serious damage, although
at six in the morning she could hardly wish the infernal thing
any good fortune. She considered rolling over, just for a moment or two, but the last time she'd done that, she awakened
to discover she was already half an hour late for work, so
instead she reluctantly dropped her legs over the edge of the
bed, the covers slipping off her nude body.

That was one of the nice things about summer: sleeping
nude. She hated bed clothes; it was so much nicer when you
could enjoy the feel of cool sheets against your bare skin, one
of the many luxuries to be taken advantage of during Minnesota's all-too-brief summers.

Blinking her eyes into focus, she looked down at herself.
Even unsupported, her breasts pushed out proudly, firmly, and
below them, her long, slender legs stretched down to the carpet.
She nudged the alarm clock with a toe; as no pieces fell off
the clock, she assumed it had survived its fall. Then her eyes
found the damned fatty roll that always appeared in her stomach
when she was sitting. Her tummy was flat as could be when
she stood, so why did the flesh have to bulge like that whenever

she sat down? She let her eyes fall a little lower, to the blond bush between her legs, and she laughed, recalling the first time Mike had seen her naked. His initial comment had been: "Well, I'll never accuse you of dying your hair."

Vanity, she thought. I'm twenty-eight years old, and I'm still as vain as a teen-ager. And that, she knew, made her a hypocrite; she had no use at all for vain women—or vain men, for that matter.

Her room was white, with a few pieces of modern furniture. Simple, functional, without any knickknacks or other purely decorative things to clutter it up, it suited her personality. It had been her room as a child, although, having never been one for developing attachments to things, she'd long since thrown out all the relics of her youth. Until a year ago, when her father was involved in the car accident, she had lived in an apartment in another part of Dakota Falls, a Minneapolis suburb of about 60,000 people. Her mother had died when she was seven—complications from pneumonia—so when the accident confined her father permanently to a wheelchair, he had needed someone around the house to do the things that could only be done by a person with two good legs. It wasn't a great personal sacrifice, really; she liked her father, and the restrictions living here placed on her social life were sometimes more advantageous than troublesome.

She stood, stretching, then snatched her blue robe off the chair, wrapped the summer-weight garment around her, and headed for the bathroom. Stepping into the hallway, she hesitated. To the right were the bathroom and her father's room, its door closed. To the left was another closed door leading to her sister's room. Actually, it was the spare bedroom now, but she'd always thought of it as Amy's room. Amy was two years older than Janice, widowed, and lived in California. And Amy, along with her five-year-old son Mark, would be here for a visit in a few days, which meant the room should be aired out. Taking two strides to the door, Janice pushed it open.

Although there were none of Amy's personal belongings here anymore, the room still had her touch. It was painted a light blue, and the matching curtains, bedspread, and even the lampshade were delicate and somewhat frilly. Not to Janice's taste at all, but then the only thing she and her sister had in common was parents.

Still, standing in the doorway of what had been her sister's room, Janice found herself looking forward to Amy's visit. All those years of growing up together had created a bond that mere differences in attitude or lifestyle could not diminish. She'd also be glad to see Mark. Although brash and a little spoiled, the boy loved his Aunt Janice dearly, even if some of his admiration did stem from his fascination with her job. Janice turned and headed for the bathroom.

Fifteen minutes later, showered, dressed in a conservative green pants suit—one that didn't emphasize her body—her short, curly blond hair combed, she gave herself a quick final inspection in the full-length mirror on the back of the bedroom door, and she was ready to face the world. She spent as little time as possible dressing, and she almost never wore makeup, in part because she thought it was foolishness and in part because her soft, healthy complexion didn't require any. Although she wouldn't go so far as to say she would never use cosmetics, she certainly didn't look forward to the day she might have to start.

In the hall, she stuck her head into her father's room and called cheerfully: "Hey! Time to get up. The sun's shining and the birds are chirping and all that crap."

Then she realized she was speaking to an empty room. There was no lump under the covers, no wheelchair beside the bed. Janice knew where she'd find him. As she stepped into the living room, she smelled the warm, friendly odors of breakfast being prepared in the kitchen. Her cat, a big gray tom named Sam, was curled up on an armchair. He opened one eye in greeting and went back to sleep.

The kitchen was modern—copper-colored appliances, built-in oven and range. She found her father, his wheelchair rolled up to the stove, an egg poacher and a frying pan on the two front burners. This was the third consecutive morning that he'd beaten her to the kitchen and taken over the cooking duties.

"Good morning," she said, sitting down at the polished-wood breakfast table. "You don't have to do this, you know. I'd be more than happy to make breakfast." She hoped he wasn't overdoing it; he tired very easily, and there was really no need for him to get up early just to make their breakfast.

Wheeling around to face her, Malcolm Anderson said: "I appreciate your good intentions, daughter, but the only thing you seem to know how to make is French toast. After all this time, I'm sorry to have to tell you this, but I really hate French toast." He made a face.

Janice laughed. "I never said I was much of a cook." Pulling over the electric coffee pot, she filled her cup, then added cream and sugar.

Even as a motherless teen-ager, Janice had not cooked. She had done other things—cleaned, washed dishes, and so on—but Amy had always fixed the meals. In fact, had Janice tried to cook, her sister probably would have resented it. The kitchen was her territory.

Because Amy had considered the culinary skills essential to catching a good husband, she had practiced them every chance she got, turning out one gourmet delight after another. It had worked, apparently; she had married a very successful lawyer who had left her quite well off when he died.

Janice sipped her coffee. She should try to improve her cooking, she supposed. She had moved back here to take care of her father, and serving him meals that were normally canned, frozen, or made with hamburger seemed a shirking of her responsibilities.

"I'll tell you what," she said, putting down her coffee cup. "I'm going to turn over a new leaf and learn how to cook. Just give me a few months, and I'll be turning out the same sorts of goodies Amy used to make. What do you say to that?"

Malcolm Anderson hesitated, his eyes finding Janice's for a split second, then darting away. "There's no reason for you to go to all that trouble," he said finally.

"What's the matter? Don't you want to eat all the screw-ups while I'm learning?"

Without answering, her father rolled his wheelchair around to face the stove. He seemed preoccupied, distant. He would tell her what was on his mind if and when he decided to, and no amount of prodding on her part would have any effect whatsoever, so she remained silent.

Lifting its lid, he gave the poacher a shake to test the consistency of the eggs, replaced the cover, then turned his attention to the bacon sizzling in the frying pan. A tall man in his fifties, he had thin gray hair and blue eyes that seemed constantly to sparkle with warmth and good humor, even when he was irritated—which wasn't often.

His eyes, Janice thought sadly, were his only physical characteristic that hadn't changed since the accident. His hair was receding rapidly, his skin was pale and sickly-looking, and on his hands were hints of discoloration that might be the first signs of old-age spots. And although she still thought of him as tall, he wasn't, not anymore. Now he just had that heightlessness that all people in wheelchairs seemed to share.

His deterioration wasn't surprising, though, all things considered. He'd spent three months in the hospital, the first two weeks in a coma, his chances doubtful. But he made it; he was too stubborn not to, even though he would never walk again. The accident was one of those things that happened but that you never expected to happen to you or anyone close to you. A drunk going seventy runs a red light just as you're entering the intersection, and that's that. The inebriated driver paid for his mistake with his life, and her father got something back from all those insurance premiums he'd been shelling out. Now the insurance companies would be paying him for the rest of his life.

Before the accident, he had been an on-site construction engineer with a Minneapolis firm, but he would never again ride up on an I-beam to check out a joint somewhere in the upper reaches of a high rise. Sometimes, Janice recalled, he would join the workers for lunch, the whole bunch of them sitting on a girder God knew how many stories above the ground. She and Amy had always feared he'd end up dead or like this, in a wheelchair, but never as a result of an auto accident. They had always felt relieved when he called from the construction site to say he was on his way home, because then they had known he was on the ground, safe.

He must have known how much they worried, although they tried not to let it show. Even when he was out of town, he'd call from the motel each evening, ostensibly to check on things at home, but at least in part to reassure his anxious daughters.

Once more facing Janice, he said: "You know, I always rather enjoyed cooking. Still do, in fact, except that I have trouble seeing what I'm cooking and I'm limited to the two front burners. My biggest problem is not being able to get at stuff—like the cupboards. And I can't even come close to reaching that damned thing." He motioned toward the microwave, which had been neatly installed above the regular oven.

Amy, who had always wanted all the latest things, had persuaded him to buy it.

"What I need is a crank on this thing," he said, patting the wheelchair, "so I can raise or lower it when I need to." He frowned. "Hell, they probably make them. They make more damned crap for us cripples than you can imagine. Most of it worthless, if you ask me."

Although it was her father's nature to be a little cantankerous at times, Janice didn't have to worry about his mental adjustment to his misfortune. That Malcolm Anderson would feel sorry for himself was unthinkable. He was a born coper.

His eyes found Janice's and held them; he was ready to tell her what was on his mind. "There's something I want to talk to you about, and I guess now's as good a time as any. I appreciate your staying here with me. It shows a lot of love on your part." He hesitated, his eyes becoming moist. "But dammit, girl, you have your own life to lead. I want you to understand that you have no obligation to stay here and care for me. None at all. The first thing the therapists told me was to learn to fend for myself and not to rely on others. If I'd stop putting down all those devices they make for the handicapped and start using them, there's absolutely nothing I couldn't do for myself. And that includes driving. I'd have to have an expensive special car—a van with a wheelchair ramp, I suppose—but I can afford one. In fact, I'm sure the therapists would cheer if I bought one. If I booted you out in the bargain, they'd cheer all the harder."

"Daddy...." She didn't know what to say.

"I just want you to understand that some day you're going to have to leave me on my own."

"Good enough," she said firmly. "But someday. Not now." And probably not for a long, long time. He was still too weak to take care of himself, and although he was noticeably stronger now than he had been a few months ago, his physical recovery was an extremely slow process.

Abruptly, he spun his wheelchair around to face the stove, obviously taking a minute to dry his eyes. When he wheeled back to the table a few moments later, his eyes were dry and he held a plate of poached eggs on toast with bacon in each hand. It did look more appetizing than French toast.

* * *

After breakfast, Janice, as usual, put off leaving for work until the last possible moment. Her father would wash the dishes, an activity that, for reasons Janice had never understood, he seemed to enjoy. It was customary for the people in her division to arrive at the office a few minutes late, and Janice saw no reason to defy the tradition. It was a liberty they felt entitled to, she supposed, to make up for all the times one was called in the middle of the night, for all the compensatory days off that had been earned but would never be enjoyed.

In her room, she went directly to her dresser and took her purse from the bottom drawer. She had carefully trained herself never to leave it lying anywhere unattended, even at home. As she did each morning, she quickly checked its contents. Her badge was there, as was her .38 snub-nosed revolver. She flipped the weapon open, checked the cylinder, then snapped it shut and set the safety, making sure the firing pin was resting next to the one empty chamber. Detective Second Grade Janice Anderson, Dakota Falls Police Department, was ready to go to work.

Dropping the .38 back into her purse, she slung the bag over her shoulder and headed for her car. In the living room, she stopped to scratch Sam, who had not moved from his spot on the chair. "See you later, Dad," she called, and she was out the door.

Like its neighbors, the Anderson house was a one-story white frame home, neither new nor old, strictly middle class. Dakota Falls was a place of commuters, people well enough off to move to the suburbs but not the ritzier suburbs. Those who didn't rise above mid-level management or professional positions stayed here; those who did moved on.

Her car was a red two-year-old Datsun, which she left in the driveway most of the time because trying to operate the cantankerous garage door was more trouble than it was worth. She was setting a bad example, she supposed. Any police officer could tell you that your car was many times safer from thieves and vandals in a garage. Well, police officers didn't always follow their own advice.

And to make matters worse, the door was unlocked.

Surprised, she withdrew her key. Talk about embarrassing! When someone's car was stolen, the cop taking the report invariably asked whether "the vehicle" was locked, always ready with that damned sardonic smile should the distressed owner say no. She could imagine what her own fellow officers would say about her—especially the male chauvinists—if she had to report the theft of her unlocked car.

Opening the door, she hesitated. She was sure she had locked it. She always locked it. Then she saw the small piece of white paper wrapped around the steering wheel, tied to it with a piece of string. Confused, she removed the paper and unfolded it. Glued to the note-pad-sized sheet were letters apparently cut from newspaper headlines. The message was brief:

NOW THE WOMAN PIG WILL DIE

Leaning against the Datsun, Janice studied the note. It was a prank. Obviously. It had to be. Yet someone had gone to a lot of trouble: cutting out and pasting on the letters, possibly even breaking into her car. Why? What was the point? That she had no answer for that bothered her. Although she didn't take the note's threat seriously, it was still a little unnerving. She'd been a cop long enough to realize it was often the things you didn't know that killed you.

She stuffed the note in her purse, slipped behind the wheel, and a moment later, she was driving down the tree-lined street, on her way to the Dakota Falls Police Department. When she arrived, she would have to turn in the note to Captain Bishop. Department policy required that all threats against officers be reported.

Pulling onto Pennington Boulevard, she passed the spacious lawn and lush landscaping that surrounded Heikkinen's Funeral Home, concealing the mortuary building itself, insulating it from the noise and confusion of the morning rush on a main artery. She followed the thoroughfare toward the center of town. Traffic was heavy at the moment, but it would thin out once she passed the freeway, as most of Dakota Falls' morning rush was on its way to Minneapolis or St. Paul.

This morning, as she passed Heikkinen's, it had given her a chill. Perhaps this was in reaction to the threatening note. Mortuaries were usually these lovely, peaceful places, but any cop could tell you that all too often there was nothing lovely or peaceful about death. If funeral homes were decrepit places that used the skull and crossbones as their logo, they'd serve as better reminders to all those people who treated death so lightly.

An unexpected shiver ran through her body, and she tried to push such morbid thoughts from her mind. She would not let some creep's sick note get to her.

She spent a few moments trying to figure out who might have left the note, then gave up. There was simply no way to work up a decent list of suspects. You arrest somebody on some minor charge or another, and the suspect's cousin swears revenge on the arresting officer. Stranger things had happened. And the world was full of cop-haters. Law enforcement had to be the only profession in which you automatically acquired a sizable list of unknown enemies simply by taking the job. Well, it was her profession, and threats, she supposed, simply went with the territory.

As she expected, the traffic thinned considerably once she had passed under the freeway. She stayed on Pennington until it reached downtown, where it narrowed and became Third Street. The central business district didn't amount to much. When people here said they were going downtown, they usually meant that sprawling cluster of office buildings and shops dominated by the towering IDS Center, downtown Minneapolis. Here in Dakota Falls, the streets narrowed for a few blocks, snarling traffic, and there were a handful of understocked, overpriced stores that were unable to compete with the shopping malls.

As did most of the city's police officers, she parked her car in the vacant lot across the street from the police station. Once, it had been the site of the Minnehaha Theater, an old brick structure where she and Amy and their friends had spent Saturday mornings at the kiddie shows. The enormous lighted marquee, the posters promoting upcoming shows, and the odor of popcorn that you could always smell half a block away were gone now, replaced by weeds and grass and cars. She slipped her Datsun in between a Dodge and a pickup with a camper. No one had ever tried to charge for parking here, but then nobody in his right mind would try to make a go of a parking lot in downtown Dakota Falls.

Having double-checked to make sure the Datsun's doors were locked, Janice hurried across the street and into the modern two-story brick police station. She waved to the uniformed man on duty at the front desk, who was busy talking to a middle-aged woman and didn't notice; then she headed down the beige hallway toward the detective division. Not only did the police department have a new and spacious building, but also it was well equipped and well staffed. Like most suburbanites, the people of Dakota Falls wanted to make sure the crime and violence of the city stayed in the city, and although they were fairly tightfisted with their tax dollars, they could be counted on to shell out generously for law enforcement.

The detective division occupied a large room with a row of desks on each side, the file room and Captain Bishop's office at its rear. A small group of men—their jackets off, revealing their shoulder holsters—stood in the center of the room, listening to Sergeant Mullins discuss—what else?—football.

"I'll tell ya," Mullins said around the fat cigar stuck in the corner of his mouth, "the Vikes are going to have a damned good season this year, now that they've got the problem with their running backs taken care of." He kept talking as Janice walked by, but his eyes followed her, lustfully taking in every inch of her, examining—almost touching—each private part. It infuriated her; it was as if she had been stripped naked and had to remain that way until his eyes had left her.

"Good morning, Janice," he said, the lust dripping from every word added for the sake of his companions. He was a heavyset man in his forties, going bald, a big potbelly. And he was a chauvinist jerk.

"Good morning, Ed," Janice said pleasantly. She stuffed her purse into the bottom drawer of her desk, then joined the others. "Ed, didn't you say you were going to lose some weight?" She tapped his potbelly. "It doesn't look like you're doing too well." She smiled cheerfully.

Mullins shrugged, but his eyes narrowed, and he chewed silently on his cigar.

"What's happening today?" Janice asked.

"Big narco bust," answered Ted Reynolds, a slender young detective with wavy dark hair. "The four of us will be on it. Gonna get 'em all—from the pushers on the school grounds right up to the major suppliers. Twin Cities guys and most of the suburbs are in on it. They're gonna hit almost everywhere in the metropolitan area today. We've got almost a hundred warrants for right here in Dakota Falls." He smiled at her warmly. Ted was a nice guy.

The other two detectives were Watson and Poldoski, both attractive dark-haired men in their thirties. Poldoski was easy enough to work with, but Watson had been cool toward her ever since he'd discovered she had no intention of allowing him to seduce her.

Although Janice had heard rumors of a big narco bust coming up, she'd had no idea it would be this big. Such things were kept as secret as possible, even within the department, as it wasn't unusual for an operation of such magnitude to develop leaks. When that happened, you wound up rounding up a bunch of small-time pushers you could have picked up anytime, only to discover the major drug traffickers had conveniently disappeared.

It was a cop's dream, this sort of operation. Warrants in hand, you had the pleasure of arresting the assholes who sold poison even to children, and even if they bonded out a few hours later, there was a great deal of satisfaction in cuffing their hands behind their backs, reading them their rights, and giving them that contemptuous little push when you put them into the car, that extra little shove that said *you're nothing but scum*.

"Is that what Collins and Green were working on?" Janice asked.

Reynolds nodded. "On the Dakota Falls part of it, yeah. Of course, each department had its own detectives working their own territory. As far as I know, only Collins, Greene, Captain Bishop, and the chief knew how big it really was." He was having difficulty meeting her eyes. He was her junior; yet he was included, and she wasn't.

Janice smiled at Ted as if to say no hard feelings, and with that she turned and headed for Captain Bishop's office, disregarding the eyes that were undoubtedly glued to her ass. She tried to control her temper, but by the time she got there, she was fuming. Bishop, a thin man in his fifties with graying brown hair, looked up from his paperwork, putting on his most official expression.

"You were late this morning," he said before she had even reached his desk. His office was small but uncluttered—standard gray civil servant's desk, a stand of filing cabinets.

He had been ready for her. Before she could even open her mouth, he had put her on the defensive. "I'm as punctual as anyone else around here," she said defiantly.

"True, but this morning you were the last one in, and the last one gets the reminder."

"What do you have me scheduled for today?" she asked.

"I thought you had an assignment you hadn't completed yet." His eyes found hers, the impartial supervisor. That he could handle her so easily infuriated her all the more.

"The child abuse case?"

"The welfare people are going to court to get custody of the boy, and they're screaming for the paperwork."

"Is that why I wasn't included in the narcotics bust?"

"That's why."

"No other reason?"

"No other reason." He leaned back in his chair. "What other reason would there be?"

"It's the biggest thing to happen around here in quite a while, and only men are assigned."

The captain frowned. "You're the only woman in the division. And as I pointed out, you were busy on an important case of your own. Or don't you think child abuse is important?"

"Of course it's important, but—"

"But you think being assigned to a big operation like this narco raid is more important than serving the community. In this case, more important than the welfare of a small child. Is that what you're saying?"

"Well, no. But—"

"But what?"

"But . . ." But she'd just lost the argument. "I'll get on the reports right away, Captain."

She was back at her desk before she remembered the threatening note. To hell with it, she decided. I'm certainly not going back in there just to tell him about that.

She busied herself with her report, pushing all else from her mind.

A solitary figure stood at the entrance to Heikkinen's Funeral Home, reading the note taped to the glass door. Neatly printed with a black felt-tip, it said: WE'VE MOVED. PLEASE SEE

US AT OUR NEW BUILDING IN BLOOMINGTON.

It was perfect. Here was a place the curious avoided, vacant without appearing abandoned, snugly nestled in the center of its own private little park. No signs of an alarm system. The one-story white building invisible from the street. And it was only a few blocks from the Andersons' house.

"Can I help you with something?" It was an old man in dirty coveralls, carrying a shovel. A grounds keeper.

"There's been a death in my family, and I'm afraid I didn't know this place had moved."

"'Fraid so. There's gonna be an expressway through here, so Heikkinen had to go somewhere else. He wants to keep up the grounds, though. Figures it would look bad, I guess, if the place went to pot."

"Will you have to find a new place to live?"

He looked confused. "No, why would I have to do that?"

"I thought maybe you lived here."

"Oh, no. My place is a few miles from here. Nobody lives on the grounds."

"That's good. I hope you won't be out of a job after the place is torn down."

"No, no. I'll be going over to the new place in Bloomington. But thank you for asking." Tipping his battered cap, he continued on his way.

Yes, indeed. The place was perfect. First Janice would suffer; then Janice would die.

Two

At noon, Janice met Mike Simpson for lunch. They sat at a corner table in Timothy's, a dimly lit place about a block from the police station, whose only specialty seemed to be mediocrity. It was fairly crowded, but then mediocrity was a notch or two above the other restaurants in downtown Dakota Falls.

Mike sat across from her, slowly—politely—spooning soup into his mouth. Janice, remembering that fatty roll that appeared whenever she was sitting, had opted for a salad, which had yet to arrive.

"Tastes like it's canned," Mike said, glancing up at Janice. "Homemade soup's become a real rarity in a restaurant these days."

Janice nodded, not really interested in small talk. Her thoughts were elsewhere: the run-in with Captain Bishop, the threatening note, her failure to report it.

Mike, apparently sensing her mood, ate his soup in silence. In his early thirties, he was a tall man, lean, with a boyish face and thick dark hair. He was the sales manager for an insurance company, his territory consisting of Dakota Falls and some of the other suburbs, but not the Twin Cities. The company had transferred him here from New Jersey. He'd grown up there, somewhere near Trenton.

They'd been going together for about six months now, a relationship that seemed to be moving slowly but surely toward marriage. At one point in her life, Janice would have stated flatly that she would remain single forever, but the closer she got to thirty, the less threatening the prospect of matrimony became. She'd had her fling, she supposed.

Suddenly, she realized Mike was staring at her. Their eyes met, and there was instantly a huge boyish grin on his handsome face.

"You look so good I could eat you up," he said.

"You have. Repeatedly."

He frowned. "That's not what I mean, and you know it."

"So why the shit-eating grin? You've seen me across the table often enough, and this is the first time I've ever seen you look like that."

The grin broadened. "I have some good news. I've been trying to force myself to hold off telling you until after we eat, but I can't contain it any longer."

"So out with it already."

"I've got another job. Three times the money I'm making now."

"Fantastic!" She leaned across the table and kissed him. "Congratulations. What's the name of the lucky company?"

"Northwestern National Insurance. I'm their new regional sales manager."

"When do you start?"

"In a month." He hesitated, his eyes searching hers. "It's in Seattle. I want you to come with me."

Janice knew she was gaping, but she couldn't stop herself. Although she'd known Mike was looking for a better job, *this* was totally unexpected.

"I know what you're going to say," Mike said. "That you can't leave your father." He reached over and took her hand. "Why don't we take him with us?"

Janice found her voice. "How do you know he wants to go?"

"Can we talk to him about it?"

"It wouldn't be fair. He might agree to whatever we suggested just for my sake." She shook her head, trying to clear it. "I don't know what to do, Mike. He told me just this morning that one of these days I'd have to move out and leave him on his own. But he's not ready yet. It'll be months, maybe a year or more. And I know he wouldn't want to leave Minnesota.

He's one of those Scandinavians who think it's God's gift to the Nordic race."

Mike's grin was gone now; he looked worried. "I really want you to come with me." His eyes were almost pleading.

"I know you do, but . . . well, you accepted this job without ever consulting me. There's more at stake than just your career. What about mine, for instance?"

He looked surprised. "But I'll be making more money in Seattle than both of us put together were making here. You wouldn't have to work."

"Mike, it's not just the income. It's my job; being a cop is what I do. And I'd make a rotten housewife. I can't even cook. And all that aside, you should have consulted me because of my father if for no other reason."

He sighed. "I'm sorry about that. You're right; I should have talked it over with you. It's just that it all happened so quickly. The vice-president of Northwestern called yesterday, said he was in Minneapolis, and invited me to have dinner with him. He'd already checked me out, liked me for the job apparently, and interviewed me while we ate. Over dessert, he made the offer."

"And you accepted it. Without ever thinking about me."

"But I did think about you, about how pleased you'd be."

"You could have asked for a few days to think it over, you know."

"Yeah, but dammit, Janice, you don't have to think about offers like that. You take them before they get away." He looked confused and a little hurt, as if he couldn't figure out why all this wasn't as clear to her as it was to him.

Janice experienced a surge of anger. But before she could tell him just how presumptuous and selfish she thought he was for assuming she would obligingly arrange her life to suit the needs of his career, the waitress arrived, bearing a plate of hot roast beef in one hand and a plate of salad in the other.

Half an hour later, they left Timothy's, both a little sullen, a little hurt.

A shadow fell across the Andersons' mailbox; then a hand slipped several letters and a magazine out from under a loose-fitting shirt and placed them in the box. With that, the shadow and the solitary figure who made it left the Andersons' doorstep, moving slowly, casually, away from the house.

Getting the Andersons' mail had been easy. You just pretend
you're knocking on the door and not getting an answer. Then,
concealing the mailbox with your body, you slip the letters
under your shirt. A little while later, you show up again, apparently checking a second time to see whether anyone's home,
and replace them.

And the mail had been very revealing. There would be some
added risk to the new plan, but it would be well worth it.

Janice left for home at five, having completed the paperwork
on the child abuse case. Although, for her, the day had been
uneventful, the station had been a madhouse.

Throughout the day, suspects rounded up in the drug raid
had been brought in, most of them having to stand in line at
the swamped booking desk. Lawyers, bail bondsmen, and relatives of those arrested had been swarming all over the building.
The roundup was still going on, and those who hadn't gotten
word in time to skip town would be arrested tonight or tomorrow.

Despite the commotion, Janice had been able to push Mike
Simpson to the back of her mind and lose herself in her work.
But now, as she drove along Pennington, negotiating the evening rush, her thoughts again turned to Mike. It had all seemed
so simple. She had been falling more and more in love with
him; in time, she'd undoubtedly have married him; they'd have
lived here, with or at least close to her father; they'd have both
kept their jobs; everything would have been fine. Well, she
thought, so much for the way things were supposed to have
worked.

She sighed. A part of her really did want to go with Mike.
But doing so involved sacrifices she wasn't sure she could
make. Or should make.

One thing she wouldn't do was make such an important
decision on her own, as Mike had done. Her father was involved; he had a right to be informed. And Janice desperately
needed to talk things over with someone.

Arriving home, she pulled in to the concrete driveway and
stopped in front of the garage door. Earlier, she'd resolved to
put the car in the garage, but now it seemed unimportant. As
she walked to the front door, sorting the house key from the

others on her ring, she noticed the wooden wheelchair ramp that took up one side of the steps. Some of the neighborhood children had been using it for a slide again. It bore fresh crayon marks and a large pink stain that was likely the result of a melted Popsicle.

She found her father in the living room, asleep in his wheelchair, an open book in his lap. He grunted, indicating he was about to wake up. Sitting there like that, still half asleep, his pale head tilted forward, his veined hands resting on the book, he seemed so frail, so vulnerable. She wouldn't discuss things with him now, she decided. She'd wait until after dinner.

Janice sat down on the couch, facing him. Sam appeared beside her, stretched, then curled up against her leg. She gently stroked his thick gray fur while she waited for her father's eyes to open. The cat had shown up on her doorstep about a year and a half ago, while she was still living in an apartment, and invited himself to stay. He was no trouble—a periodic cleaning of his box—and woman and cat got along fine, usually by ignoring each other.

Janice had always liked this living room. It was a plain yet warm and comfortable place with dark paneled walls, solid furniture, and a deep-pile brown carpet.

"Hi, daughter," her father said, rubbing his eyes. "I thought I heard you come in."

"How are you feeling?"

"Fine, except that these afternoon naps always leave me so damn groggy." He covered his mouth while he yawned. "Excuse me."

"The steaks thawing?" She had called after lunch, asking him to take them out of the freezer.

"They sure are. And they look delicious. Even uncooked."

"I'll tell you what. As soon as I change, I'll put some potatoes in to bake; then we'll take the steaks out back and do them on the grill. Sound good?"

He grinned. "Sounds excellent." Abruptly, he wheeled over to the end table beside the chair where Sam usually slept. When he wheeled back again, he held a letter in his hand.

"From Amy," he said. "She finally made her reservations, and her flight will get in at two-ten on Sunday afternoon." He turned the envelope over, examining it. "It's all wrinkly, as if it was steamed open. I wouldn't put it past Amy to seal up a letter, then change her mind and steam it open again, but all the mail's that way—the bills and all."

"Let me see," she said, taking the envelope from him. The wrinkles were there, heaviest right around the flap, as if it had indeed been steamed open. "Let me see the others."

Spinning his chair around, her father rolled back over to the end table and returned with the rest of the mail, which he handed to her. The envelopes were all the same: wrinkled and, in some cases, water-stained around their flaps. Based on the evidence, she would have to say their mail had been opened. By someone. Was there a connection—first the note and then this?

She shrugged. "No harm done, I guess. The postman probably dropped them in a puddle or something." Still concealing her uneasiness from her father, she slipped Amy's letter out of the envelope.

"There's something I should tell you about that letter," her father said.

"What's that?" Janice asked, looking up from the expensive blue stationery.

"Well, never mind. You'll see it."

She continued reading. Mark would again be attending the exclusive private school in which he'd done so well his kindergarten year. Amy was still sampling all the latest California crazes, which seemed to change faster than people could tire of them. The most recent mud slides and brush fires around Los Angeles had spared her split-level modern home with the lovely view of the Pacific. Then, turning to the last page of the letter, Janice had to suppress a gasp.

Amy had only used the top half of the page, and on the bottom half was a drawing in purple crayon. A drawing of a pig, clumsy, as if a child had done it. Beside the picture, in what could have been a child's scrawl, was her name, an arrow extending from it, pointing at the pig's eye. Beneath the drawing, in shaky capital letters, were the words THE WOMAN PIG.

"I don't know what Amy was thinking of, letting Mark draw that on there," Malcolm Anderson said. "Knowing her, she probably thought it was cute, but I think she should have known better. I hope that's not what they teach him in that expensive school."

The book was still in his lap. He pulled a bookmark from his shirt pocket and slipped it into place, closing the hardbound volume with a thump. It was Hardy's *The Mayor of Caster-bridge*.

Janice dismissed the issue with a casual flip of her hand. "Amy's a typical parent. Thinks everything the kid does is cute. I'm sure Mark meant no insult. He probably got the idea from watching TV."

Malcolm Anderson nodded sagely. He hated television.

"I'll tell you what," Janice said, rising. "I promised myself today that I would start putting the car in the garage when I got home. Naturally, I did my usual and left it sitting in the driveway. Let me take care of that; then I'll change and we'll see about dinner."

"Hurry. My mouth's been watering ever since I looked at those steaks."

Outside, Janice paused by the front door, her eyes taking in the neighborhood. Grass, flowers, well-maintained middle-class homes with TV antennas on their roofs, trees casting elongated shadows in the late-afternoon sun. Partway down the block, a pair of boys played catch in the street. It looked peaceful, totally unthreatening. Yet somewhere out there in that quiet suburban setting was someone who was going to a lot of trouble to frighten her. Someone who—and she felt she could no longer dismiss the possibility—who might truly want to kill her.

Fishing her keys from her purse, she headed for the garage. Separate from the house, although not more than ten feet away from it, the one-car garage had always reminded Janice of a small white frame barn. Its only door was made of hinged wooden panels that rolled up on metal tracks and usually jammed with the door halfway open. The lock was in the center, about three feet above the driveway.

When Janice tried to insert the key, she discovered she'd selected the wrong one. Then, as she flipped through them, attempting to recall which one unlocked the garage, she dropped them. Irritated, she snatched up the ring of keys and tried again, finally finding one that fit the lock but wouldn't turn it. When she tried to pull it out again, it jammed. She tugged, twisting the key back and forth; then, exasperated, she pulled with all her strength, and the key came free. And Janice stumbled backward, sitting down hard on the concrete driveway.

She glanced quickly around to see whether anyone had been watching. No one had. At least she didn't think so. Her vision was too fuzzy for her to be certain, blurred by the hot tears running down her cheeks. She picked up the keys and flung them at the lock.

Why the hell did she have so many goddamn keys anyway? She didn't even know what half of them were for. They just accumulated.

Stop it! she thought. I won't let some warped creep get to me. I won't, dammit. I won't.

She stood up, brushing herself off, and picked up the keys. Spotting one that looked right, she tried it, and the lock turned. To her amazement, when she twisted the handle and pulled up on the door, it rolled neatly up on its metal tracks, not even hesitating at the spot where it normally jammed.

The tears were all gone now, and she let her eyes wander through the garage. The grease stains on the concrete floor had come from a whole succession of her father's cars. His most recent one, a red station wagon, had been demolished in the accident. The garage was full of things her father would probably never be able to use again: rakes, shovels, an axe, a wheelbarrow.

She unlocked her car and climbed in behind the wheel. She had no idea why she was being threatened or by whom, but she did know that crying in the driveway wasn't the way to deal with it. She had to remain alert, aware of who and what was around her. If she was being threatened, then she had to be prepared to defend herself. And should her tormentor keep at it, maybe, just maybe, the creep would slip up and do something to reveal himself.

In a shabby motel room on Pennington Boulevard, a solitary figure lay on the bed watching the black and white TV set that was chained to the wall. Beside the bed, on a small cigarette-scarred table, were a number of poker-chip-like coins of various colors.

Called "funny money" by many of the patients at Elk Ridge, the coins could be used only at the institution's canteen and were given as a reward for cleaning your room or even yourself in some cases, depending on how bad off you were, on what behavior the doctors wanted to reinforce. Being obedient and cooperative guaranteed a patient a pocket full of coins. And other rewards. Like bus rides in the woods.

The funny money should be thrown away. But not here, not where a maid might see it, find it curious, associate it with the occupant of the room. Disposing of it was a thing forgotten too many times. Other things always seemed to take precedence; there simply hadn't been an appropriate opportunity to drop the coins from a bridge or toss them into a storm drain somewhere. Well, no matter. It was a minor detail.

The new, more daring plan was much better than the first. Much. The next step would be to check out the place. If it proved to be as ideal as it had appeared, the plan could shortly be shifted into its final, most deadly stages.

Janice and her father sat at the metal table on the patio, steak bones and potato skins all that remained on their plates. Janice wished she hadn't eaten the potato; she just knew all those carbohydrates would head straight for that damned fatty roll. Christ, she thought. Even when you had the big things to worry about, your mind never let you forget the little ones. Troubles didn't replace each other, apparently; they just added up.

Her father, who had rolled back a foot or two from the table, was staring off at the yard, looking quite contented. Janice followed the direction of his stare. The yard was looking pretty scruffy, flower beds choked by grass, the lawn full of weeds and badly in need of mowing. The boy her father had hired to take care of the yard had unexpectedly gone to camp for the summer, and no replacement had been found, which left the job to Janice, and she was no gardener.

The sun had just set, but the early evening seemed as sticky as the day had been. Considering that winter temperatures here dropped well below zero and stayed there for days at a time, the summer heat seemed unfair, somehow. Up north, especially around Lake Superior, the summers were beautifully cool, but in this part of the state, you froze in the winter, sweltered in the summer.

"Haven't seen Mike in a while," her father said. "What's he up to these days?"

Well, there it was. She'd been trying to think of a way to

broach the subject, but her father had just done it for her.

"I've got to talk to you about Mike," she said. She tried to see his face, but his features were fading in the dusk.

"I could tell something was on your mind, daughter. Let's hear it."

"I suppose you figured out that some day we'd probably get married. At least it seemed to be moving in that direction. Well, something's come up. He just got another job. In Seattle. So much more money that he couldn't turn it down. . . ." She trailed off.

"And he wants you to marry him and go with him. But you have doubts, one of which is me. Well, forget that one. I've already told you that I have to learn to fend for myself. If you want to go with Mike, then, by God, girl, you go with him." His face was a blur now, but his voice was firm, commanding.

"Daddy, it's not that simple. I do have doubts about leaving you, but they're not the only doubts I have. It would mean giving up my job, being a housewife if I couldn't find another one, having no say about where I live. Hell, what do I know about Seattle? . . . Uh, maybe that was the wrong thing to say because the next thing I have to ask you is how you'd feel about going with us."

He didn't answer immediately, and when he did he spoke slowly. "I'd miss you, daughter, but this is where I belong. If you want to go—and that's completely up to you—you go ahead. But I'm staying here. I'll be fine."

"But how do I know you're not just saying that? How do I know you'll be fine?"

"You don't, but I'll tell you this. The therapists would be so happy they'd probably throw me a party."

"I don't believe that, Daddy. They probably do want you to learn to be independent, but I can't believe they want you to be all alone."

"No, they don't. But they want me to behave as normally as I can, considering my disability. You wouldn't have this problem—at least as it relates to me—if it weren't for *my* problem, would you?"

"Daddy. . . ."

"Don't deny it, because you didn't live here before I had the accident. Only since. According to the therapists, you should do just as you would have done before. And I should make some new friends, instead of hanging around the house all the time. There's all sorts of organizations I could join. Right now. I don't even need a special van. There's an outfit that will pick me up and deliver me. All I have to do is call. That's how it should be, Janice. If you have other reasons for being reluctant, fine. You'll have to weigh them and decide. But if I think for a minute that you're hesitating on my account, I swear I'll boot you right out of here. Clear?"

Her eyes damp, she went to him and kissed him. "It's clear," she said.

It was after midnight when a flexible nail file slipped into the narrow space between the door and the jamb, found the tapered edge of the bolt, and teased it back, unlocking the rear door at Heikkinen's Funeral Home. It was dark here, the only lights in front, illuminating the grounds and not the building, maintaining that serene mortuary look even at night. The building was totally without security, but that seemed reasonable. The contents of such a place would be of little interest to the average burglar.

The intruder stepped inside, letting the door close by itself, then clicked on a flashlight. It was safe to use the light, for this part of the building had no windows. The things that had gone on within were not meant to be seen by those on the outside.

The light showed a hallway with a number of doors leading from it. The intruder's footsteps echoed off the tiled walls. It was a hollow, lonely sound. The place had the silence of death about it.

There was a hint of what seemed to be disinfectant in the air, a vague chemical smell. Perhaps it was the odor of death.

The rooms were empty, stripped of whatever equipment had been there. Like the hallway, they had walls of light green tile. Many had double doors of the sort a gurney could be rolled through. This was obviously the portion of the building friends and relatives of the deceased were never allowed to see.

Then one room in particular caught the intruder's attention. Covering the face of one wall were numerous metal drawers, as if it were an enormous filing cabinet. Entering the room, the intruder switched on the light, and, choosing one of the drawers at random, pulled it open. It was a filing cabinet, all right. For corpses. Here in this coffin-sized compartment had lain someone's Aunt Sarah, someone else's Uncle Joe. And like a filing cabinet, each drawer had a thumb-operated latch on the outside, a mechanism to insure that, once closed, it would not slide open of its own accord.

Of course, this was not a filing cabinet but a refrigerator. The face of the drawer was thick and edged with a heavy rubber seal; the latching mechanism was hefty. These could be useful. Quite useful.

Yes, indeed. This place would again be put to the purpose for which it was intended. There would again be death here.

But not now, not for a few days yet. Money was the next order of business. The man who had picked up a hitchhiker outside Duluth—the man who had died—had provided some money. Now that it was used up, someone here in Dakota Falls would have to provide some more.

Janice lay awake in her room, watching the shadows on the ceiling move mysteriously as a gentle summer breeze stirred the leaves on the trees. Unable to shake the feeling of forboding that had nagged her since discovering her mail had been tampered with, she had tossed and turned, dozing for brief periods, waking again.

Despite her resolve to deal with this thing in the logical, clear-headed manner of a trained detective, she couldn't rid herself of her apprehension. Something terrible was going to happen. Maybe not tonight or tomorrow, but soon.

And she had a new problem now. Her mail had been tampered with, and that, without question, should be reported. But doing so meant admitting her negligence in not reporting the note. And that would mean a lecture from Captain Bishop. After making a fool of herself over the narcotics raid, she was in no hurry to upset her boss again.

She rolled over and buried her face in the pillow. Still unresolved was the question of whether to marry Mike and accompany him to Seattle. She was no closer to making that decision since talking to her father than she had been before.

Dawn was only half an hour away when sixty-eight-year-old Charles Nordin pulled up to the small men's clothing store on Pennington Boulevard and began giving it the once-over with the car's spotlight. On a clear night like this, he didn't need a watch to tell him it was nearly dawn. He could tell by the stars. They were dimmer now, just slightly, and soon the first traces of gray would appear on the horizon.

Since taking this job with the Dakota Falls Merchant Patrol ten years ago, he'd become a part of the night. He knew her and all her little idiosyncrasies. He loved her the way some men loved the sea, and like the sea, the night could caress you and pamper you one moment, then turn violent and sinister the next. So far this shift, she'd been friendly, seductive.

It was warm and humid tonight. Soon, the mosquitoes would be out in force. Already he had a bite on his arm and another on his ankle.

Dummies wearing sports jackets and slacks stared back at him as he ran his spotlight over the display windows. It had occurred to him that someone might slip into one of the dummies' outfits, hoping to be taken for a mannequin. It was silly, he supposed, but he always checked. Tonight all the dummies seemed genuine.

Switching off the light, he dropped the car into gear and headed for the rear of the store. Although it was only one of about half a dozen businesses in the small shopping center, he paid little attention to the others, as only the clothing store was his employer's client.

A narrow alley ran behind the shopping center—rear entrances to the shops, trash bins, and stacks of empty cartons on one side, a high block wall on the other. Illuminated by a few weak and ineffective lights near the roof of the building, the alley was filled with patches of blackness that vanished when the car's headlights hit them and crept back as he drove on. There were homes on the other side of the wall, but it was too high for the people living in them to see into the alley. Through good fortune—and little else, it seemed—the clothing store had never been hit.

At the rear entrance, he stopped the car, grabbed the flashlight lying beside him on the seat, and got out. Although a cursory inspection was fine for in front, here he had to be more meticulous. A tall, wiry man with long limbs, he often felt cramped sitting in the car; it was good to stretch his legs. Pushing down his gun belt—it tended to ride up when he was driving—he strode briskly to the clothing shop's rear entrance and switched on his flashlight. A twist on the knob showed the door to be securely locked. The small wire-mesh window in its center was intact; there were no signs of forced entry. Moving his flashlight to the left, he checked the only other likely spot for a burglar to gain access: a barred window in the wall. It, too, was undisturbed.

Then he heard a noise to his right. Instantly alert, he whirled, the beam of his flashlight poking into the shadows. The sound had come from the vicinity of a big, gray trash bin about fifteen feet away—a plink, as if someone had dropped a bottle cap. A rat perhaps, or a stray cat.

Then a new thought began to form in his mind, the idea that someone might have tossed something over there to get him to turn in that direction. But before he could act on that notion, he felt a sudden and sharp pain in his back.

Dropping the flashlight, he tried to turn and draw his revolver, but his legs suddenly seemed unable to support him, and he was falling, the official-looking badge painted on the door of his car momentarily filling his vision, then blurring. As if through a haze, he saw a face above him, and his mind seemed to tell him there was something unusual about that face, something unexpected, but the thought refused to register.

Then he saw the knife coming down, and he was instantly surrounded by blackness, as if the night were clutching him to her bosom, about to take him into herself and share with him all her secrets.

A pair of hands rolled Charles Nordin's limp, bloody form over, removing first his handgun, then his wallet. This was apparently the sort of man who liked to carry large sums of cash, as the billfold contained nearly eighty dollars. Both the money and the weapon would be needed, and it had been a stroke of luck to find them both on the same person.

Three

Janice arrived at work early. She'd decided to tell Captain Bishop about the note and the steaming open of her mail; and first thing in the morning, before any of the others came in, seemed the best time to do it. Fortunately, the captain usually came in early.

"Well," he said as she stepped into his office, "my little reminder yesterday must have done some good." He looked pointedly at the clock on the wall. It was 7:45, fifteen minutes before her workday officially began.

She gave him her most polite, subservient smile. The good subordinate. He eyed her skeptically.

"Captain—" She was interrupted by the phone.

Bishop picked it up, listened a moment, then said: "Oh, shit! Okay, I'll be right there." He slammed the phone down, hurriedly shuffled through the papers on his desk, extracted one, and shoved it at her. "One of Dakota Falls Merchant Patrol's men is in the hospital. He was mugged last night."

With that, he rushed past her into the larger office, looking around to see who was there. Just then, Ted Reynolds, who was still green enough to come in early, appeared from the hallway. Captain Bishop grabbed him. "Let's go, Reynolds. One of the narco suspects we missed yesterday's holding some kids hostage, and he's got a shotgun."

Both men disappeared out the door, and Janice was alone

in the office. She stared at the empty doorway a moment, then turned and headed for her desk, feeling the heat of anger rushing to her face. Well, fuck you assholes, she thought. Maybe I will go to Seattle.

She understood what had just happened, although the knowledge did little to ease her hurt. It had happened before. The time a burglar was trapped inside a warehouse and Mullins had ordered her to stay in the car while he and Greene went inside. The time she and Collins had been assigned to pick up a teenage robbery suspect and Collins had called for backup from patrol, then left her to watch the rear door. The time she and Watson had been in the car closest to a robbery-in-progress call and Watson, who would have ordinarily rushed to the scene, had driven in the opposite direction, saying patrol could handle it.

Oh, yeah. She understood all right. You went into a potentially dangerous situation knowing you had to place your full trust in the officers who went in with you, for a mistake by one of your companions could easily cost you your life. Simply put, she was asking these men to trust her with their lives, and they wouldn't do it. Not one of them would choose to have a woman at his side when facing a crazed killer.

Not that she'd ever failed under such circumstances; she'd never had the opportunity to fail. Even as a patrol officer, she'd been carefully excluded from dangerous situations. If she remained a police officer, it would happen, though. Some day. And that thought was every bit as frightening for her as it was for any of the officers who might have to depend on her.

Still, she knew that, until it happened, she could never be truly accepted. And even if she did prove herself, she would remain an unwanted intruder in the eyes of many. But she could handle being unwanted. It was not being trusted that hurt.

Standing beside her desk, she sighed. Her blanket condemnation had been a little unfair. She had a good working relationship with Reynolds and Poldoski. Whether they trusted her with their lives, *truly* trusted her, she couldn't say. At least if they didn't, they never let it show.

When she sat down at her desk, her stomach did a quick flip, giving her a second taste of the Canadian bacon and scrambled eggs she'd had for breakfast. Her father had again prepared the morning meal, an arrangement that seemed likely to become permanent, especially now that he had a need to show her how well he could do things on his own.

Turning her attention to the report Captain Bishop had handed her, she read that the victim was sixty-eight-year-old Charles Nordin of Dakota Falls. Stabbed twice, once in the back and again in the abdomen. Unconscious when found. Admitted to Brookwood Hospital in critical condition. Location: an alley behind the Plaza Shopping Center, near the rear entrance of Ed's Men's Apparel. Victim, a merchant patrolman, robbed of his sidearm, weapon described by his employer as a Smith and Wesson .38. Wallet abandoned at scene, credit cards apparently untouched, contained no cash when found. No indications of a break-in at shopping center. Victim's local next of kin: none. The report was signed by Officer J. Edwards, who, while on routine patrol, noticed what appeared to be an unattended merchant patrol car in the alley and investigated. Time: 4:16 A.M.

Janice sighed. Muggers were rarely caught. A shadowy figure surprises someone in the alley, a park, along a dark street, the victim frequently the only witness and often too shaken and confused following the experience to provide much useful information about the mugger.

Well, the only known witness to this mugging was in the hospital, at last report in critical condition. She picked up the phone and, a few moments later, was speaking to a Dr. Burke at Brookwood Hospital.

"You can talk to him briefly," the doctor said. "I'll tell you, the old guy's got one hell of a constitution. When he came in, it was touch and go. If you'd asked me what his chances were a couple of hours ago, I'd have said doubtful. But he's over the hump now."

"I'm glad to hear I won't be investigating a homicide. When can I see him?"

"You'd better hold off until late this afternoon. He's asleep now, and I don't think he'll be awake until then. He'll still be under the effects of his medication, so he may not be able to talk too coherently, but you're welcome to try. Give us a call first, to make sure he's awake."

Fifteen minutes after ending her conversation with Dr. Burke, she learned that the man holding the children hostage had surrendered without incident.

Later that morning—Franklin Ross, the fingerprint man, in tow—Janice surveyed the scene of Charles Nordin's mugging. The blood stains, dark brown smears now, were readily discernible from the other splotches on the filthy concrete. She examined them a moment, then turned to Ross, who said:

"If it was necessary to dust here, why didn't patrol call for someone at the time?" He was a slender, distinguished-looking man in his forties with black hair graying at the temples and cold blue-gray eyes. He'd already dusted Nordin's wallet. It had been wiped clean.

"Patrol obviously didn't think it was necessary."

The look on his face showed he agreed with patrol. "So where shall I begin?"

"I don't know yet," she answered, studying the alley.

"You got me out here without even knowing whether you'd need me?" There was no surprise in his voice; he'd worked with her before. It was just his nature to complain.

Ignoring him, she turned to face the block wall that made up one side of the alley, then jumped, trying to see whether she could catch a glimpse of the homes on the other side. She couldn't. Next, she stepped over to the rear door of Ed's Men's Apparel and studied the alley in both directions. To her left—Nordin's right if he'd been facing the building—was a big metal trash bin of the type that had to be dumped by a special truck. One corner of it came within a few inches of touching the wall; not a good spot from which to attack anyone standing here. In the other direction, the alley was clear for twenty-five feet or so, until it reached a group of battered metal garbage cans. But much closer—ten, maybe twelve feet away—was a recessed doorway.

"Frank, would you please stand here while I check something?"

Ross obliged, and Janice eased herself into the recess. "Can you see me?" she called.

"No."

"Okay, thanks." She was standing beside a rusty metal door set back a foot and a half or so from the alley wall. Its purpose eluded her, but it was clearly not used very often. A thin film of rain-spotted filth covered the metal uniformly, except for two spots where it had been recently smeared. One was the sort of mark someone might make by leaning against the door; the other was smaller, the type of smudge that might have been made with a hand as someone pushed himself out of his hiding place.

"Okay," she said, stepping from the doorway. "Here's what I want dusted."

Ross, who had not moved from where she'd positioned him, headed for the car to get his equipment.

"You're in luck," Janice called after him. "It looks like you won't have to print all the employees in the shopping center after all."

"Was that what you had in mind for me?" he asked, unlocking the trunk of their unmarked brown Ford.

"Of course."

"You're a real friend, Janice. A real friend."

Within five minutes, Ross had two fingerprints neatly preserved on sticky plastic. Still squatting by the metal door, he examined his find. "Only partials," he said. "Not much use unless we know who we're looking for."

Well, Janice thought, it's better than nothing. She stepped back from the doorway and looked off down the alley. This wasn't too far from her father's house, she noted. The alley continued in the next block, running behind a gas station, a laundromat, and some other small businesses. But then it ended, and beyond, lush and green in the June sunshine, were the grounds of Heikkinen's Funeral Home.

It was after six when Janice left her unmarked car in a no-parking zone in front of Brookwood Hospital and headed up the wide flower-lined walk toward the building's main entrance. An old four-story brick structure, Brookwood was private, expensive. Still, serious emergency cases were usually brought here because the alternative was a half-hour emergency run to Minneapolis.

As instructed, she checked in with the second-floor nurses' station and was escorted to room 212 in the intensive care ward. The old man was on his back, an IV tube taped to his arm, his eyes closed.

"There's someone here to see you," the nurse said. She was middle-aged, stocky, and had copper-colored hair.

Nordin opened his blue eyes, taking a moment to focus on the two women. He had smooth skin for a man nearly seventy, his thin white hair the only thing that revealed his true age. He tried to smile, but the corners of his mouth wouldn't work right.

"This is Detective Anderson," the nurse said. "She'd like to speak with you, if you feel up to it."

"Sure," he said, his voice weak.

The nurse nodded and left the room.

"What did I do to deserve such a pretty detective?" he said slowly, mouthing the words with difficulty.

"The captain picked me out for you special." She winked.

Another lopsided grin.

"Can you tell me what happened to you?" Janice asked.

"Tricked. Tossed something—a bottle cap maybe—so I'd turn my back."

"Did you get a look at the person?"

He hesitated, his eyes fixed on a point above his head. "Saw him, but . . ."

"You said 'him,'" Janice prompted. "Was it a man who attacked you?"

Again, he hesitated. "Not sure. Can't remember. Something about the face." And then with surprising lucidity he added: "When I try to see the face, the same words always come to me: an angel of the night. But I don't know what it means. You see . . ." He was starting to slur his words again now. "You see, I see the night like that . . . as a woman . . . like the sea."

Janice tried again. "When you see that face, do you see a woman or a man?"

"Don't know. Blurred. Must have been a man."

"What color was his hair?"

"Blond . . . I think. Yes, blond."

"Long hair or short?"

"I'm not sure. Long, I think."

"You said there was something about the face. Do you remember what it was?"

"Just . . . just an angel of the night. I'm sorry."

Janice decided this was getting her nowhere. The old man

was still too groggy to be much help. There was nothing to do but wait until he could think more coherently.

"I'm sorry," he said weakly.

"Don't worry about it. We'll talk again later, when you're feeling better."

"You'll come back? I mean you personally?"

"The captain wouldn't dream of sending anyone else after picking me out special the way he did."

Once more, the lopsided grin.

Janice turned the unmarked car in at the police building's underground parking facility, then walked up the ramp to the street and hurried across it to the department's unofficial, above-ground parking facility, the vacant lot that had once been a theater. Her Datsun was surrounded by a new set of cars now, those belonging to swing-shift officers, and she wondered where the police force would park should someone decide to build on this site.

She unlocked the door and slipped behind the wheel, glad to be heading home. When the car failed to start on the first try, she tried again. And again. She was on the verge of running her battery down to the point of uselessness when she finally gave up, got out, and raised the hood, thinking she might attract the attention of someone who knew something about cars. No, dammit! What she was really thinking was that some man—mechanical geniuses that they all were—would come to the aid of the mechanically inept but pretty woman. She very nearly slammed the hood in anger with herself.

By God, she knew a little bit about engines, and if she couldn't fix it herself, she'd call a garage. She would *not* be rescued.

It took her only a moment to spot the problem: a disconnected coil wire. Christ, she thought, and here I was, ready to do the helpless-woman-in-distress bit. In the next instant, she had a very good reason for being distressed, as she had just noticed what was attached to the dangling coil wire. Wrapped around its black insulation, covered with grease so it wouldn't be too noticeable, was a piece of paper.

Her hand shaking, she carefully slipped it off the wire and unfolded it, smearing grease on her fingers. She was looking at another crude drawing of a pig, clearly the work of the same person who had made the childlike picture on the last page of Amy's letter. Apparently, Janice was supposed to have been in doubt about the origin of the first drawing, and this one was designed to confirm her worst fears. Well, she was smarter than her tormentor gave her credit for being. Yet it was a trivial victory, for the words written on the paper were every bit as unnerving as their author had undoubtedly hoped they'd be. In wobbly, childlike capital letters, the message read:

THIS COULD HAVE BEEN A BOMB. THEN THE WOMAN PIG WOULD HAVE BEEN ALL BLOWN UP.

She jumped when she heard footsteps behind her. Panic momentarily numbing her mind, she operated on instinct, whirling to face a potential attacker, one hand desperately trying to unzip her purse, find her weapon, the other coming up to ward off the blow.

"Jesus! You out of your mind?" It was Mullins. Mullins with the potbelly. Mullins the intolerable sexist. Mullins the fellow officer. He stood there a few feet away, looking at her in awe.

"Christ," he said. "I thought you were going to pull a weapon on me."

She stared at him, not knowing what to say.

"Hey, are you all right? You look like you're scared shit-less."

Forcing herself to muster some composure, Janice said: "I'm fine. Really. I was just thinking about the case I'm working on. I, uh, I was thinking about how the offender sneaked up behind the victim, and just then I heard you behind me. Sorry." She smiled. "I didn't mean to overreact. You just startled me."

"Yeah, it's okay," he said, but he was eyeing her with obvious uncertainty. "I saw you with the hood up on your car, and I thought you might be having some problems."

That brought her back to reality. He was going to rescue her. Oh, shit, it would be Mullins. And of all the people to make a fool of herself in front of, she had to choose the biggest sexist in the division. Well, she'd recoup what she could.

"No problem," she said, turning back to the engine. "Just a loose coil wire." She waited until he had stepped forward to see for himself, then casually inserted the wire back into its hole in the center of the distributor cap. "All fixed," she said, slamming the hood.

Mullins actually stared at her with total disbelief on his face. "You sure that's all it was?"

"That's it," she replied confidently. But Mullins wasn't leaving until he saw for himself, so she slipped behind the wheel and reached for the ignition key. If it doesn't start, she thought, I'll kill myself.

It did start. On the first crank.

Mullins, looking almost hurt, gave her a halfhearted wave, then turned and headed for his own car. Realizing she'd dropped the note when Mullins had come up behind her, she got out of the car again to look for it. She found it resting against the left front tire. The paper, springy from having been wrapped around the coil wire, had curled itself loosely into a cylinder. She scooped it up, deciding against putting the filthy thing in her purse. Then she noticed the condition of her purse. The brown leather was covered with black, greasy finger smudges.

Again sitting behind the wheel, she felt her face flush, her vision suddenly blurred by tears. "Goddamn it," she sobbed. "Goddamn it."

More than 150 miles to the north, Dr. Andrew Eklund, the chief pathologist at the St. Louis County Medical Center in Duluth, was still at work in his small basement office. Spread out before him on the desk were the files on the twenty-eight victims of last week's bus crash, the county medical examiner's office having given him the grim task of trying to identify the remains, many of which were burned beyond recognition. He wanted very badly to dispose of the matter, to get back to the neglected routine matters of his department. But he couldn't. Because he was unable to get the twenty-eight names to match up with the twenty-eight bodies.

He was having all the usual problems that went with something of this scope. Missing dental records. Charred hands that could provide no fingerprints. At least the numbers were correct: five state hospital employees and twenty-three patients, twenty-eight bodies. They had been on the way to an outing in the woods, part of a program to reward those patients who had been exhibiting the desired behavior. None of them had survived the flash fire that followed the crash.

He stared at his long, slender fingers, noting what good hands he had for delicate work. And his work was delicate, despite the good-natured ribbing he took from some of his colleagues. Of late, they had taken to chiding him about the fact that none of his patients would ever sue him for malpractice. Well, he didn't mind. To him pathology was fascinating, and often he'd find himself approaching a new case as if he were a detective about to begin work on a complicated and challenging puzzle. And, what the hell, he might as well say it: He'd never lost a patient.

It was past his dinner time, and he was hungry. Unlike many of his colleagues, who jogged or dieted to stay trim, he had the opposite problem. He looked something like a fifty-two-year-old, six-foot, walking pencil and had to stuff himself at meals just to keep from getting even thinner. He ran a hand over his bald head and picked up the file folder labeled "Bus Crash, 13."

This one, number thirteen, was going to be the most difficult. The badly burned remains seemed to be those of a young woman, possibly a teen-ager, tall, probably slender. At least that was the profile worked up from the physical evidence. The trouble was that according to the records provided by the mental institution, no one on the bus had had those physical characteristics.

Closing the folder, he sighed. This, he was afraid, could turn out to be one of those instances when you simply had to guess, to state confidently that A was Mr. Smith and B was Mr. Jones, having no idea which was really which. You had no choice, really. You weren't allowed to keep the remains forever while you tried to make up your mind, and telling the truth of the matter—that you didn't know—was satisfactory to no one. So you did what you had to do, knowing nobody would be the wiser. Still, he hoped it wouldn't come to that. It was a last resort that violated both his scientific and his moral principles.

He picked up the phone to let his wife know he was on his way home. He could tackle the problem again tomorrow, after a good night's sleep.

Four

It was drizzling the next afternoon when Janice arrived at Brookwood Hospital to have another try at getting Charles Nordin to describe his attacker. She again parked illegally in front of the building and, buttoning her lightweight raincoat, ran up the walk to the entrance. It was the end of the week, Friday, TGIF and all that.

This morning, she'd interviewed a rape victim, who'd decided not to prosecute, then helped Watson on an investigation of an armed robbery at a Seven-Eleven store. *Accompanied* Watson would be more accurate. He'd asked all the questions and had barely even spoken to her. She was uncertain whether his behavior stemmed from lingering hard feelings over her refusal to be seduced or his dislike of woman cops. Since he wouldn't talk to her, she was unlikely to find out.

At least her car hadn't been tampered with again. She'd checked it over thoroughly—including the engine compartment and anywhere else a bomb might be hidden—before dashing home at noon to put a frozen roast in the microwave. Her father had protested that he could have prepared it in the regular oven, which he could reach, had he been told far enough in advance to thaw it. Then he said he would have the microwave moved so he could get at it. It was only a matter of time before she would start arriving home to find dinner already under way.

He seemed determined to show that he was quite capable of taking care of himself.

In any event, the microwave was programmed. Later this afternoon, it would automatically finish thawing the roast, then cook it to perfection.

She hoped whoever had been threatening her had had his fun and was now ready to leave her alone. So far, she had mentioned the threats to no one. If they had stopped, she wouldn't have to, and that would suit her just fine.

Nordin was in a room on the third floor now, having been removed from the intensive care unit. He wasn't sitting up—he probably wasn't allowed to—but his eyes were bright, and he greeted her with a pleasant smile this time rather than a lopsided grin.

"Well, how are you today?" she asked, pulling a chair up beside his bed and sitting down.

"A lot better now that you're here." He grinned. Both it and his speech were normal.

Fumbling in her purse, Janice took out a small pad and a ball-point. "I'm glad I can bring a little pleasure into somebody's life," she replied pleasantly. "It doesn't always work out that way when you're a police officer."

"I couldn't imagine your presence being anything but pleasant, believe me."

"Be careful. Police officers aren't supposed to blush—at least not while they're on the job. Now, before you make me break that rule, let's get back to the person who attacked you."

He wrinkled his brow. "I'm sorry, but I still can't help you. I've thought about it and thought about it, but all I get is a fuzzy image of a face hovering over me . . . and those same words again. An angel of the night. I'm sorry. I don't know what it means."

"I think you know more than you think you do. For instance, the face. What race was it?"

He closed his eyes, apparently trying to picture it. "It was white," he said. "At least it wasn't Negro, I'm sure of that."

"You see, we've already eliminated a portion of the population." Although not a sizeable one. There weren't many blacks in Minnesota generally and almost none in Dakota Falls. "Now let's try another general category. Was your assailant male or female? Yesterday, you didn't seem too sure."

He sighed. "I'm still not, I'm afraid. I think it was a man, but I don't really know why I think so."

"Did the attacker say anything?"

"No, nothing. I heard a noise over by the trash bin, and when I turned to see what it was, I was attacked from behind. I fell, and I saw this blurry face above me, then a knife . . . and that's all."

After another ten minutes of questioning, Janice decided there was nothing useful that Nordin could tell her and that the case would most likely go down as unsolved. She reviewed with him the contents of his wallet, determining that he'd had about eighty dollars in cash, which of course was missing. Apparently, nothing else had been taken, except his weapon.

Nordin watched her go. Pretty young thing. And nice. Seemed quite competent, too, although he was traditional enough to wonder whether she shouldn't be home with the kids instead of out chasing criminals. But then, society changed, and one had to go along.

These thoughts reminded him of his Maggie, with whom he'd lived for thirty-six years before she died. He pushed her image away, for whenever he recalled those wonderful times they'd had together, he was forced to realize they were gone forever.

Closing his eyes, he tried again to remember that face he'd seen looking down at him in the alley. It was a shimmery, almost spectral image, a face without features, without substance. Yet there was something wrong with his perception of it, something he could almost grasp but not quite. Something important.

He allowed the image to drift away, his thoughts wandering, and a few moments later he was asleep.

Concealed from the house next door by a tall, unkempt hedge and from the street by a lilac bush, a solitary figure peered through the window, into the Andersons' living room. The old man was asleep in his wheelchair, an open book in his lap.

But he wasn't old, not really. The accident had aged him, an accident that had been reported in the Twin Cities papers, to which some of the patients at Elk Ridge subscribed. One of the papers had even mentioned that Malcolm Anderson was the father of Detective Janice Anderson of the Dakota Falls Police Department. He seemed almost feeble; when the time came, he would be easy to handle.

The window was open, only the screen blocking entry. The rain wasn't heavy enough to close the windows, the weather muggy enough to want them open.

From the back pocket of a pair of tight-fitting blue jeans, the solitary figure removed a screwdriver.

Mildred Dieryck and Katherine Fox lived across the street from the Andersons in a small two-bedroom house. Both widows in their seventies, they had moved in together in part for companionship but mainly so they could combine their meager incomes. At the moment, each was in her customary spot, Mildred in the antique rocker, reading a romance, Katherine perched on a small wooden stool by the window, spying on the neighbors.

"I thought I saw someone prowling around the Andersons' house," she said, easing the lace curtain back into place. "Just from the corner of my eye, and then it was gone."

"Katherine, come away from the window before you get arrested for peeping." Mildred flipped another page in her book. The big sex scene was coming up, and she was reading eagerly.

"I'm sure I saw someone. Do you think I should tell the police?"

She patted her curly gray hair, something she did when she was undecided, which was often. Unlike Mildred, who was tall and slender, she was a squat woman with a round face.

"His daughter is staying there now, and his daughter is the police." Mildred was beginning to get annoyed with the distraction; the big sex scene would begin any page now.

"Well, she isn't there at the moment, and poor Mr. Anderson is so helpless in that wheelchair."

"If you call the police, they'll know you've been peeping, Katherine."

"Well, it's not against the law as long as I do it from my own house."

"It's probably just the meter man."

Katherine looked doubtful. "I think the meters are on the other side of the house."

"If you're really worried about it, why don't you call Mr. Anderson and make sure he's all right?"

Katherine headed for the phone, and Mildred turned another page in her book.

It took a few rings for the phone to bring Malcolm Anderson out of his sleep. Trying to blink his surroundings into focus, he groggily wheeled through the living room toward the kitchen, where the phone was mounted on the wall.

Between rings, he thought he heard a noise, as if someone had opened the back door. Then he was in the kitchen; the door was closed, the phone still ringing. He answered it.

"Mr. Anderson?"

"Yes."

"I just wanted to make sure you were all right. This is Katherine Fox, across the street."

"I'm, uh, I'm fine," he replied sleepily.

"Well, I'm sorry I bothered you. It's just that I thought I saw someone prowling around your house."

He remembered the sound that might have been the door closing. Stretching the phone's cord as he went, he rolled over to the door and checked it. It was locked. Besides, had anyone entered the house that way, the intruder would have run into him in the kitchen. It was nothing, he decided.

"Everything's fine here," he reassured her. "But I appreciate your concern. Listen, why don't you and Mildred come over sometime? We can have dinner, and maybe Janice would consent to being a fourth for bridge."

She agreed that was a good idea, but, as was typical of such arrangements, they ended the conversation with no date having been set. As he replaced the receiver, the small red light on the microwave blinked on, indicating that the oven had begun its work on the still partially frozen roast.

The rain had stopped and the sun was shining when Janice left for home at five. Unless called in, she would be free until Monday, and as Poldoski and Mullins were the on-call detectives this weekend, it didn't seem likely she would be. And Sunday, of course, Amy and Mark arrived.

She followed Fourth Street out of downtown, then cut over to Pennington, passing the Seven-Eleven store that had been robbed earlier that day. Forty-seven dollars had been the take, and for that a young man who'd worn a stocking over his head faced an armed robbery rap if he was caught.

Glancing in the rearview, she noted that the orange Pinto that had been behind her on Fourth was still there. Ordinarily, she wouldn't have noticed whether a particular car was behind her, but this one had such a bright orange paint job, you couldn't miss it, even in the Friday afternoon rush.

As was usual for Fridays this time of year, there were a number of pickup campers and trailers on the road, people heading for the north woods to fish, camp, start forest fires.

Her gaze drifting to the mirror again, she observed that the Pinto was still there, three or four cars back. Absently, she thought that such a car would certainly be useless for surveillance; it very nearly glowed.

Her own car had again survived several hours in the parking lot unmolested. It seemed likely her tormentor had given up, and she was just as glad she hadn't taken the matter to Captain Bishop. It would have just complicated further an already complicated situation.

Mike would be picking her up this evening. The Guthrie Theater, drinks, then back to Dakota Falls and his apartment for the night. She'd be home early in the morning to check on her dad. She and her father had never discussed her sleeping elsewhere on the weekends—which she'd done even before she met Mike—and they probably never would, as both realized it was her business. Actually, her father demanded nothing of her; caring for him was an obligation she'd taken on voluntarily, her father always appreciative but never behaving as if it were his due.

The subject of Seattle would come up again tonight; it was unavoidable. She had no answer for him yet. She needed more time, more than she had.

Pulling off Pennington, she glanced in the rearview again, finding the orange Pinto right behind her now, the driver's face obscured by the glare on the windshield. Now that she was in a residential area, she tried to switch her awareness from brake lights and turn signals to children, dogs, balls that rolled out into the street.

Suddenly, the Pinto was alongside her, matching her speed, the driver wearing a ski mask, a gloved hand holding a gun, aiming it at her through the open window.

Hitting the brakes, Janice reached for her purse, for the weapon inside it, just as the bag tumbled off the seat, spilling its contents on the floor. The car came to a stop. As she frantically tried to separate her service revolver from the papers, pencils, hair brush, and other things that had fallen from her purse, for some reason the thought flashed through her mind that this wouldn't have happened if only women's clothes were designed to allow for shoulder holsters.

The weapon finally in her hand, she cautiously raised her head enough to see out the window. The orange Pinto was gone. Then she saw it, partway down the block, speeding away. She hurriedly started the Datsun, which had stalled; she could still catch the Pinto.

Driving with her .38 in one hand, she sped along the street, the Pinto now a full block ahead of her. But she was gaining on it. By the time she passed her father's house, she'd narrowed the gap to half a block, not quite close enough to make out the license number. Suddenly, just ahead of her, something small and black darted out from between two parked cars, and Janice jammed on the brakes, the Datsun's tires squealing.

Sitting in the middle of the street, wagging its tail at her, was the Tyler's cocker spaniel. The orange Pinto had disappeared.

It wasn't over, she realized. Her tormentor had simply switched tactics. The orange car had been chosen so she'd *know* she was being followed. No shots had been fired; this had not been an attempt to kill, only to frighten her. And it had very nearly backfired. Had it not been for the dog, she would have had him. Damn, she thought, slamming the steering wheel with the palm of her hand. I could have had him. I could have had the son of a bitch.

With a shaking hand, she grabbed the ignition key and restarted the engine. Not wanting to bother her father with any of this, she decided to drive around until she was calm enough to walk in the front door as if nothing had happened, cheerful because it was the weekend.

Half an hour later, she breezed into the living room and greeted her father with a kiss. She was still somewhat flustered, but she had an excuse now. She'd just spent ten minutes un-jamming the garage door.

"You look rather bedraggled," her father said, slipping a bookmark into the volume on his lap. "Hard day?"

"Not until I got home," she lied. "We've really got to do something about that garage door."

"Stick again?"

"Did it ever! I must have been quite a sight, swinging from the handle with both feet off the ground. At least it finally came down again, but one of these days it won't." She hadn't shed any tears of frustration in the driveway this time; she hadn't let herself.

"I'll call the repairman first thing Monday. You don't usu-ally use the garage during the summer, so I've been putting it off."

Janice said she thought that was a good idea, then headed for the bedroom, where she tossed her raincoat on the bed, then stashed her purse in the bottom dresser drawer. That she should report the threats was totally beyond question now. Whatever excuses she had been using not to do so—and she wasn't certain exactly what they were—would no longer stand up. And even though the harassment had become quite serious, she had the feeling now it wasn't the extent of what her tor-mentor had in mind.

It was a prelude. To something worse.

On the bed table was the extension she'd had installed when she moved back in with her father—one of the few certainties of life as a police detective was being called out in the middle of the night. With a sigh, she lifted the receiver and dialed Captain Bishop's home number. After letting it ring about fifteen times, she decided no one was going to answer and slowly replaced the receiver.

No one would be in the detective division's office right now. If something came up over the weekend, dispatch would phone the on-call officers at home. If she called patrol, a uni-formed officer would be sent out to take a report, and there seemed little use in that. Besides, the captain was the one she needed to talk to. All she could do was wait and call again later.

After a quick stop in the bathroom to freshen up, she headed for the kitchen to see how the roast had come out.

"Strange thing this afternoon," her father said as she stepped into the living room. "Katherine Fox across the street called me to say she thought she saw a prowler over here."

Janice froze. "A prowler?"

"Nothing to it, as far as I could tell. Do you know Mrs. Fox?"

Janice shook her head.

"No, I guess you wouldn't. She and another elderly woman bought the Holtons' house while you were living in that apartment over on Seventeenth Street. She's sort of the neighborhood busybody. Spends all her time at the window spying on people. I think her imagination plays tricks on her sometimes."

That was good to know. The snoopy Mrs. Fox just might have seen someone at the mailbox the other day. As a detective, she'd more than once had good reason to be grateful for the keen-eyed neighborhood busybodies of this world.

"I'm sure it was nothing," Janice said casually. But was it? Had someone been here? With great effort, she managed to manufacture a smile. "Just to be on the safe side, let me give the place a professional once-over. After all, how often do I get to use my talents at home?"

Her father went back to the ever-present book in his lap. He obviously wasn't concerned.

Janice began with the living room, her eyes searching for anything out of place, anything unusual. Then she moved to the windows, most of which were open, checking the screens to make sure they were latched, scrutinizing them for any signs of attempted entry. She repeated the process in the three bedrooms, the bathroom, the kitchen, finding nothing.

Next, she went out the back door and walked around the house, seeing nothing suspicious until she squeezed between a lilac and the high hedge that ran along one side of the property. The unmowed grass here had grown quite tall, and just ahead of her was a spot where it had been flattened. Directly below a window. Someone had stood there and done something.

Moving to the spot, she peered through the window and found that she was looking into the living room. Her father was sitting in his wheelchair, reading, unaware that anyone was watching him. Her father! He was alone here all day and sometimes even at night, a cripple, entirely vulnerable. Heretofore, she'd seen the threats as being entirely against her.

Would someone get at her through him? It could be so easily done. And quite effectively. Oh, God, she thought. Oh, God.

Then her eyes fell to the lower portion of the window frame, and she shivered. It was an aluminum storm window, and with the outer glass raised, as it was now, the screen became accessible. It had a pair of sliding latches, one on each side, that could be used to lock it in the open or closed position. By each one, the metal had been pried back, probably with a screwdriver, which could then be used to slide back the latch.

What had happened? Had someone climbed in through the window while her father was asleep or in another part of the house, closed the screen again, then left, disturbing nothing? There would be no point. If this was the work of her tormentor, why had the evidence, invisible from the inside, been so hard to find? She couldn't be threatened by things she didn't know about, and she wouldn't have known about this at all had it not been for the nosy Mrs. Fox.

Then, too, it could have been a burglar. A man alone and in a wheelchair would be quite tempting to the sort who preyed on the weak or the elderly—as would the two women across the street, now that she thought about it. A burglar, or her tormentor—either could have been scared off by a passing patrol car, a barking dog, anything. There was no way to know exactly what had happened here, except that someone had tried and, judging by her inspection of its interior, presumably failed to gain entrance to the house.

She turned, studying the hedge and the lilac. The shrubbery concealed this spot from the street and the neighbors. Precisely the situation the police department was always urging homeowners to avoid.

Again, she faced the window, watching her father. Should she tell him? Yes, she had to. At least about this. He had to be alert, keep the doors and windows locked, and be cautious when he answered the door. And it was imperative now that she reach Captain Bishop. She headed for the back door.

Her father looked up from his book as she returned to the living room. "Well," he asked, "find any signs of hanky-panky?"

"Someone tried to break in."

He closed the book, forgetting to mark his place. "You're kidding."

"There are pry marks on that window." She pointed to it.

"Oh, my goodness," Malcolm Anderson said, staring at the window. "I was in the middle of one of my afternoon naps when Mrs. Fox called. I guess I slept through the whole thing."

She put her hand on his shoulder, and his eyes slowly swung up to meet hers. "Listen, Daddy, there are people out there who prey on people like you—people who might not be quite as able to defend themselves. It's no secret that you're here alone, and the fact that you're a cop's father wouldn't discourage them at all." She squeezed his shoulder more tightly. "I want you to start being very careful whenever I'm not here. Make sure the doors and windows are locked, and make sure you know who's on the other side before you open the door. In my job, you learn just how much of this stuff goes on— and what kind of animals do it. Will you be extra careful for me? Please."

His eyes remained fixed on hers. "You're really worried about this, aren't you?"

"You're the only father I've got."

"I'll do what you say, daughter." He smiled, then patted her hand. "Now go and see about that roast. I'm starving."

"Okay, but first I've got to call in and get someone out here to investigate this. There may be some nice incriminating fingerprints on that window frame." And she hoped like hell there were, especially if it was the work of the asshole who'd been threatening her.

In the kitchen, she called dispatch. "This is Detective Anderson at two-one-three-eight Maple Grove Drive. I've had an attempted signal five here, and I need the on-call fingerprint man."

"Ten-four," the young woman answered. For some reason, the radio room was staffed almost entirely by women who only spoke in police radio code.

"You might let him know that this is my home ten-twenty."

"Ten-four on that. Shall I send a thirty-four to take a report?" There was no code for report. Thirty-four meant a uniformed officer.

Janice hesitated. She didn't especially want a patrol officer to come, but she could hardly handle the report on an incident at her own home. "Uh, is Poldoski available? I know he's on call."

"Negative. Him and Sergeant Mullins are out on a signal

eight." They were investigating a shooting. Probably a family fight. A typical Friday night in surburia.

"Okay, send a patrol unit."

"Ten-four."

After hanging up, she reached for the phone again to call Captain Bishop, then hesitated. Her father was watching from the living room, and the call to the captain should be made in private.

"I guess you heard," Janice said, joining her father. "A patrol car and a fingerprint specialist are on the way."

"Is all this really necessary?"

Janice nodded. "If we're to have any chance of catching the person who tried to break in to this house with you in it, it is."

"You do what has to be done. Will you have time to eat before Mike gets here?"

She'd forgotten about dinner and Mike. Fortunately, the microwave had been programmed to keep the roast warm. But what about Mike? How could she leave her father here alone tonight?

"Let me clean off some of the dirt I picked up poking around outside," she said. "Then I'll see what I can do about dinner."

After washing her hands in the bathroom, she slipped into her room and called the captain. Again, there was no answer.

Before she could make it back to the kitchen, the doorbell rang. It was the patrol officer, a young man in his early twenties, a rookie.

"You Detective Anderson?" he asked, eyeing her curiously. Although they hadn't met, the look on his face said he knew who she was.

"Yeah," she replied, joining him on the stoop and closing the door. "Come on. I'll show you where the entry was attempted."

As the patrolman followed her around the side of the house, he identified himself as Officer Mercer. He was a pale-skinned young man, tall and thin, and he carried the customary clipboard under his arm. He gave the window a cursory examination, then followed her into the house, took her statement and her father's, noted the address of Mrs. Fox, and left, his eyes clinging to Janice's body just a fraction of a second too long to be inconspicuous.

Within a minute of the patrolman's departure, Franklin Ross showed up with his fingerprint kit. "Janice," he said, standing in the doorway, "I had just cut into a gorgeous hunk of porterhouse steak when the call came." He sighed. "Presumably, my wife and son are finding theirs most enjoyable."

"You on the take, Frank? Cops can't afford porterhouse steak." She stepped outside. "This way to the scene of the crime."

Walking beside her, he said: "Just so you don't get the wrong idea, my brother-in-law owns a small meat market. I get my steaks wholesale—although I don't suppose it matters because I never get to eat them."

At the window, Ross put down his equipment case, withdrew a jar of fingerprint dust and a brush, and set to work. Janice's father, who had rolled his wheelchair up to the window, was observing the operation from inside.

"Just like they do it in mystery novels," he commented, as Ross carefully applied dust to the aluminum sash.

It took the fingerprint man only a few minutes. He held up the square of sticky plastic, looking at it against the white of the building. "It's your week for partials," he said. "Get me a suspect, and there might be enough here for a match, but otherwise . . ." He shrugged.

Janice nodded. If only she did have a suspect.

"Any need to do the inside?" Ross asked.

Janice shook her head. "Doesn't look as though entry was gained."

"Good enough," he said, closing his equipment case.

After Ross had gone back to his now cold steak and Janice had explained to her father what the fingerprint man had found, she made another trip to the bathroom, ostensibly to wash up again, then ducked into the bedroom, where she tried once more to reach Captain Bishop at home. There was still no answer. She put the receiver down slowly, reluctantly, as if there was somehow security in being connected to a phone in her superior's house, even if no one answered it.

"Well," she said, joining her father in the living room, "are you ready to eat?"

"Whenever you are," he replied, glancing up from his book. Thomas Hardy had been replaced by the latest Robert Ludlum thriller, but then he'd always had varied tastes in reading.

As she turned toward the kitchen, he said: "Why don't you let me eat by myself tonight? I'll slice some roast, cook a canned vegetable to go with it, and you can grab a hamburger or something on the way." He glanced at his watch. "Mike will be here any minute."

"Oh, I really don't feel much like a hamburger." Nor would she be going anywhere tonight. She still had to get in touch with Captain Bishop, and she'd decided there was no way she could leave father here alone. The theater and sex with Mike were out for this weekend. She could tell Mike the truth; he'd understand. They'd tell her father . . . something.

"You'd better hurry then," her father said.

"There's plenty of time."

In the kitchen, she dumped a can of green beans into one saucepan and ran water for instant mashed potatoes in another, putting both on the stove.

"If you get a chance sometime this weekend," her father said from the living room, "I'd appreciate it if you'd move some of those things in the kitchen cabinets down to where I can reach them."

"You planning on doing some more of the cooking?"

"Oh, you never know." Which meant he was.

Grabbing a pair of potholders from a drawer, she switched the microwave from warm to off and yanked open the door, reaching inside for the roast. Because the microwave was high, above the regular oven, getting steaming-hot things out of it was tricky even for Janice, who was fairly tall. She had the glass roasting pan out, gripping it with the potholders, before her eyes forced her mind to accept what was really in her hands. She heard herself emit a sound that was part gasp and part shriek, the roasting pan and its hideous contents falling to the kitchen floor.

Five

"*Janice, are you all right?*" *her father called from the living* room. Then he was there, beside her in his wheelchair, and when he saw what was on the floor by her feet, he exclaimed: "Oh, my God!"

Too stunned to speak, Janice simply stared at what she'd just removed from the microwave. There on the floor, amid pieces of the shattered roasting pan, steaming, was her cat, his gray fur untouched by the tiny electromagnetic waves that had passed harmlessly through his flesh only to cook him from within. Then she felt her father's hand on her arm, pulling her away from the sight, and she allowed herself to be led out of the kitchen. In the living room, he steered her to the couch, and she sat down, only vaguely aware that tears were streaming down her cheeks.

Leaning forward in his wheelchair, watching her anxiously, her father waited until she'd had a good cry, then addressed himself to the problem. "It appears someone did get inside this afternoon."

Forcing herself to regain some composure, Janice dried her eyes. The threats, the constant hassles of her job, Mike's new job in Seattle, and now this. An innocent animal horribly murdered for no purpose. And then she realized there was a purpose. To let her know her father was just as vulnerable as Sam had been.

"I have to call Captain Bishop," she said. She went to the bedroom, where her father couldn't overhear her conversation, where she wouldn't have to see what was in the kitchen. Sitting on the bed, she dialed the number, and to her relief, this time someone answered.

"Hello," said a teen-age boy's voice.

"This is Detective Anderson. May I speak to Captain Bishop, please?"

"Sorry, Dad's not here right now."

"Do you know when he'll be back?"

"Not till late Sunday, probably. Him and the deputy chief went fishing together up north."

"Will you tell him I called, please?"

"Sure. Anderson, right?"

"Right."

She replaced the receiver; her hand was shaking. Oh, God, she thought, why of all weekends did he have to choose this one to go fishing? She had to call someone. Technically, the second in command in the division was Sergeant Mullins. Oh, God, she really didn't want to call him. The captain's superior was the deputy chief, whom she didn't know very well and whom she probably shouldn't call. Still, the alternative was Mullins. Damn! What was the matter with her? The kid had just told her that the deputy chief, too, had gone fishing. Christ, she thought, why don't they just hang a sign on the goddamn police station that says *gone fishin'?*

She was reaching for the phone to call Mullins when the doorbell rang, startling her. "Dad, don't answer it! I'll be right there."

She hurriedly got her purse from the dresser and removed her .38. Switching off the safety, she returned the weapon to her bag, then, slinging the purse over her shoulder, went to the door. She parted the curtains of the window nearest the stoop and was relieved to see a tall, dark-haired, and very familiar figure. It was Mike.

When she opened the door, he reached for her to give her the customary kiss, then hesitated, the smile slipping from his face.

"Janice, what's wrong?"

Her eyes were bloodshot from crying, she supposed; no

doubt she looked terrible. "Come into the living room, and I'll tell you all about it."

He followed her, looking worried. "How are you, Mr. Anderson?" he asked politely.

Her father, who was sitting in his wheelchair, facing an empty couch, simply shook his head.

Janice moved into his field of vision and sat down. "Before you sit down, Mike, go look in the kitchen. Then I'll tell you both what I know about it."

This had changed things. The situation had to be considered very serious now, and anyone involved with her could be affected. Both her father and Mike should hear the whole story.

Looking confused, Mike did as she had asked. When he returned from the kitchen, he was pale.

"Who . . . why . . . ?" He sat down in the overstuffed chair, facing her.

"Okay," Janice said, "I've been receiving threats. I haven't told you about it because . . . well, I didn't want to worry you."

"My, God," Mike said, leaning forward, "you should have told me. I—"

She cut him off. "Mike, please. Let me tell this." As she explained what had been happening, her father listened attentively, while Mike listened tensely, almost angrily, as if he wanted to find the culprit and stomp him.

"Why didn't you report this when it first started, honey?" her father asked.

Janice hesitated, then said: "Oh, hell, I'm not sure I know. Maybe it was because I was afraid of being treated as a threatened woman instead of a threatened officer."

"That's ridiculous," Mike said. "If you'd reported it, it might not have ever gotten this far. Your captain could have assigned someone to watch the house, and this sicko would have been caught by now."

"Look," Janice snapped, "I *didn't* report it, so let's just drop it, okay?"

Mike pressed on. "I think you should marry me and come with me to Seattle. You'd be safe there, and you'd be away from that job."

"Mike," Janice said, becoming exasperated with him, "the job is my chosen career—even if it does have more than its share of hassles. And I obviously can't leave until this is over."

"But why? You'd be safe in Seattle."

"Because my leaving won't end someone's desire for revenge—if it is revenge. There are other ways to hurt me than by attacking me personally."

"She means," her father explained, "that she's afraid this person, whoever it is, will come after me." He frowned. "Janice, honey, I don't think you need to worry about me."

"Believe me, Daddy, what happened to poor Sam"—she shuddered—"was designed to show me how easily something could happen to you. Shit, Daddy, he was right here in the house with you, and you didn't even know it." She fixed her eyes on his, driving home the point.

He nodded. "Okay, daughter. You're the expert, and I'll leave myself in your hands."

"Good. Mike—obviously, we're not going anywhere this weekend. I have to stay here."

"I'll stay, too," he replied, meeting her eyes. "Just in case you need me."

She had mixed emotions about Mike's staying. Although one part of her resented his protectiveness, another part felt relieved knowing he'd be here. And it certainly showed he cared. She smiled. "Okay, thanks, Mike. Now I've got to call dispatch and get them to send over Sergeant Mullins."

Again, she made the call from the bedroom.

Mullins and Poldoski arrived about half an hour later, having just finished booking a suspect in the shooting they'd been investigating. As Janice led the two detectives into the living room, Mullins was explaining what had happened.

"Family fight," he said. "The broad wanted to put the kids in a nursery school or a day-care center or some other such thing and get a job. Her old man says no, and they start screaming at each other, and then apparently he starts slapping her around. So, what does she do? She goes and gets a twenty-two automatic and empties the clip at him. Sure as hell wasn't much of a shot. She only hit him twice, and neither one did much damage." He snorted. "Kinda makes you wonder, though." He paused, apparently waiting for someone to ask him what he was wondering about. When no one did, he went on. "Makes you wonder whatever happened to motherhood."

No one said anything. Poldoski looked a little embarrassed. An attractive, dark-haired man in his thirties, he resembled Mike in some respects, but whereas Mike had the all-American-boy sort of good looks, Poldoski's were more rugged, his strong features giving his face a look of incorruptibility.

Janice made the introductions, then sent the two detectives into the kitchen to see the remains of her cat, again taking her seat on the couch.

When the two detectives returned to the living room, Poldoski said: "I examined the cat, Janice, and I thought you might like to know its neck was broken. It was already dead when . . ."

Janice nodded. At least poor Sam hadn't been cooked alive, thank God.

"Okay," Mullins said, sitting down beside Janice on the couch and pulling out a small notebook, "tell me the whole story."

When Janice finished, he flipped the notebook closed and took out a cigar, looking around the room. "Got an ashtray?"

Malcolm Anderson wheeled over to a small table, pulled one from a drawer, and set it on the coffee table in front of Mullins. Neither he nor Janice smoked.

"Thanks," Mullins said, lighting the cigar. "How much of this has been reported?" White smoke filled the air.

"I tried to call Captain Bishop after the incident with the gun this afternoon, but he's gone fishing for the weekend. Patrol took a report on the break-in, but it was put down as an attempted. At that time, there was no reason to believe entry had been gained."

"Before that. When did you first report the threats?"

"I didn't," Janice answered weakly.

Mullins rolled his eyes. "Okay, so this is the initial report." He sighed. "I'll have to get Ross back over here. I bet he'll be delighted."

"I'll call him," Poldoski said, heading for the kitchen.

"Got any idea who's doing this?" Mullins asked around the cigar, which hadn't left his mouth since he'd lit it. A few ashes fell, landing on his potbelly. He brushed them away.

Janice shook her head. "I've got the usual number of enemies any cop does, I guess, but I can't think of any one really good suspect."

"Any threats at the time of arrest?"

"No."

"Anybody sent up for a long time who was protesting like hell how innocent he was—not that they don't all say that?"

Again, Janice shook her head. "Do you want to see the notes and the letters?"

"No point in handling them any more than they have been until they're dusted." He glanced pointedly at her. "Just give the stuff to Ross, and I'll get it from him when he's done."

Returning from the kitchen, Poldoski announced that Ross was on his way. "Do you want any pictures in there?" he asked Mullins.

The sergeant frowned. "Naw. Don't see any need."

"Where can I find a garbage bag?" Poldoski asked Janice.

"Under the sink. Why?"

"I thought it might be a little easier for you if I . . . well, Animal Control's on our way."

"Thank you," Janice said. He returned to the kitchen, and a few moments later, she heard the back door open and close, Poldoski thoughtfully not bringing the bag with its obvious contents through the living room.

Mullins sighed, brushing away more cigar ashes. "Well, I guess we got to go across the street and talk to this Mrs. Fox." Then, to no one in particular, he added: "Sure glad tomorrow's my day off. Taking my boy up to see the Twins play."

"Jesus!" Mike exclaimed. "Here one of your own officers has been threatened, had her house broken into, and you can think about baseball!"

The sergeant took the cigar out of his mouth. "Just calm down now. We know how to handle these things."

"Okay, so what are you going to do about protecting Janice and her father?" Mike demanded.

"What do you want me to do?" He glanced up as Poldoski returned.

"What do you mean, what do *I* want you to do?" Mike asked, his face reddening. "You're the expert. What are *you* going to do?"

Jamming the cigar back into his mouth, Mullins stood up. "Right now, I'm going across the street and talk to an old lady."

"I'm coming with you," Janice said, rising.

Mike, too, was on his feet. "And so am I," he said defiantly.

Janice went to him. "Please, Mike, just calm down. I want you to stay here with my father while the rest of us are across the street."

He hesitated, then sat down again, giving Mullins a smoldering look.

"Incidentally," Poldoski said, joining Janice and Mullins as they headed for the door. "I found the roast. It was in the garbage, under some other stuff."

As the three detectives walked across the street, Mullins flipped his cigar into the gutter. Though early evening, it was still bright daylight outside, and with Minnesota's northerly latitude and daylight-saving time, it would remain that way for a couple of hours yet.

The house in which the two elderly women lived was a relatively nondescript white frame home, as indistinctive as the Andersons' or any of the others on the block. A pudgy woman in her seventies with curly gray hair greeted them at the door, said she was Katherine Fox, and led them into a living room that looked like something from another century. It was ornate throughout, down to and including the gilt frames of the pictures and the oval mirror on the wall, and filled with strange-looking furniture that might have come from an estate sale at a mansion a hundred years ago.

Katherine Fox seemed thrilled to have three police officers here to ask *her* questions. She introduced her roommate, Mildred Dieryck, a tall gray-haired woman who nodded politely to each officer as the introductions were made. She sat in a high-backed wooden rocker, a paperback book in her lap.

"Sit down, sit down," Katherine Fox said excitedly. Janice and Poldoski lowered themselves onto a hard couch with flowered upholstery, and Mullins and Katherine Fox into uncomfortable-looking wooden-legged chairs.

"I haven't been here since the Holtons left," Janice said. "It looks quite different than it did then."

"The furniture was all mine," Katherine Fox said proudly. Mildred rather pointedly gave the room a disapproving look, which Katherine ignored. "Now then, what is it you want to talk to me about? Is it about the prowler I spotted across the street?"

"Tell us what you saw," Mullins said, taking out his notebook.

"Well, I was looking out the window—it was drizzling if that's important—and I thought I saw someone over by the left side of the Anderson's house. So, of course, I called Mr. Anderson to make sure—"

"You *thought* you saw someone?" Mullins interrupted.

"Oh, I *did* see someone. I just caught a glimpse, but I saw him all right."

"Him. It was a man you saw then."

"Well, I think so. Whoever it was was wearing blue jeans and a baseball cap. And had blond hair . . . I think."

"How could you see the hair if the offender was wearing a baseball cap?"

"It was long hair, long enough to stick out from under the cap. You know the way men wear their hair these days. Well, some of them anyway. I'd say this was shorter than shoulder length but still long enough to stick out from under the cap."

"Okay, so the offender was a male Caucasian, is that right?" She nodded.

"What else was he wearing, besides jeans and a cap?"

She frowned. "The top was blue also—or something dark that blended with blue. I'm not sure if it was a shirt or a jacket."

"No raincoat, huh?"

"It wasn't raining that hard," she replied a little defensively.

"Yeah, okay. Any writing on the jacket—if it was a jacket?"

"Really, Sergeant Muggins, I—"

"Mullins."

"Pardon me." The correction seemed to have flustered her somewhat. "What was I saying? Oh, yes. I can assure you, Sergeant. I would have mentioned it if there had been anything on the jacket."

"Okay. How tall was the offender?"

"Not too tall. But not extremely short either. A little below average, I guess."

"Five-seven, five eight?"

She shook her head. "I didn't have the chance to measure him, Sergeant. He was on the slender side, I think. And I'd say he was young, but I'm not sure how young. Older than eighteen but younger than thirty, I guess. I'm sorry, but that's the best I can do. I only caught a glimpse, you know."

"I think you've done very well," Janice said. "Many people

can be face to face with a suspect and not recall as much as you did."

Katherine Fox smiled, pleased with herself.

Mullins scowled, apparently irritated by Janice's interruption. "What about the way the offender moved? Any limp or anything like that? Or a slouch?"

"Not that I noticed in the brief glimpse I had, no."

"Okay. . . ." Mullins flipped through the pages of his notebook. "On Wednesday morning, did you see anyone in the vicinity of the Andersons' mailbox?"

"Not that I recall. Of course, we go grocery shopping on Wednesday mornings. The supermarket over on Welby still gives double stamps on Wednesdays, you see. Not many places give stamps anymore, you know."

"Yeah. Have you noticed any strange cars around the neighborhood lately?"

"Well, only those cars down at the end of the block by the Johanson's house. But most of those belong to teen-age boys, I think. You see, the Johansons have two teen-age daughters, and it seems there's always boys over there. Always different boys. Both parents work, you see, and sometimes I wonder just what—"

"That'll be all, Mrs. Fox." Mullins closed his notebook. "If you think of anything else—or if you see anything else—please call us."

"Oh, I certainly will," she said, smiling and looking important. "Uh, it might help if I knew what to look for. Just what is this all about?"

"Look for strangers in the neighborhood or anything suspicious."

"I see. Specifically around the Anderson house?" she prompted.

"Or anywhere else in the neighborhood. Like somebody parked down the block, watching."

"I'll certainly do my best." Her eyes swung from the sergeant to Janice. "Is everything all right, dear?"

"Just some things we have to look into," Janice replied politely.

"Well, if there's anything I can do to help, you just let me know. And don't worry. I'll keep a close watch on things."

At that, Mildred, who hadn't said a word, chuckled.

When they returned to the Anderson house, Franklin Ross was there, busily dusting the living room window—from the inside this time.

"Find anything?" Mullins asked.

"A few." He turned to face the three officers, who were standing in the middle of the room, watching him. "Ordinarily, I'd have a few choice words about being called back here a second time on a Friday night, but even I've got to admit there are no indications that entry was gained. And believe me, I looked. Failing to check the oven, I think, is forgivable."

"Mighty white of you to forgive us," Mullins said.

Ross grinned. "I certainly thought so."

Mullins lit another cigar.

Twenty minutes later, Ross was finished. He'd found numerous prints around the microwave oven and back door, most of which, he said, would turn out to be Janice's or her father's. He then inked the fingers of Malcolm Anderson and Mike Simpson, explaining that he needed their prints so he could isolate any that shouldn't be there. Janice's, of course, were already on file. After collecting the two warning notes and those of the steamed-open letters that were still on hand—which included the one from Amy—he left, reminding the detectives to call Kline, the other fingerprint man, if anything came up tomorrow. When Mullins and Poldoski left a few moments later, Janice accompanied them to the car, which was parked at the curb.

"We'll have patrol keep an eye on your place," Poldoski said, climbing into the passenger side of the unmarked car.

"Thanks," Janice replied, squatting by his open window. She waited until Mullins had slipped in behind the wheel, then said: "My father needs protection. He's completely alone when I'm not here, and as you can see, he's helpless."

Mullins grunted. "You mean you want a patrol guy—twenty-four hours? Then you'd better find somebody who knows how to reach the captain. *I* sure as hell can't authorize it."

"I've got a better deal for you than that. I'm officially requesting protection for my father. That gets you off the hook on that. Now, I'll be the official protection. All you've got to do is change my status on the call list at dispatch to unavailable, assigned. That way I wouldn't even be called in an emergency."

Mullins thought about that for a moment, then said: "Yeah, okay. Until the captain gets back. Then you'd better work this out with him." The tone of his words added an unspoken footnote: *And he's gonna be pissed at you.* Well, she could deal with that when the time came.

Mullins started the car and drove off. As she headed back toward the house, the door opened, and Mike stepped out, waiting for her on the stoop. She collapsed against him, welcoming the security of his embrace, certain the old woman across the street was watching. She didn't care. She was glad he'd refrained from snapping at Mullins; it would have angered them both, accomplishing nothing.

"I'm so sorry about all this, Janice. And about Sam."

"Poor Sam," she said weakly. "He was a good old cat. He really was." Feeling the tears that wanted to come, she held them back. She'd done enough crying in the past few days.

"Janice, how many guns do you have in the house?"

She stiffened. "Guns? Why?"

"Well, I just thought it might be a good idea if I knew where one was . . . in case . . . well, just in case."

"Mike, let me explain something to you." She pushed herself back, out of his arms. "If I have to fire a weapon in the course of doing my duty, that's one thing. If you go and get trigger-happy, that's another ball of wax entirely."

He gave her his little-boy-hurt look. "I'm just trying to be helpful."

"I know you are, but I've seen what can happen when people with good intentions start playing with guns."

"Janice, I know how to use one. I made marksman in the Army with a forty-five."

"Sure, Mike, fifteen years ago. Trust me, I'm trained to know when to shoot and when not to, and I have to go to the range and qualify every few months. Besides, the only firearm that's ever in the house is my service revolver, and no one is allowed to use that except me. Come on, let's go in. I don't like leaving my father alone."

"Wait," he said, grabbing her arm. "What about the sleeping arrangements?"

"You can sleep with me." She smiled. "After all, I just put clean linen on Amy's bed, and I don't want to change it." And she really didn't want to sleep alone, not tonight.

"But your father...."

"What do you suppose he thinks we do on all those weekends we spend together?"

Mike shrugged. "Well, I certainly won't argue the point."

As they stepped into the house, Janice's mind was on Amy's visit. Her sister, she thought gloomily, couldn't have chosen a worse time to come. But then she realized that Amy's being here would have its bright side as well—and not just that Janice would be glad to see her sister. There would be someone in the house with her father.

In room eighteen at the Falls Motel on Pennington Boulevard, a solitary figure sat on the bed, thinking. It had been foolish to risk the incident with the gun this afternoon. Had it not been for the dog that had forced Janice to stop...

No harm done, in any case. And Janice would have been excited, nervous when she arrived home. Just the right condition for her to be in when she discovered the surprise awaiting her in the microwave oven. It would have been fantastic to have been there, to have seen her reaction.

And another minor detail had been taken care of. The funny-money coins had been swept down a storm drain before the stolen orange Pinto had been abandoned miles away in another suburb. How nice it had been of the Pinto's owner to leave the keys in the ignition. And just the kind of car that had been needed. A nice, bright, noticeable one.

For a day or two now, Janice would be left in peace, just long enough for her to gain a false sense of security. Then, with one quick, devastating stroke, the main event would begin.

Six

For Janice, Saturday morning passed slowly, torturously. They
sat in the living room, Janice and Mike watching television,
Malcolm Anderson reading, all of them hoping nothing further
would happen, yet knowing it was all too likely that something
might. Hanging in the air like a cloud of Mullins' cigar smoke,
the forboding in the room was almost tangible.

Early that afternoon, Franklin Ross called. Janice took the
call in the kitchen.

"I've gone over the prints I got at your place last night,"
he said, "and I thought I'd let you know what I found. Most
of them were either yours or your father's, but I did come up
with a few I can't identify. Those were on the letters and, of
course, the two partials I found outside the window. It's going
to be tough to sort them out. There's your sister, whose prints
would be on her letter, employees at the companies the bills
came from, and the postman, to name just a few possibilities.
I can tell you this though; none of those other prints appear to
match the partials. Oh, and the only prints on the threatening
notes were yours."

Janice winced. "What you're saying is there's a good chance
we've got no prints of the suspect except the partials."

"That's what I'm saying."

"Okay. Thanks for calling, Frank. I thought you were off
today."

"I am." He hung up without explaining. Despite his constant complaining when they worked together, Frank was clearly on her side. Poldoski, too, was on her side. But she wondered whether anyone else in the Dakota Falls Police Department was. Many of them, she was certain, would be quite happy to see her assigned as a meter maid.

The afternoon passed as the morning had, stretched into the evening and then the night. Last night, Janice had lain awake, alert, listening, so she could protect her father. Mike, she knew, had done the same, wanting to protect her.

As she and Mike climbed into bed, she knew tonight would be no different. And tomorrow, Amy and Mark arrived.

The occupant of room eighteen at the Falls Motel also lay awake that night, worrying, every little slipup—either real or imagined—a torment. What if one of the funny-money coins had been dropped somewhere, in the orange Pinto, for instance? And what if the merchant patrolman had not died as he should have and had provided a description of his attacker? And the gloves, which were always to be worn, had been twice forgotten. In the alley with the merchant patrolman, and again outside the Andersons' house. They'd been slipped on before climbing in through the window, but how many stray fingerprints might have been left by the uncovered hands that had worked on the screen? At least it had only happened twice. The notes, the mail, the stolen car would not provide the authorities with the fingerprints they needed.

So many chances had been taken, so many. The risk of threatening Janice with a gun at close range, the risk of entering the house while the old man was asleep. Had he awoken, he would have recognized the intruder, and he would have had to die. And that would have ruined the plan because he had not been meant to die, not then.

Though soon. Very soon.

So many months of waiting, hoping for a chance to destroy Janice, always doing what the doctors wanted, earning funny-money coins, and never, never letting the name Janice slip out during therapy sessions. And then the unexpected opportunity when the bus crashed. Fate had granted this one chance to be free of Janice, to be whole.

It was important that Janice be *destroyed*—not merely killed, but demolished. Oh, no, just slaying Janice was not nearly enough, for you could not eradicate the powerful thing she had become just by killing it. First, she had to be brought to her knees, toppled, crushed. Only then could she be slain, her death the final act, the culmination of the soon-to-begin main event.

Hers would be the last of several deaths and, if a way could be devised to accomplish it, the most horrible.

It was in the hospital that the knowledge had come, the realization that destroying Janice was the only way to be whole. Janice, beautiful, popular Janice who took it all, leaving nothing for others. Only when Janice was destroyed would the hell finally end.

If only the plan didn't involve so many risks, so many chances of a fatal slipup. But then, even if mistakes had been made, it would take the authorities time to figure things out, more time than they had. Although the occupant of room eighteen found that thought comforting, the night was too charged with anticipation to allow for sleep.

The sun was up when Janice rolled over, slipping her arms around Mike.

"Hi," she whispered.

"Hi," he answered, working his arms around her.

It felt good having him here, his body beside hers. Neither their mood nor the proximity of her father had encouraged them to make love, but now, holding each other, their bodies touching, she was becoming aroused. A moment later, she realized the arousal was mutual because she felt him stiffening against her leg.

"None of that," she cautioned. "My father."

"He knows we're in here together," Mike protested.

"True. But I don't care to have him awakened by grunts, groans, and squeaking bedsprings."

Mike said nothing, although the stiff thing against her leg gave no indication of his losing interest.

"Amy arrives today," she said, hoping to get his mind off sex.

"Ummmm."

"Is that all you can say?"

"Um-hum." A hand worked its way between them and found a breast.

She pushed the hand away. "Stop it."

He sighed. "Okay. You were saying."

"We have to go to the airport this afternoon to pick up Amy and Mark."

"And?"

"I'd like you to stay here and keep an eye on the house."

"Stay here? I'm not interested in protecting the house. It's you I'm worried about." The thing against her leg was shrinking.

"And what surprises might be here waiting for us if we leave the place unattended?"

"Well, get the cops to watch it. Jesus, you're one of them. Don't they protect their own?"

"There are things you don't understand about the way police departments work. In any case, I can protect my father, but I don't want to leave the house unattended. I'd feel a lot safer with you here."

"It's comforting to know you'd feel safer with me here than with you."

"Please, Mike."

He sighed. "Okay, I'll do it."

Neither spoke for a few moments; then Mike broke the silence. "Will you marry me and run away to the West Coast with me? If you will, I promise to make love to you three times each weekday and continuously all weekend." A hand began gently stroking her leg.

"I might."

"Do you want a sample?" The hard lump was back, pressing into her leg again. And she did want a sample. Badly. When the hand found her breast once more, she let it stay there. Close your ears, Daddy, she thought.

Janice, her father, and Mike were finishing a late Sunday breakfast in the kitchen when the phone rang. Janice, being closest to it, answered it.

"Janice, Poldoski. Things okay over there?"

"No further problems."

"Good. Listen, I'm just calling to let you know that we've

found the orange Pinto. It's gotta to be the right one. Christ, there couldn't be two cars that color. Anyway, it's on the hot sheet. Stolen here Friday afternoon. Turned up in a shopping center parking lot in Edina. Kline's on his way over there now to dust it."

"Where was it when it was stolen?" Janice asked.

"Uh, let's see. . . ." She could hear him rustling papers. "Okay, here it is. On Pennington, seventy-two hundred block. I think that would put it a block or two east of the mortuary."

"That's only a few blocks from here." Janice pointed out.

"Yeah, but what does that mean? And why was the car abandoned clear over in Edina?"

"You going to check out the places in that block to see if anyone got a look at whoever took the car?"

"That's up to the captain. There's nothing we can do about it today, in any case. It's all businesses in that area, and most of them would be closed on Sunday."

After ending the conversation, Janice told her father and Mike what Poldoski had reported.

Fifteen minutes before Amy's flight was due to arrive, Janice parked her car in the lot at the Minneapolis-St. Paul International Airport, pulled her father's collapsible wheelchair from the trunk, helped him into it, then wheeled him into the terminal.

Flashing her badge, she passed through the metal detector without being searched, although the device unfalteringly sounded its high-pitched warning when it registered the .38 in her purse.

Amy's plane, the flight-information screens said, was five minutes late. While driving to the airport, Janice had kept a close watch on the rearview mirror; as far as she could tell, she had not been followed. Now, sitting outside the gate at which the jet carrying Amy and Mark would arrive, her father beside her in his wheelchair, she studied the faces around her, looking for eyes that darted away before they met hers, for someone who seemed vaguely out of place, perhaps trying too hard to blend in with those waiting to greet incoming passengers, possibly staring too intently at something that should not have been that interesting. And as she scanned the faces, she also looked for one that might trigger a memory, a recollection of something seemingly inconsequential, forgotten. Something that had not faded from the memory of her tormentor. For she realized that she and her tormentor were different individuals, and one person's easily forgotten episode could be another's private hell.

Suddenly, she was staring into a pair of intense brown eyes that immediately jerked away, breaking the contact. It was a dark-haired young man in a rumpled suit who stood about ten feet away. She'd spotted him earlier sizing up the more attractive women. His eyes had not been threatening, though; rather, they seemed to ask: *Are you available? Would you like to be picked up?* She hoped the look she'd given him in return had answered his question. Although it seemed unlikely he was her tormentor, she'd keep an eye on him just in case.

Continuing to observe the people at the gate, she spotted no one who seemed familiar, threatening, or out of place.

Amy and Mark were among the first off the plane. Spotting his aunt and grandfather, the five-year-old scampered around the other arriving passengers and flung himself at Janice, who had stood to get a better view of the people emerging from the jetway.

"Hi, Aunt Janice!" he squealed happily. Then, before she could respond, he practically bounced off her legs and was hugging his grandfather. Then Amy was there, and still more greetings were exchanged.

Like Janice, Amy was slim, blond, and very fair-skinned. Unlike Janice, she was quite fond of cosmetics—lips red, eyes shadowed, so on—and she wore expensive, usually eye-catching clothes. At the moment, she was dressed in red and black, the skirt short enough to show off her long, shapely legs, the blouse's V neckline just barely dipping into the space between her tiny breasts. On Janice, that spot would have been a cleavage; on Amy, it was a space. Other than Janice's being half an inch taller, breast size was the main physical difference between them.

Mark had the Anderson ski-jump nose, but beyond that he'd apparently acquired most of his looks from his father. Dark-haired and tanned—a feat of which no sun-sensitive Anderson was capable—he was on the stocky side and had brown eyes. Except for noses, Janice decided, Andersons must be made up almost entirely of recessive genes.

The greetings over, they headed for the luggage area. Janice noticed that the young man who'd been staring at her earlier was ahead of them, accompanied by a plump, middle-aged woman who appeared to be his mother. She was chattering continuously and waving her arms, while the young man silently nodded.

Mark talked about the plane ride, Amy about life in California. The jet had gone so high, so fast, was so powerful, made such neat noises. California was *the* place, where all the latest things were happening, where Amy had received three marriage proposals, all of which she'd turned down because now that she no longer needed a man to support her she wasn't sure she needed one at all on a permanent basis. Living with another person, after all, did have its inconveniences.

And so it went. All the way to Dakota Falls.

Mike greeted them in the driveway and offered himself as the official porter for the luggage. Suddenly, Janice realized the grass had been cut, the jungle transformed once more into a lawn. Mike had done it while they were gone.

She helped her father into the folding wheelchair, and the two of them joined the others at the trunk, where Mike was unloading bags.

"Are you a cop, too?" Mark asked him. "Do you have a gun?"

Janice intervened. "Let me make the introductions. This is my friend Mike Simpson, and he works for an insurance company by the way."

Mark looked disappointed, and Mike said: "Actually, I'm her friend and potential fiancé." He grinned.

"In any case," Janice continued, "this is my sister Amy Withers and her son Mark."

"We both have names beginning with *M*," Mark pointed out to Mike. "Are you a . . ." He hesitated, looking for the right term. "Are you an insurance investigator?" he asked finally.

"No," Mike said. "I'm in sales."

"Oh." He turned to Janice. "You shoot any crooks lately?"

"I'm sorry, Mark. I've never shot one. Do you still like me?"

He looked worried. "Oh sure, I still like you. It would just be neat if you had, that's all."

Neat for whom? Janice wondered.

"Mike," Malcolm Anderson said, "if you'll put a suitcase in my lap, I'll carry it inside." Mike obliged him with a small one.

"I'll carry mine," Mark said. He identified it, and Mike gave it to him.

Once the luggage was inside, Mike went back out, put the car in the garage, and locked the door. If he was trying to become indispensable, Janice decided, he was doing a good job of it.

They settled in the living room, Janice and Mike on the couch, Amy in a chair, Mark on the floor.

"Thanks for doing the lawn," Janice whispered to Mike.

He shrugged. And if he'd asked her at that moment whether she'd go to Seattle with him, she wouldn't have hesitated to say yes. But at that moment, he didn't ask.

"Since I got here," Amy said, "I've been telling you all about what *I've* been doing. Now it's your turn. What have you been doing? How are things at the police department, Janice? Have you made lieutenant yet—or colonel or whatever?"

"We do have some things to tell you," Janice said cautiously. "But they'll have to keep for a while." She glanced pointedly at Mark, who was lying on the floor, staring at the blank TV screen, kicking his heels together.

Amy nodded. "Mark, you want to go out and play in the yard?"

Almost instantly, the boy was on his feet, headed for the door. Janice and Mike exchanged nervous glances.

"Hey, Mark," Malcolm Anderson called, "don't leave the yard, okay?"

"Okay." The door slammed, and he was gone.

Janice's father rolled over to the window, where he could keep an eye on things. "He'll be all right," he said.

"It would be a good idea if you kept a pretty close watch on him, Amy," Janice said. She realized now that she should have called Amy and had her cancel her visit. What if it had been Mark rather than Sam? She shuddered.

Her sister looked puzzled. "What's going on here?"

Janice took a deep breath and plunged in.

Mark poked around awhile in the front yard, finding nothing interesting. Just grass and a tree with no swing on it. Every so often, he'd look toward the house and see Granddad watching him from the window.

Mommy had said it was sad that Grandpa was in a wheelchair, but he didn't seem sad. It would be fun to roll around in a chair like that. You could pretend it was a car. Vroom! Beep, beep! Screech!

But you couldn't go outside and play very well. Maybe that's why Grandpa was watching him. Because he wanted to come outside and play, but he couldn't. That part was kinda sad.

He lay down on the grass and began rolling. Dizzy time! As soon as he was sure he'd rolled over enough times, he stopped and stared at the house, which was spinning and seemed upside down. But then the house was soon rightside up again, and dizzy time was over.

Bored, he wandered, following the magic zigzag course that grown-ups knew nothing about, toward the side of the house, where he found a hedge high enough to be the wall of a fort. A magic hedge if ever he'd seen one. Or maybe it wasn't a hedge at all but a wall of cordonite, the strongest thing in the universe. Maybe it was disguised as a hedge so nobody would know it was a cordonite wall.

Oh, oh, here comes a missile. Sploooom! It hits the wall and does nothing. Now for some missiles of our own. No, laser guns. Suddenly, Mark hit the ground, rolling under a bush, debris falling all around him. Oh, no! The enemy had a new secret weapon that was stronger than cordonite!

The only thing to do was to use the new secret intensifier that made the laser guns superpowerful. It was dangerous to use, but . . . but what was this?

Reaching for the intensifier, he had grabbed a round plastic thing from the dried leaves beneath the bush. It was red, had the number ten on one side, some writing on the back:

ELK RIDGE STATE HOSPITAL

He'd learned to read, a little, but he'd never seen any of these words before. Oh, oh, it's a missing part for the intensifier. Better get it back where it belongs quick. Pocketing his find, he dashed off for the back yard, the only one who could save the universe from the evil Kruptors.

Malcolm Anderson rolled back from the side window and aimed his wheelchair toward the kitchen, shaking his head.

"What's he doing?" Amy asked worriedly.

"He's okay. Just dug up an old poker chip from under the lilac bush, put it in his pocket, and he's headed for the back yard. And I'm headed for another window, so I can keep an eye on him." He disappeared into the kitchen.

"All this is just terrible," Amy said. "And to think that someone would do something like that to your poor cat."

"I think that things are under control now," Mike put in reassuringly. "The police are investigating it, and there's a little old lady across the street who watches the place like a hawk."

Amy fidgeted. "Do you think this . . . this madman might attack Mark or me?"

"It's just a good idea to be cautious," Janice said. "All we know is that someone has been putting a great deal of effort into tormenting me. We don't know who or why. I'm sorry I didn't tell you about this before you got here, but it all happened within the last few days, and I didn't know just how serious it was until the day before yesterday."

"And nothing's happened since then?"

"Nothing. I hope it's over." If she could only truly believe it was. But she was still unable to shake the feeling that all this fit into some elaborate plan, an insane scheme that was as yet incomplete.

Amy did not look reassured.

"Hey," Mike said, "there's no reason to let some sicko mess up Amy's visit. Let's forget about him, what do you say?"

Amy forced a smile. "You're right. Let me tell you about this new group I joined. It's called CLS, and it operates on the theory that your mind gets contaminated by certain thoughts and experiences, so it needs to be cleansed, purified. In a way, it's like draining the old, dirty oil from a car, except in this case, you drain the old, contaminating thoughts from your mind." As she told her captive audience in detail about the wonders of CLS, the worry drained from her face.

No longer having to fulfill the obligations of a successful

man's wife, and well off financially, Amy had become fad happy. And Janice couldn't help but wonder whether it was a defense against boredom. Despite the big house with the view of the ocean and the special school for Mark and the rest of it, Janice would never trade places with her sister.

Amy finally wound down, and Janice decided to attempt changing the subject. "You remember those Saturday mornings at the kiddie shows at the Minnehaha Theater? Did I ever tell you that's where I park, where the theater used to be?"

Amy shook her head. "But I certainly remember the Saturday mornings. Let's see, there were the two of us, Becky Styles, Sue Grindy, Lora somebody-or-another—"

"Lindgren," said Janice.

"Right, Lindgren. And who was that boy that used to sit behind us and pester us all the time?"

"Bruce Bunning." Janice laughed. "When I think about him, I want to go *yuk!* just like I did when I was a kid."

"Whatever happened to him?"

"Who knows? Sue Grindy now weighs about two hundred and fifty pounds, and she's some kind of a nurse supervisor at a hospital in St. Paul. Becky, the last I heard, was on her third husband and about ready for a trip to the sanatorium to dry herself out. Lora I lost all track of years ago. She was kind of weird, wasn't she? Always so quiet and sort of nervous. And she was so skinny."

"She wasn't really our friend," Amy said. "She was just always there. Made it a point to be with us if we wanted her to be or not. Anyway, she wasn't nearly as weird as Bruce Bunning. That kid used to carry knives, long ones, and his favorite pastime, as I recall, was frying ants with a magnifying glass. I'm sure he pulled the wings off flies, too. And he never went to the show without making it a point to sit behind us."

"He had a thing for you, Amy."

"His thing you can keep." She giggled.

They went on reminiscing: Amy as head cheerleader, both sisters among the most sought-after girls in school, the boys they rejected, the boys who rejected them—although there weren't many of those—the heartaches, the learning, the growing, and finally the separating, each having become a unique individual, different from the other.

The conversation came to an abrupt halt when Mark dashed

in, holding an enormous fuzzy caterpillar, which he tried to present to Amy. "Look at the big worm I found, Mamma!"

Amy, who'd always been frightened by bugs of any sort, blanched. Janice told him to take his worm back outside and to leave in the yard any other creatures he might find out there.

A few hours later, Janice and her sister were in the kitchen, preparing dinner. Amy had long since lost her teen-age interest in cooking. She said she was thinking about hiring a house-keeper to take over that duty. She was happily describing the better restaurants in the Los Angeles area when the phone rang. It was Captain Bishop, back from his fishing trip, and he wanted to see Janice in his office immediately.

Mike was more insistent this time. "I'm going with you, Janice," he said flatly.

He had accompanied her from the house and opened the garage door for her, which had jammed even more stubbornly for him than it usually did for Janice. They stood beside her car, its driver's side door open.

"Please, Mike, stay here and look after Daddy and Mark and Amy. Besides, you can hardly accompany me into Captain Bishop's office."

"No, but I can wait for you outside. It'll be getting dark by the time you get back."

"I can take care of myself, Mike. It's them I'm worried about." She nodded in the direction of the house.

"It's you I'm worried about."

"Dammit, Mike, I'm trained to handle violent situations. If something happened and you were with me, you'd be in the way. My first concern would have to be your safety because my principal obligation—above and beyond anything else—is to protect the citizens of this community. I couldn't do anything until I got you out of danger."

For a moment, he stared at her, a puzzled expression on his face. "You win," he said finally. "Back the car out and I'll close the door."

Christ, she thought, as she pulled into the street, why does the male ego have to be so damn fragile?

"Sit down," Captain Bishop said, closing the door to his office. Still in his khaki fishing clothes, he had a weekend's growth of whiskers on his face. He looked tired.

"Okay," he said, sitting down behind his desk, "let's hear it. From the beginning."

After she'd told him the whole story, he asked the inevitable question: "Why didn't you report it before things got out of hand?"

"I tried, Captain. I came in here the morning after I discovered my mail had been opened, and you threw a report at me and ran out the door."

"The matter was rather urgent as I recall."

"So urgent that you ran right past me, looking for an officer to go with you." What the hell, he'd always tried to put her on the defensive.

"Who I did or did not take with me is not an issue here, Miss Anderson. At issue is why you failed to report the threats. On that particular morning, I was back here within half an hour. You had the rest of the day to tell me about it. Why didn't you?"

He was staring at her, his eyes hard. She met his gaze and held it. "Look, I fucked up, all right? I can't offer you an explanation you'd understand, but I know now it was a dumb thing to do, and I'll never do anything like it again."

He was silent a moment, his eyes still locked on hers; then he said: "Good enough. The matter's closed."

"Thank you, Captain."

"I am going to tell you one thing though, something you should already know. In a police department, any police department, cops may fight like hell among themselves, but that's strictly an internal thing, a family matter so to speak. And anytime anyone outside the family threatens one of its members, we immediately forget our little quarrels and start sticking together. Understood?"

"Understood."

"Do you think you need protection?"

"I don't, but my family does. My father, as you know, is confined to a wheelchair. Ordinarily, he's alone all day, but at the moment, my sister and her five-year-old son are visiting. At first, I thought their being here would be good. Safety in numbers, I suppose. But now I'm not so sure."

"More potential victims?"

"Yes, sir. Something like that."

"I'll arrnage a watch on your house, starting early tomorrow morning before you leave for work. Poldoski's the detective in charge of the case. I've pulled Mullins off. First thing tomorrow, I want you to start going through all the records of your past cases, looking for anything that might give us a lead. If anyone looks like even the remotest possibility, pull the prints and send them over to Ross for comparison with the partials he got from your window." He stood up. "I'm going home and try to make up for all the sleep I didn't get this weekend. Remember what I told you. Nobody messes around with a member of the family and gets away with it."

"Yes, sir."

That night, the occupant of room eighteen at the Falls Motel sat on the edge of the bed, the items that would be needed arranged on the bedspread. The merchant patrolman's revolver, two throwaway syringes containing a powerful knockout drug— these had been removed from the pocket of one of the orderlies accompanying the patients on the bus—a flexible nail file, scarves of various colors, a roll of white clothesline, a stick-on blond moustache.

Everything was ready for tomorrow.

Seven

Janice spent the morning at her desk, going over a computer printout summarizing her past cases. Hers was the kind of job in which anytime the phone rang you could be sent out on something, and whenever that happened, you got your name in the official records—as either investigating or assisting officer—and the computer had dutifully typed out all this information on a stack of folded paper the size of a book manuscript.

Assisting officer on a vandalism—car windows smashed throughout neighborhood, three teen-agers arrested, suspended sentence after plea bargain. Investigating officer on smash-and-grab, no arrests. Assist on a homicide, a rape, a residential burglary. Investigator on a hot check case, a rape, two child abuse cases. The list went on and on.

Leaving the house this morning, she'd spotted Reynolds in an unmarked car partway down the block, and they'd waved. It was a relief, knowing the house would be watched. Mike had complained that it should have been done immediately. Janice had explained that there was really no need to have another officer watch the house while she was there. Mike, damn him, had seemed doubtful. It had taken a great deal of persuasion to convince him to spend last night at his own apartment. Not that she was prudish about such things, but it had seemed inadvisable to have Mike there at night when there were so many people in the house—especially when one of them was a young child.

Mike, as usual, had given in mainly to avoid an argument, and that was the wrong way for two people to reach a decision. Although she didn't want to think about it, not now, she knew it was a facet of their relationship that would have to be dealt with.

Unfolding another layer of computer printout and flipping it back, she sighed. So far, she had found nothing even to hint at the possibility of someone's being upset enough to seek revenge.

The blue van had a raised roof, as if the top portion of another van had been added to it, making it look awkward and top-heavy. On its side in white letters were the words: SERVICES FOR THE HANDICAPPED.

It was coming down the street, a residential street lined with trees and bushes. Concealed by the shrubbery, a solitary figure watched the van approach. It was coming because it had been called for a pickup, an old woman in a wheelchair, a passenger who did not exist.

It stopped about ten feet from the observer's hiding place, the driver, a dark-haired man in his late teens or early twenties, peering out the window, apparently trying to read the numbers on the houses. The observer moved silently along the row of bushes, then slipped out behind the van, quietly yet casually approaching the driver's open window. Unaware of anyone's presence, the young man behind the wheel was still scanning the houses. Apparently having decided this was the right place, he reached toward the ignition key.

He might have felt the prick of the needle as it entered his arm, but if so, that was all. He slumped over the seat, unconscious, the motor still running.

Slipping on a pair of gloves, a solitary figure climbed into the driver's seat, straining to shove the unconscious body out of the way.

Franklin Ross sat at his desk, alone in his small office adjacent to the department's lab.

Before him on the desk was a stack of fingerprint cards, arches, loops, and whorls of the guilty, the innocent, the unidentified. Some were prints obtained simply by applying ink to fingertips; others were latents, lifted from some surface somewhere, their telltale patterns revealed by the painstaking application of dust.

He began arranging the cards in stacks approximating the way he wanted to file them. This, he decided, was a very impersonal way to deal with crime. He rarely saw the perpetrators or the victims. If the parties involved weren't on their way to jail or the hospital or the morgue, or if they hadn't long since fled the scene, they were kept well out of his way while he worked. To Frank Ross, everything boiled down to these small but intricate patterns in black and white. And they told absolutely nothing of the one person to whom they were unique. A given print could as easily belong to a mass murder as to a potential candidate for canonization.

Suddenly, he stopped sorting the cards and picked up two of them, his eyes darting from one to the other. Taking a magnifying glass from the desk drawer, he examined them more closely. Both had two prints, two partials. What appeared to be the same print was on both cards. At least he thought it was a match; you could never be certain with partials.

Again, he moved the glass from card to card. The two remaining prints, which definitely didn't match, could have been made by different fingers of the same hand. A pair of partials wasn't much to go on, but both were clear, covering approximately the same portion of the fingertip. The possibility that the same individual had made both prints was certainly strong enough to be passed along.

He picked up the phone and dialed Janice's number. She would undoubtedly be interested to learn that the person who attacked a merchant patrolman in an alley might well be the same person who had broken into her house and killed her cat.

Stunned by Ross's news, Janice replaced the receiver, now even more worried about her father. True, Ross wasn't absolutely certain, but even the possibility disturbed her, for the attack on Charles Nordin had involved a second and probably unnecessary thrust of the knife, one that had come after the victim was down and dazed, unable to offer any serious resistance to the robber.

The person who had left the notes and killed Sam was sick, deranged. Whoever had attacked Nordin was ruthlessly violent. Combining the two did not make for a pleasant picture, especially when you tossed in the merchant patrolman's stolen gun.

Blond hair and a pair of blue jeans. She tried to picture the slender young man described by Katherine Fox and found it impossible. Who the hell are you? And what the hell do you have against me?

Shoving the printout aside, she looked around the room. Only Watson, who was busily typing reports, was at his desk; everyone else was out. Poldoski was checking the places in the area where the orange Pinto had been stolen. He'd been gone for more than an hour.

She decided to call home, just to make sure things were all right. As she reached for the phone, her eyes caught the clock on the wall. It was 11:15.

There was no answer. She let it keep ringing, twenty, maybe

thirty times. And still there was no answer. Thinking she might have misdialed, hoping she had, she tried again, getting the same result.

Very worried now, she quickly punched another button on her phone, breaking the connection, and dialed the radio room.

"Dispatch," a woman said.

"This is Detective Anderson. One-eighty-seven's on surveillance on Maple Grove Drive." The number was Reynolds' radio code identification. "Tell him no one answers the phone at the ten-twenty he's watching and for him to go inside and make sure everything's all right. Have him call me here at the office right away."

"You want one-eighty-seven to give you a ten-twenty-one from that ten-twenty, is that ten-four?"

"Yes, ten-four." She wanted him to phone her from the house.

Hanging up, she waited. When her phone finally rang, she grabbed it so hurriedly she nearly dropped the receiver.

"Detective Anderson?" It was the woman in dispatch.

"Yes."

"No response from one-eighty-seven."

"Get the nearest patrol unit over there. Have him go in and check. It's two-one-three-eight Maple Grove Drive. Then call one-seventy-two"—Poldoski's number—"and advise him of the situation on Maple Grove Drive: that no one answers the phone and that there's no response from one-eighty-seven. If you don't get him, keep trying."

Grabbing her purse from the desk drawer, she glanced into Captain Bishop's office, saw it was empty, and dashed out of the office, hoping there was a reasonable explanation, fearing there wasn't.

She was on Pennington in her unmarked car when she heard the patrol unit report in.

"Two-Adam to PD."

"Go ahead, two-Adam."

"Be advised there is no one at this ten-twenty. The door is unlocked."

"Any signs of problems there?"

"Negative. Just an empty house."

Oh, God, Janice thought. What could have happened? They

couldn't have just left, not with Daddy in a wheelchair.

"Two-Adam," the woman dispatcher said over the radio, "there's supposed to be a detective unit there, watching that ten-twenty. Any sign of it?"

"Stand by."

A minute later, the patrolman was back on the radio, his voice urgent. "Two-Adam, PD. I found the detective unit. The officer inside appears to be unconscious. Better send rescue and a fifty-five." An ambulance.

Possibilities tumbled frantically through Janice's mind, her brain desperately searching for one that would hold up, that would give her hope.

Switching on the siren, she placed the removable red light on the car's roof, her thoughts a whirling jumble of horrors.

Checking his watch, Detective Ted Reynolds yawned. It was 11:04 A.M. He was bored and suffering the curse of men on surveillance everywhere: the need to go to the bathroom. The thermos of hot coffee his wife had insisted on making for him sat beside him on the seat, untouched. He'd learned early in his short career as a detective that drinking anything on these kinds of jobs was a serious error.

His unmarked white AMC was parked across the street from Janice's home, about two houses away, giving him a clear view of the front and one side of the house. Although someone could presumably sneak up on the place from the rear, he felt the Anderson house was fairly safe with him on watch and so close at hand in the event he was needed. From this vantage point, he could see the telephone wire where it entered the house. It could not be cut without his knowing it, unless someone climbed the pole from which it ran to the house, an act that required a certain amount of expertise and could not be done inconspicuously. One phone call, and the need for assistance would be relayed to him over the radio within seconds.

He'd been parked here when Janice left for work early this morning. She'd waved at him. He liked Janice, and he thought she was a good detective, although that opinion was not shared by everyone in the department. To those—and there were many of them—who felt women didn't belong in a police force, except as secretaries, radio operators, or meter maids, Janice was an anathema, the first of the department's handful of female officers to make detective. They made it rough for her sometimes.

The trouble was she was so damned noticeable. Plain Janes, like most of the women in the patrol division, probably got by with fewer problems. But Janice... well, to quote Sergeant Mullins, she was stacked. And in a male-dominated, macho organization like a police department...

Hearing a vehicle approaching from behind him, he shifted his eyes to the rearview mirror, where he saw an unusually tall blue van coming toward him. He'd seen the blue vans on other occasions; they were used for picking up people in wheelchairs and were specially equipped with ramps and things like that. The reason for their unusual height, he presumed, was to give the passengers needed headroom. As the van passed him, he caught a quick glimpse of the driver, a blond man with a moustache. It continued down the block, slowly, as if the driver was looking for a house number. No problem there, Reynolds decided; anyone up to no good would have enough sense not to use such a unique and easily recognized vehicle.

A few moments later, he was beginning to have vague misgivings about the blue van. It was, after all, used for picking up people in wheelchairs, people like Janice's father. And the driver had been blond, as had the prowler spotted at the Andersons' house. He reached for the microphone hanging from the dash; it wouldn't hurt to make sure the van had legitimate business in the neighborhood.

He hesitated, hearing another vehicle behind him. It was the van again, coming faster this time, more purposefully. Suddenly, it braked and pulled in behind him. In the mirror, Reynolds could see the driver's door open, but not the driver himself. Replacing the microphone, the young detective freed both his hands, one of which he rested near his shoulder holster.

Then a checked shirt filled his window, and a hand thrust a note at him. When he didn't take it, the hand waved the folded paper up and down urgently. Accepting it cautiously, he read: *I'm a mute and can't talk. Could you please tell me how to get to Maple Grove Court?*

Reynolds relaxed a little. It stood to reason the handicapped would be hired to drive such a vehicle. But he'd never heard of Maple Grove Court.

"I'm sorry," he said handing the note back. "This is Maple Grove Drive, but I've never heard of a court. You might try—"

His brain registered that something had just been jabbed into his arm, and something somewhere in his head was trying to sound an alert, a warning. His hand dutifully moved toward his shoulder holster, finding nothing, as if he'd reached into a vacuum, and then all of him was following the arm, plunging downward, into nothingness.

Mark stood in front of the dresser in the room he and his mother were using while they visited Grandpa and Aunt Janice. In his hand were the goodies he'd found around the house and yard: a stick that would make a neat slingshot, a spring, a large nail, and the big plastic coin he'd found under the bush. These were important things that had to be well hidden. So the evil Kruptors couldn't find them and destroy the universe.

The nail and spring he put under his clothes in the bottom drawer of the dresser. The Y-shaped stick he decided to keep out until he had a chance to ask Grandpa for a big rubber band. But he needed a special place for the red disk because that was the secret part for the intensifier that would fix the laser guns so the good guys could beat the Kruptors and save the universe.

Then he had it. He went to the closet and took out his small brown suitcase. Opening it, he found the torn piece of material at its bottom and carefully slipped the intensifier into the lining. Except it showed. You could see there was something under there. Well, he knew what to do about that. Dragging the bag over in front of the dresser, he began piling clothes in the suitcase.

He hesitated. Was this going to make Mommy mad? She'd told him to pack the suitcase before they left California. He was just early this time. Mommy might even be proud. You never knew for sure about Mommy.

He stopped when he heard the doorbell ring. Then he heard Mommy say: "Daddy, did you call for—hey! What are you doing?"

This sounded interesting. Abandoning his packing and his slingshot stick, he hurried into the living room to see what was happening. He found a stranger in the room with Mommy and Grandpa. Mommy was standing there, looking funny. Her face was all white. And Grandpa looked funny, too. And the stranger had a gun!

Mark's mind had trouble with this for a moment. People on TV had guns, not real people. Kids had guns, play guns, but grown-ups didn't use them. Then the realness of the situation, the danger here, dawned on him, and he dashed across the room to his mother.

"Okay," the stranger said, pointing the gun at Grandpa, "you do exactly as I tell you, or I shoot him. And remember, he can't get away. If you run or scream, you'll be killing him." He was a man with a moustache, kinda skinny, and his voice was funny somehow.

Mark's mother clutched him to her tightly. "W-what about about the boy?"

"He goes, too."

"Look," Grandpa said, "you don't need all of us. Why risk it with the others? Just take me. There's no danger in that."

"I'm taking all of you." He looked at Mommy. "Get him into the other wheelchair, the folding one. I know you've got one. I saw it when I was here the other day."

Mark's mother was gripping him so tightly it hurt. He could feel her body shaking. "Don't hurt us," she whimpered. "Please. We've done nothing to you."

"Move!" the stranger screamed. "Or I'll shoot the kid now!" Suddenly, the gun was pointing right at Mark.

"Do it, Amy," Grandpa said softly. "We've got no choice. The other chair's in the closet."

Mommy got it and helped Grandpa into it.

"Let's go," the man ordered.

Then the stranger was behind the wheelchair, pushing Grandpa toward the door, and Mommy was leading Mark by the hand. Suddenly, the phone rang, but nobody answered it. Though confused and frightened, Mark instantly realized this was a way to get help. There would already to someone on the other end. All he'd have to do would be to pick up the receiver and say it: help. They were almost to the door. Mommy was crying.

Mark did it. Breaking from his mother's grasp, he dashed toward the kitchen, the ringing phone on the wall getting closer and closer, his hand outstretched, reaching for it. Behind him he heard a shout and the word kill, and then he was standing below the phone, disappointment flooding through his small body. He wasn't tall enough to reach it.

Suddenly, his mother was there, scooping him up off the floor, carrying him back into the living room, sobbing: "Don't hurt him. He's just a little boy. He didn't know what he was doing."

Mark saw that the stranger was pointing the gun at Grandpa's head. He'd done his best, but it really didn't matter anymore. Tears filled his eyes, and he began to cry. In the kitchen, the phone was still ringing.

For Mark, the rest was a blur. His mother leading him out the door, then waiting for the stranger to roll Grandfather down the wooden ramp that took up one side of the steps. A moment later, they were in a truck, watching as Grandpa was rolled up another ramp and inside with them, the gun having been stuck in the stranger's belt, hidden so nobody could see it. The door slammed closed, and he and Mommy sat down on the floor, and they were moving, going somewhere.

Granddad looked sad. Mommy started crying again, and so did he.

Katherine Fox was perched in her usual spot by the window. She'd been there since the van had pulled up, and now she observed as the driver wheeled Mr. Anderson out of the house, accompanied by his eldest daughter and her son, who were visiting. It was good to see Mr. Anderson getting out of the house. He'd been cooped up there ever since his accident.

The blue van, she knew, was owned by a charitable organization. If you were confined to a wheelchair, all you had to do was call, and one of the special trucks would come and pick you up, taking you anywhere in town you wanted to go. It was a wonderful thing, she thought, that someone had cared enough to start such a program.

It seemed Mr. Anderson was going out to enjoy himself with his daughter and grandson. Except they didn't look very happy about it. She wondered why. An argument? Some bad news arriving just before they left? Strange they should all seem so distraught when they were going on an outing. Could it be something sad they were doing? Going to a funeral perhaps? No, they weren't dressed for it. She hoped there hadn't been any more trouble over there. As yet, she had been unable to find out just what that trouble had been, which was frustrating. None of the neighbors she'd spoken to had known a thing.

They were all in the van now, and the driver climbed in behind the wheel. A slight young man with blond hair and a moustache, he looked vaguely familiar. No, she decided, she'd never seen him before.

The van pulled away.

Ron Poldoski was just leaving a small shop that made picture frames when he saw Janice speed by on Pennington Boulevard, going code—using red light and siren. The framing shop had been the last place to check in his effort to locate someone who had seen the orange Pinto stolen Friday. No one had.

He hurried to his unmarked car, which was parked in front of a pet store partway down the block. Starting the engine, he grabbed the two-way-radio microphone.

"One-seventy-two, PD."

"Go ahead one-seventy-two. Be advised I have traffic for you."

"Give me the traffic."

"Concerning Maple Grove Drive, that ten-twenty was found to be vacant, and rescue and a fifty-five are en route for Detective Reynolds."

"Ten-four, PD. I'm en route."

Oh, Jesus, he thought, pulling away from the curb. What the hell could have happened?

Janice brought her car to a stop outside the house and rushed inside, frantically going from room to room, to her relief finding no overturned furniture or telltale red stains on the floor. There had not been a struggle. In Amy's room, she discovered Mark's suitcase on the floor, partially and haphazardly stuffed with clothes. Quickly checking the drawers and closets—cautiously, so not to disturb any latent prints—she found that, apparently, no clothes had been taken. So why the partially filled suitcase? In her father's room, it was the same: nothing taken.

Hurrying back to the living room, she stopped in front of

her father's wheelchair. It stood there, looking so empty without him in it, the kind of a picture one might expect to see in a sad movie: the empty chair, collecting dust now, signifying that its occupant was . . . She refused to complete the thought. Why was it here? How was her father taken from the house without it? Then, scanning the room, she noticed the open closet door, the missing collapsible wheelchair.

Oh, God, what had happened? What?

She ran outside, hurrying toward the car containing Ted Reynolds. A blue and white patrol unit was parked in front of it, the uniformed officer standing beside the cruiser, talking into his microphone, its cord stretched out the window. Sirens screaming, first the rescue truck then Poldoski's car appeared at the end of the block and came rushing toward her.

Reynolds was slumped on the front seat of his car, his eyes closed, his expression peaceful, as if he were sleeping soundly. Janice stepped out of the way as the rescue firemen rushed up to tend him. Without regard for any prints on the handles, they opened both doors, leaned inside, and began checking his pulse, his eyes.

After a moment, one of them looked up at Janice and said: "Out cold, but he should be okay. I think he's been drugged."

The other fireman was talking over a portable two-way radio, saying something about Reynolds' vital signs. Poldoski was standing beside her now.

"You hear what he said about Ted?" Janice asked, dazed.

Poldoski nodded. "That's a relief anyway. Have you been inside?"

"No signs of violence. Nothing taken, but the boy's suitcase is partially packed. That might or might not figure into it, I don't know."

"Call for a print man?"

"No."

He took her arm, squeezing it gently. "You okay?"

Janice nodded. She could function. Barely.

The ambulance arrived, siren blaring, and the attendants loaded Reynolds onto a collapsible gurney while Poldoski radioed for a fingerprint specialist. Janice watched all this, feeling strangely detached, as if it weren't really happening, not to her.

* * *

The van had stopped. Its side door slid open. Their abductor pointed the gun at them.

"Out," their captor commanded.

Dazed and afraid, Amy slid the ramp into place and wheeled her father out, Mark followed her.

"Stop."

Amy stopped. Everything seemed a blur. She was carrying out their abductor's commands mechanically, obeying simply because there was nothing else to do. Her mind was numb, no thoughts at all being preferable to considering the horrors of the present reality.

Things seemed to register only as hazy impressions. Dimly, she was aware that they were now in the woods somewhere, that they were in danger, that something about the kidnapper was not as it seemed, not as presented. But just what it was was too dangerous to be dealt with, too apt to break the fragile shell in which she'd encased herself, letting in the terror it kept at bay.

"Get him in the car."

A car? Yes, a car, a green one. The same color as the trees. No wonder she hadn't noticed.

"Hurry up."

Amy complied. Struggling to roll the chair over the rocky ground, she finally succeeded in moving her father the fifteen feet or so to the green car. She opened the door, then helped him to stand erect on his useless legs, turned him, and eased him into the rear seat.

"Amy," he whispered, "are you all right?"

No, no, no. Don't answer. Too dangerous. She closed the door and faced the man with the gun, awaiting further instructions. If she did everything she was told, he might like her. And it was important that he like her. Otherwise . . . no, no, no.

Mark was at her side now, hanging on to her. Sweet little Mark. He'd be good from now on, and the stranger would like him, too.

The man waved the gun at the wheelchair. "Fold it up and put it in the trunk. I'll unlock it."

Again, she did as instructed.

Slamming the lid, he said: "Get in the car. You in front

with me, the kid in back. And remember, your father can't get away. I'll kill him if you try anything."

Oh, no. She wouldn't. Never. He'd see. He'd like her.

As their captor drove them along a narrow road through the woods, a new impression flitted across Amy's consciousness. The man was familiar, someone she had known long ago, someone she and Janice had both known. She pushed the thought away. He wouldn't like her if she had thoughts like that.

Katherine Fox opened the door, looking excited and all but bubbling with curiosity. "Come in, come in," she said. "What happened?"

"You might as well know," Janice said as she and Poldoski stepped inside. "My father, sister, and nephew have apparently been abducted."

"Oh, my!" Katherine Fox exclaimed. "Please come in and sit down."

In the living room, they found Mildred as she'd been before: in her rocker and with a book in her lap.

"Did you hear?" Katherine Fox asked her. "Mr. Anderson and—"

"I heard, Katherine. I heard." She closed the book.

Janice and Poldoski sat on the couch; Katherine Fox, apparently too excited to sit, remained standing.

"Did you see what happened?" Poldoski asked her.

"Oh, yes. I saw it all. Except I didn't know it was an ab— a kidnapping." She told them about a blue van and the young blond man driving it, describing both in detail. "I thought they were going on an outing. It never occurred to me that anything might be wrong."

Poldoski stood up. "May I use your phone?"

"Of course. It's in the hall." To Janice, she said: "Was that important, what I just told you?"

"Very important, Mrs. Fox. He's phoning in that information right now."

She beamed, her chubby body swaying from side to side. Then, apparently thinking better of her reaction, she said: "I'm so sorry to hear about the kidnapping, Janice. I do hope they'll be all right."

"Thank you. Before the van came, did you happen to see anything happen to that white AMC parked down the street?"

Katherine Fox looked puzzled. "What white AMC, dear?"

"Two houses down." She pointed out in which direction. "There's a white car parked there."

"Oh, I see," Katherine Fox said, sounding relieved. "That's in my blind spot."

"Blind spot?"

"Come, I'll show you."

Janice followed her to the window, where the older woman parted the curtains and pointed. From this angle, a large evergreen tree completely obscured Reynolds' car and even the patrol car parked in front of it.

"You see," Katherine Fox said, "I wasn't negligent. You told me to watch, and I watched. But I can't see through trees, dear."

"I didn't mean to imply—"

"No, no, of course you didn't. I'd have had that tree cut down if I could, but it's just across the property line, in Mr. Swensen's yard."

Returning from the hallway, Poldoski said: "They've got a priority locate out on the van, and they're checking with the outfit that owns it right now. Captain wants to see us as soon as we're done here."

Janice nodded.

Eight

"Reynolds is okay," the captain said, looking across his desk at Janice and Poldoski. "He's a little groggy yet, so the doctor sent him home to sleep it off. Should be good as new tomorrow."

After the horrors of the last couple of hours, Janice was glad to hear some good news. "Did he add anything useful to what we already know?" she asked.

Captain Bishop shook his head. "Same description of the truck and driver as the witness across the street gave you. In fact, the woman got a better look at the driver than Reynolds did. Made a slow pass down the block as if he was looking for an address, then came around again and parked behind Reynolds. Got out and handed Reynolds a note saying he was a mute and needed directions. I think we can scratch the mute angle right off the top, though. The note was probably intended to distract Reynolds. As soon as he finished reading it, he got a needle jabbed into his arm."

"Or so the kidnapper wouldn't have to speak," Janice suggested. "Maybe there's something wrong with his voice—a speech impediment or something."

"It's possible," Bishop said thoughtfully. "But I think it's more likely the note was a distraction. Anyway, let's keep the notion of a speech impediment in the backs of our minds."

"Anything on the van?" Poldoski asked.

"Yes. It's missing. Got a call to pick up a woman a few blocks from Janice's place. Mullins has already checked with the people at the address. The call was a fake."

"So the driver could be dead or a hostage," Janice said.

"Or drugged and left somewhere. No sign of the van so far, which probably means it's hidden somewhere—either the same place the hostages are being held or a place where a car was waiting." He paused, rubbing his face. "I think your family's okay, Janice. He wouldn't have gone to all this trouble if he'd simply intended to . . ." He trailed off, the point made, the awful thought left unspoken. "The question is: Just what does he want?"

"Revenge," Poldoski said, shifting his weight in the skimpily padded chair. "Or something like it. There's obviously no ransom involved."

The captain frowned. "For whatever reason, he wants Janice to suffer. So, unless we catch him, I think we'll be hearing from him." His eyes swung from Poldoski to Janice. "He'll probably let you stew awhile; then he'll send you a message, something to let you know they're still okay but whether they stay that way is up to his whim. It seems unlikely he'll demand anything from you, but you never know. We're obviously up against a very determined, very crazy individual."

Forcing herself not to think about what might happen to three people in the hands of a determined lunatic, Janice said: "Before all this happened, I got a call from Ross. He said it's possible a print he got outside the window of my living room matches one we found in the alley where the merchant patrolman was attacked. He's only got partials to work with and only one possible match, so he can't be certain. Also, the victim, Nordin, was unable to describe his attacker."

The captain absorbed that, then said: "Yeah, but Ross is good. If he thought it was important enough to mention it to you, then there's a damn good chance the same person was in both places. What does it tell us?"

"Nordin was apparently left for dead," Janice answered. "It tells us that the man who did this is quite capable of killing. It also tells that the gun that was pointed at me was quite likely Nordin's."

"And something else," Poldoski put in, leaning forward. "It's another event that happened not too far from the Anderson house. The spot where the orange Pinto was stolen. The address where the van was sent on the fake call. Now the attack on the merchant patrolman. Everything within a few blocks of Janice's house."

"Hmmm." Bishop rubbed his chin. "So we could be looking for someone living in that area. Or at least staying in that area."

"But not the typical middle-class citizen you'd expect to find in that neighborhood," Poldoski added. "Why would one of them have to roll a merchant patrol guy for eighty bucks and a handgun?"

"Someone who's out of work?" Janice suggested. "Maybe losing his job is what set him off."

The captain sighed. "We're just guessing. Let's start with what we know for sure and go with that. The hunches and guesswork can keep until we've used up the facts. Put the description into the computer and see what you get back. Janice, keep going through your past cases. Pull the prints of anyone matching the description and anyone who's ever been involved in a mugging even if he doesn't match the description. Have

Ross compare them with the partials."

Janice nodded.

"There's one thing we haven't mentioned," Poldoski said. "The knockout drug. What does that tell us?"

"That whoever pulled this off was prepared," Captain Bishop replied. "And that he had access to the drug, although I'm not sure how much that helps us at this stage. Drugs like that are used for subduing animals as well as people. Tranquilizer darts, for example. Zoos, veterinarians . . . lots of places would have them. Hell, for all I know, you can walk in off the street and buy tranquilizer darts. You can buy ammo that way, and the darts are sure as hell less deadly."

By late afternoon, Janice had sent more than a dozen sets of prints to Ross for comparison with the partials. None of them matched, but then she hadn't expected them to. No one in her case records even came close to being a good suspect.

Ross had also compared the partials with the prints lifted from the orange Pinto. None of those matched either, but of course the hand aiming the gun at her through the Pinto's window had been gloved. Though disappointing, the absence of any matching prints in the orange car proved nothing.

Pushing the pile of folded computer printout to the side of her desk, she leaned back in her chair. At least the activity had kept her mind safely engrossed in the task at hand rather than letting her thoughts torment her with possibilities it would do no good to dwell upon. She was grateful that Captain Bishop had not taken her off the case because of her personal involvement, as she had feared he would. She would have argued, the result predictable. She'd have lost.

It was nearly five, and most of the desks were occupied now, a rush of activity in progress as detectives tried to get rid of as much paperwork as possible before calling it a day. She was thankful that, like the captain, most of them had refrained from giving her any special attention. They were by no means one big happy family, but the captain had been right in saying they were a family of sorts. They knew each other as only people whose lives depended on each other could. You could have little use for your partner personally; liking each other was nice but unnecessary. Trusting each other professionally was essential. So they knew her, as she knew them. And because they knew her, they let her get on with her job, sparing her from unwanted sympathy or special treatment.

Then, unbidden, another thought bobbed momentarily on the surface of her consciousness. They knew her, but would they ever truly trust her? Would any of them, even those who might resent the out-and-out sexism of officers like Mullins, care to step into a really hairy situation with a woman for backup? She pushed the question aside, a little ashamed that she would worry about such things when three members of her family had just been kidnapped.

The office was emptying out now, one by one the desks being vacated. Janice picked up the phone to call Mike. She'd put off doing so because he would be worried and upset and she didn't need that right now. But the time had come. She didn't want to be alone in that house, for one thing. For another, she needed him, especially tonight.

Before she'd finished dialing, Poldoski, whom she hadn't seen all afternoon, was standing beside her desk, looking somewhat pleased with himself. Janice replaced the receiver.

"I've got a possible," he said. "I had the Twin Cities PD's run what we've got through their computers, and the machines came up with one Eddie Clipp." He pulled out a small notebook and flipped it open. "Age twenty-six, blond hair, five-eight, one hundred and forty pounds. Now get this. He spent two years at Stillwater for attacking woman police officers in St. Paul. And he got out six weeks ago."

"Jesus Christ," Janice said.

"There's more. He was a member of one of those weird fundamentalist religious groups that thought for women to do anything but stay home and have babies was a sin. To prove the point, he interfered with woman officers while they were making arrests—even freed a guy who'd just been busted for DWI. Anyway, the purpose, he said, was to demonstrate how ineffective women were as officers, how easily overpowered by a man, I suppose. At his trial, he offered no apologies and said that when he got out he'd do even worse things to woman officers. God's will and all that." He flipped the notebook closed. "No prints or photo on him yet, not until morning, but I've got an address on him. You ready for a trip to the city?"

"I sure am," Janice said, grabbing her purse from the bottom drawer. She knew that on cases like this, with no immediate suspects, it was usually a matter of first finding some suspects, then eliminating them, and that the first one you found was rarely the one you sought. Still, turning up a young, blond fanatic who hated woman cops...

It was a run-down neighborhood, the grimy streets lined with old brick or stone buildings. They parked in front of a brick triplex with a rusty tricycle lying on its side in the weed-choked front yard. The apartment they wanted was on the right. As Poldoski rang the bell, Janice unzipped her purse, then rested her hand casually on the bag, the butt of her .38 within an inch or two of her fingertips.

The door was opened by a slight young woman who eyed them warily, waiting for them to state their business.

"Is Eddie Clipp at home?" Poldoski asked.

"No. Why?" Wearing jeans and a loose-fitting blouse, she had stringy blond hair and a face plagued by pimples. Behind her on the worn carpet, blocks and other toys were scattered.

"We'd like to see him," Poldoski replied.

"Why?" She said it defiantly this time. You answer my question before I answer yours.

"We're police officers," Janice said. Poldoski flashed his shield.

"Figures," the young woman said. "What did he do this time?"

"He's not charged with anything," Janice explained. "We just want to talk to him. May I ask who you are?"

"I'm his ex-wife." She stood firmly in the doorway; no invitation to come in was forthcoming.

"I didn't know he was divorced," Poldoski said.

"We're not. Not officially anyway. I told him to get out and take his religious freaks with him. I thought the time he spent in jail might have put some sense in his head, but it just made it worse. He's crazier now than he was before."

"Does he still want to attack women police officers?" Janice asked.

The woman hesitated, taking in all of Janice, then their eyes met. "He says he's going to pick one this time and really mess her up." She shrugged. "If you haven't figured it out by now, he's crazy. He belongs in Elk Ridge or one of those places."

"Did he mention any officers by name?" Poldoski asked.

She shook her head. "That's all I know. He quit talking about it around me after I told him what I thought."

"What about his friends?" Poldoski asked. "Do you know any of their names?"

"Those creeps? Hell no, I don't know any of their names."

"Does Eddie have a job?" Janice asked.

"Ha! Who'd hire him?"

Poldoski, who'd been jotting down the major points in his notebook, asked: "Where is he now?"

"Went to live with his uncle."

"Do you have an address?"

"No, but it's on his father's side, so it's the same name. Clipp. Somewhere in Dakota Falls."

Janice and Poldoski exchanged glances.

It was dusk when they pulled up in front of the modest yellow house owned by Harold Clipp. Located in another section of town, it was several miles from the Andersons' house. The place was well cared for—lawn mowed, shrubs trimmed, no peeling or faded paint to be seen anywhere. Finding the right Clipp had not been difficult; there was only one in the city directory.

This time, the door was opened by a middle-aged man in khaki work clothes. Behind him, in the dimly illuminated living room, a TV screen flickered.

"Yes?" the man asked.

Poldoski held up his badge. "Police officers. Are you Mr. Clipp?"

"Yes. What's wrong?"

"May we come in, please?"

"Yes, of course." He pushed the screen door open and ushered the two detectives into a small but spotless living room, simply furnished. A heavyset middle-aged woman sat on the couch, facing the TV screen. She got up and turned down the volume. Above the set on the wall was a picture of Jesus praying in the Garden, a light shining on him from above.

"This is my wife Sheila," Clipp said. The officers introduced themselves, declined her offer of coffee, then sat down in the chairs Mrs. Clipp had hurriedly dragged over.

"Does an Eddie Clipp live here?" Poldoski asked as soon as their hosts were seated on the couch.

The Clipps exchanged worried looks. "I don't know how to answer that," Sheila Clipp said. She had curly brown hair, a motherly face. "He came here to stay with us a few weeks ago. He, uh, he had just got out of prison and had a falling-out with his wife, and he needed a place to stay."

"What she means," her husband said, taking over, "is that he had a falling-out with us too and left, saying he was going to stay in a motel."

"Do you mind telling us about this falling-out?" Janice said. "It might be important."

"Well," he said slowly, "I guess there's no harm in telling you. I got him a job where I work—Henderson Plumbing and Heating—and he quit after one week. It was just washing up the service trucks, but at least it was a job. I'm afraid I got pretty upset with him."

"Why did he quit?" Janice asked.

Harold Clipp sighed. "He said it was too time-consuming. It interfered with the Lord's work, as he put it."

"Did he say what that work was?"

"Not to me." He looked at his wife.

"He wouldn't discuss it," Mrs. Clipp said. "I asked, but he said he wouldn't tell me because it would be better if I didn't know." Her eyes saddened. "We're religious people ourselves, but there can be too much of anything, I think. Even religion. Too much of it's a sickness." Then, meeting Janice's eyes, woman to woman, she asked: "What's he done? Please tell me. His father—Harold's brother—is dead, and his mother wants no part of him, I'm afraid. She's remarried and lives in New Mexico now. You see, we're all the family he's got."

Janice smiled reassuringly. "He's not charged with anything, Mrs. Clipp."

"But he's suspected, isn't he?"

"He's a possible suspect. I really can't say any more because that's all he is, and if it turns out he's not involved in what we're investigating, we don't want to have damaged his reputation unnecessarily." Not that Janice really gave a damn one way or the other about Eddie Clipp's reputation.

Mrs. Clipp nodded. "I never thought of that. I guess you have to be very careful, don't you?"

"Yes, we do," Poldoski said. "When did Eddie leave here?"

They exchanged looks again, as if trying to decide who should answer; then Sheila Clipp said: "A week, maybe ten days ago." Her husband nodded.

"And you've had no contact with him since?"

"No." She hesitated, glancing at her husband, then added: "He has fantasies, you know. He sees things in the news or reads them in the papers and thinks he's really part of what happened. Once, I remember, he was watching a show on the Kennedy assassination—a special looking into whether or not there might have been a conspiracy like some people say there was—and Eddie started laughing. He said the investigators were stupid because they'd never know it was him . . . that he was the one who assassinated Kennedy. For that moment anyway, I really think he believed it. At the time President Kennedy was shot, Eddie was just a little boy."

"Did he ever receive psychiatric treatment?" Janice asked.

"Only in his mind. He told me once that when he was in prison he'd sometimes pretend it was a mental institution because that was the only way he could make life there understandable. It was the only thing he ever said about prison."

Poldoski glanced at his notebook, which he'd taken out as soon as he sat down. "Did he have his own room while he was here?"

"Oh, yes. He took most of his things when he left, of course. Would you like to see it?"

"Please."

Mrs. Clipp led them into a small bedroom, which, like the living room, was simply furnished. Everything was tidy, the bed made, the furniture recently dusted. Having found the closet and wastebasket empty, Janice looked under the bed, finding nothing, not even dust. Poldoski was going through the dresser drawers. He pulled a stack of magazines from one of them and spread the publications out on the bed.

"That's all he left behind," Sheila Clipp said. She had remained in the doorway, watching the detectives search.

As Poldoski flipped through Eddie Clipp's reading material, Janice noted that most of the publications were extreme right-wing, generally anti-ERA and antihomosexual in their emphasis.

"This was it for the dresser," Poldoski said. "You find anything?"

"Nothing." She turned to Mrs. Clipp. "The last time you saw Eddie, did he have a moustache?"

She seemed distracted.

"Mrs. Clipp?"

"Oh, I'm sorry. What was your question?"

"Eddie—did he have a moustache?"

"Oh, yes. Grew it while he was in . . . in jail."

Before leaving, the two detectives learned that Eddie's aunt and uncle didn't know the names of any of his friends and that he didn't own a car. The Clipps promised to call if they heard from Eddie.

Poldoski driving, they headed for the station in their unmarked gray Plymouth. For a while, functioning as a detective had enabled Janice to forget her deep personal involvement in the case. Going from place to place, asking questions, these things were routine, and she had temporarily shifted into the role of the impartial investigator. But now, as she and Poldoski drove along the tree-lined streets, past block after block of frame homes, houses like her father's, the professional detachment was beginning to wear off, being replaced by pain. Regardless of what she hoped, the truth had to be faced, and the truth was that all three of them—her father, her sister, her nephew—could die before all this was over, could be dead already.

Resisting the impulse to push the thought aside, she held it, trying to handle it simply as a thing that had to be dealt with. I'm strong, she told herself. I can do what must be done. And at that moment, she realized she could. She wouldn't crumble.

Strange, she thought, how she had cried in the driveway that day, then again in the parking lot. Over minor things. Threats, a car that wouldn't start, a door that wouldn't unlock, the possibility of embarrassing herself in front of Mullins. Yet she had not cried once since she'd recovered from finding Sam in the microwave oven. Tears were a luxury, apparently, reserved for those who had time for them.

When this was over, whatever the outcome, she could and likely would bawl her eyes out—either in happiness or in grief. But only then and not before.

Poldoski slowed for a red light, then picked up speed again as it turned green. It was nearly dark now, the windows of the houses becoming squares of light in the blackness, the trees silhouettes against the gray-black sky. Traffic was light. A typical Monday night in suburbia.

"Well, what do you think?" Poldoski asked.

"About Clipp? I think he sounds pretty damn good, although it's hard to believe we'd get so lucky with the very first suspect."

"True. We don't really have anything on him yet. And we won't get the prints or photo from St. Paul PD until tomorrow morning. As soon as we have them, I'll have Ross compare Clipp's prints with the partials, and we'll have Reynolds and Mrs. Fox take a look at the photo."

"There's another thing we don't have that would be quite helpful," Janice said. "Clipp."

"As soon as we get in, I'll put a locate out on him. We've got enough for that, considering that . . ." He trailed off.

"That lives are at stake," Janice said, finishing his sentence.

Poldoski said nothing.

Slamming the door of his battered pickup, Rick Kaminsky staggered toward the shack he called home. A one-room wooden structure on the edge of a wood, it was cold in the winter and hot in the summer, but no one had ever complained about his having erected it here, so it was rent-free, which made it ideal for Rick Kaminsky. Now fifty-seven, he hadn't worked at a regular job in nearly fifteen years and hoped never to do so again. He'd been an executive, a vice-president, at a paper products company. White shirt, tie, ulcers, the first heart attack at forty-two. Last one, too. Taught him that life was more important than so-called success.

Clearing his throat, he spat. To hell with the bastards, he thought. His vegetable garden kept him fed in the summer; shoveling snow earned him enough to keep going in the winter; the junk he collected and sold to scrap yards kept him in booze. Too much booze tonight. He should have left Pogo's sooner.

He shook his head to clear it. Pop Jones was buying. Couldn't leave with Pop Jones buying. Besides, it was only ten o'clock or so.

He stopped at the crude door, surveying his domain. Didn't look like much, not made of logs and scrap lumber the way it was. Damn good location, though. Right on the edge of Dakota Falls, yet hidden by the woods. Not a house, car, or ulcer-ridden vice-president in sight. He'd been gone all day; it was good to get home.

Raising his hand to push open the door, he froze, his spinning head suddenly sober. Something had just crashed to the floor inside. Rats? He'd killed some last year. In the next instant, he knew it wasn't rats because he heard a moan. A very human moan.

Quickly he scanned the area for a weapon, spotting a three-foot length of one-inch pipe lying in a small pile of scrap he'd collected. He crept the fifteen feet or so to the scrap heap and silently slipped the pipe out of the pile. Then he returned to the door and, taking a moment to steady his nerves, kicked it open.

Inside, he could see nothing but darkness. Raising the pipe, he said: "All right, you son of a bitch, come out of there before I bend this goddamn pipe around your head."

Silence.

"If I have to come in there, you'll wish to hell I hadn't."

Silence.

Kaminsky realized the pipe was shaking in his hand. There was sure as hell someone in there. Why wouldn't he answer? What the hell was going on?"

Then he had an idea. He hurried back to his truck and switched on the lights. Returning to the door, he peered cautiously inside, the light from the truck dimly illuminating the interior. There, on the floor, was a man, tied, gagged, blindfolded, and from the looks of things out cold. Kaminsky dropped the pipe and quickly lit the oil-burning lantern. No electricity here—or electric bills.

He untied the ropes that secured the man's arms and legs, then removed the gag and blindfold. He was looking at a man of about twenty with wavy dark hair. On closer examination, he found the bump on the man's head. Must have fallen just as I came up, Kaminsky decided. Hit his head on that damned old cast-iron wood stove, maybe. That would have knocked anybody out.

What the hell was this all about? How did this guy get here all tied up like this?

The man on the floor groaned.

Nine

Janice and Poldoski were within a block of the station when the call came.

"PD, one-seventy-two," the female voice said through the speaker.

Poldoski grabbed the microphone. "Go ahead, PD."

"Be advised the driver of that van taken this morning has been found in the county. Sheriff's office is there now. Subject appears to be ten-four."

"Ten-twenty, PD." He glanced at Janice.

"Go south on Gitche Gume off Pennington. About half a mile. Go left on a dirt road when you see a mailbox marked Kaminsky."

"Ten-four, PD. Advise county we're en route." At the next intersection, he turned left, heading for Pennington Boulevard.

They found a black and white sheriff's unit parked outside a shack surrounded by small piles of junk. A pickup beside the county cruiser looked as if it belonged in one of the piles. Inside, they found two uniformed deputies, a man in his late fifties whose worn clothes were in roughly the same condition as the pickup, and a young man who was apparently the driver of the ill-fated van. He sat on a wooden chair, a cup of coffee in his hand, looking shaken.

The deputies introduced themselves. One was stocky, middle-aged, going bald, and his name was Aho. The other was dark-haired, slimmer, and younger. His name was Baldwin. The older man, they discovered, was Rick Kaminsky, the occupant of the place, a one-room shack with no electricity and a wood-burning stove for heat. The driver was named Vincent Cooper.

"That's all I know," Cooper said. "I was getting ready to kill the motor, and all of a sudden I felt this prick in my arm, and then whamo! I was out. I woke up here all tied up."

"You never saw the guy?" Janice asked.

He shook his head. The oil-burning lantern flickered, causing the shadows to waver throughout the room.

"Did he speak to you?"

Again, Cooper shook his head. "From the corner of my eye, I saw a hand, but before I could turn my head it was all over." He frowned. "All I've got's a weird impression, but I don't know if it's the drug or what."

"Tell us about it," Poldoski said encouragingly.

"Well, I don't know why, but I thought—when I first saw the hand—that it was a kid, a child." He shrugged. "I don't know why I thought so. All I know is that that one impression registered. That a kid was there. Doesn't make much sense, does it? No kid would drug me and tie me up like that."

"What made you think it was a child?" Janice asked. "The size of the hand? Its shape? Something it held?"

He smiled weakly. "Hell, I know what it held. That's how I got here." He thought for a moment, then sighed. "I don't know. I only caught a glimpse of it. I really don't know what made it look like a kid's hand. Hell, it'll probably turn out to be a guy seven feet tall with mitts like a bear."

Janice felt the excitement she'd experienced earlier, when she'd learned the driver had been found alive and well, slipping away. This was a dead end. The first of many probably, but they were always disappointing. And in this case . . . She checked the thought.

"What happened next?" Poldoski asked. "After you were drugged."

"Well, when I woke up, I was here, except I didn't know I was here, if you know what I mean. I was blindfolded and tied up. I didn't know where I was. I spent hours that way. Then I heard someone drive up outside, and I thought it was the same person coming back for me. I got scared and tried extra hard to get the ropes undone. I stood up and tried to move—I don't know what that was supposed to accomplish, but that's what I did. Anyway, I tripped over something and fell and hit my head and knocked myself out cold. When I came to, he"—Cooper looked at Kaminsky— "was leaning over me, and the blindfold was off, and I wasn't tied up anymore."

Kaminsky, who was standing beside the two deputies, picked up the story from there. "He looked kinda scared at first, but then he must have realized I was the one who'd untied him because he told me to call the police. Got no phone here, so I ran out to my truck and drove over to the Shell station on Pennington, where there's a booth."

Pointedly leaning around Janice, Deputy Aho handed Poldoski a paper bag. "That's the stuff he was tied up with."

Poldoski gave the contents a cursory inspection, then handed the bag to Janice. Aho looked away. Inside were several pieces of rope and two scarves, one red, the other blue.

"The blue one," volunteered Kaminsky, "was used for the gag, the red one for the blindfold."

None of these items would be very helpful, Janice decided. The rope was white clothesline; one scarf was made in Hong Kong, the other in Korea. These things could be obtained at almost any department store.

"Look," Cooper said, "doesn't anyone want to tell me what this is all about now? Why the hell was I drugged and left here like this? And have you caught the son of a bitch that did it? These guys"—he waved in the direction of the deputies— "wouldn't tell me anything. Kept saying to wait until the Dakota Falls cops got here. Okay, you're here."

"The van you were driving was used in the abduction of three people this morning," Janice explained. "The abductor and the van and the three hostages are all still unaccounted for."

Cooper slowly let out his breath. "Wow," he said.

* * *

Deputy Jack Peterson drove his cruiser slowly along the narrow country road. He'd heard all the radio traffic about the driver of the van having been located at old Kaminsky's shack, and the area he was currently patrolling wasn't more than three miles from there.

He'd also heard what had happened. Three people abducted from a woman cop's home, including her father who was a cripple in a wheelchair. Although Peterson didn't much believe in woman cops, she was still an officer, and he knew every lawman in the vicinity was keeping a close lookout for that van. And they'd all like to get a piece of the son of a bitch responsible. You do something like that to one cop, he thought, and by God, it's a personal affront to all of us. When they did catch the asshole, he'd arrive at the station hurting. No marks, of course, and no witnesses. Though only in his thirties, Peterson was of the old school. Doing away with the rubber hose and the back room had been a mistake.

Pushing those thoughts aside, he let his mind drift. The woods were damned spooky at night. The headlights barely penetrated the wall of trees, occasionally picking out the eyes of some animal, two glowing spots peering at him from the shadows. Go very far in there at night, he thought, and all the trees begin to look alike. You can stumble around for hours a hundred feet from the road, not having any idea where the hell you are.

At a dirt side road, he turned right, bushes and tree limbs scraping the sides of the car as he drove deeper into the woods. Ahead was a clearing where teen-agers liked to park at night. There hadn't been any trouble in the spot that he knew of, but he liked to keep an eye on it. Through the trees, he caught a glimpse of his own headlights, reflected back at him by glass or metal. Someone was here.

Then, as he drove into the clearing, he saw it plainly, maybe fifteen feet ahead of him. A tall blue van. For hauling people confined to wheelchairs. *The* van.

He grabbed the microphone from its holder on the dash.

"I've got all of them," Franklin Ross said, emerging from the side door of the van. "And believe me, there were hundreds of them." He set his box of fingerprint equipment on the ground and stretched. "It's all yours."

Deputies Aho and Baldwin had accompanied the two Dakota Falls detectives to the scene. They'd hung around for a while, then left, although Deputy Peterson, who'd discovered the van, was still with them.

"You need a hand?" Peterson asked. He was a lanky man with light brown hair and cold blue eyes.

"We can handle it," Poldoski said. "But thanks."

Peterson grunted and joined Ross, who had picked up his equipment box and was stowing it in the trunk of his car.

Janice and Poldoski climbed into the van, he in the rear, she in the front. Using a flashlight, she checkd the floor, the ashtray, the glove compartment, then got down to her knees and looked under the seat, where she found the moldy remains of a hamburger, straws, an unpaid parking ticket.

The van had been discovered with one front door and the side wheelchair entrance open, the ramp in place. Wheelchair tracks led from the ramp to a spot where another vehicle had been parked. Ross had photographed the tire tracks.

Seeing those wheelchair marks in the earth and knowing they had been made by her father had very nearly shattered the professional detachment Janice had worked so hard to maintain. She had preserved it only by forcefully reminding herself that she would be able to do her family no good at all if she crumbled.

"Find anything?" Poldoski asked from the rear of the van.

Janice was still on the floor, looking under the dash now. "Nothing. You?"

"Same here."

When they climbed out of the van, Peterson and Ross were leaning against Ross's car, waiting. Poldoski shook his head.

"I'll need the driver's prints," Ross said. "So I can at least eliminate him." He sighed. "If you need me, I'll be at the station. This is going to be an all-night job."

"Frank," Janice said.

"Yes?"

"Thanks."

Officer Martin Edwards of the Dakota Falls Police Department sat in his cruiser, which he'd positioned just off Pennington on a residential street so that he had a clear view of the boulevard. He was waiting for the nightly drag race.

Night after night, the shift commander, in his briefing, had mentioned complaints about drag racing along this stretch of Pennington, looking at Edwards pointedly. And night after night, Edwards had failed to be in the right place at the right time. But not tonight. This time he'd get them.

Then, to his left, he heard the squeal of tires and the roar of loud mufflers. Starting the car, he inched up to the intersection. They flew by, engines roaring. A gold Pontiac and a red Dodge, neck and neck. He turned on the red light and pulled onto the boulevard, pushing the accelerator to the floor. Then he hit the siren.

A few moments later, ticket book in hand, he was confronting two carloads of somewhat frightened teen-agers. He paid little attention to the green car with four people in it that passed on the other side of the street, heading in the direction of Heikkinen's Funeral Home a few blocks away.

"How do you figure it so far?" Poldoski asked as he drove into town on Merit Boulevard, a through street that paralleled Pennington a few blocks to the north.

Janice had been staring out the window, absently watching the homes and small businesses they were passing, deliberately suppressing any thoughts of her family. That her father, sister, and nephew were somewhere out there in the night, possibly dead and most certainly in danger, was a fact that did not need to be dwelled upon.

She shifted her thoughts to Poldoski's question. "It looks like he unloaded the driver right after taking the van. That shack of Kaminsky's doesn't seem too lived in. Probably seemed a good spot."

"I'll buy that," Poldoski said. "The driver would have been in the way. Also, that would account for the driver and the van being found in two different places. Cooper will never know whether he was present during the kidnapping, that's for sure." He was silent for a moment, then said: "That spot in the woods had been carefully picked as a place to stash the car. Peterson said lovers go there at night sometimes, but that no one ever goes there in the daytime."

Something registered in the back of Janice's mind. Something had happened to someone she'd known in a spot like that, perhaps that very place. Who and what hung at the edge of her subconscious, just out of reach.

"When I was in high school," Janice said, "that certainly wasn't one of the main spots in my circles, but I suppose anyone who grew up around here could know about it. Each little group had its own places to park."

Poldoski snapped his fingers. "Gee, if I'd known that at the time, I'd have talked my family into moving here. Things weren't nearly so lively in St. Cloud, where I went to school. With all that parking, I might not be single now."

"A hunk like you? The only reason you're still single is because the waiting list of women wanting to sleep with you is still ten pages long."

"If you expect me to respond to that, you're crazy."

"Ummm. Do you think the car was left there ahead of time, or that there was someone waiting for the van, an accomplice?"

"There's no way of knowing. My gut feeling is that the car was stashed there. The spot's isolated but still within easy walking distance of town."

"So you think there's only one person involved."

"That's what my gut feeling says."

"Mine, too," Janice said. "This is the second case of his using drugs now. First Reynolds, then Cooper."

"Once is the same as twice, I think. We already knew he had access to the drug."

"Okay. What about the locations of the sites where he left the driver and the van? A few miles apart, on the edge of town, in the woods."

"I'm not sure that tells us anything. Both were secluded spots that were handy."

"But has he shown a preference for the woods? Do you think that might be where he's holding the hostages?"

"I don't know, Janice. Let's face it, if it's woods he's interested in, then he should have taken them up north. There's places up there where there's nothing but woods. For miles."

That was true. There was no reason to assume the kidnapper had stayed in this area. Or even this state. Her family could conceivably be in Wisconsin or South Dakota or Iowa or God knew where. Yet she didn't buy that, somehow. Something told her her family was here, close.

She studied Poldoski for a moment, his handsome face dimly illuminated by the light from the dash. He was a friend, a true friend. And in the next instant, she heard herself speaking before her mind had a chance to censor the words.

"Ron, when this is all over, I'm going to show you one of those spots I was talking about, one of those places where people go to park."

"Whenever you'd like," he said warmly.

Sitting beside Mark in the rear seat, Malcolm Anderson watched as the green Chevrolet turned off Pennington, traveled partway down the block, then pulled onto a small road entering the grounds of Heikkinen's Funeral Home. Here the grounds were not illuminated as they were along the boulevard, the serenity of lush green replaced by sinister shadows—a big-city park, dark, filled with muggers. But Malcolm Anderson had no fear of muggers. Muggers he could understand. What the person driving the car had in mind he did not understand at all.

That he thought he recognized their abductor only added to his confusion. Why the fake moustache? And why were they on this little-used entrance to a mortuary? And why would a former friend of Janice's hate his daughter enough to do this? What, for God's sake, had Janice done?

Seeing the police car with its red lights flashing had been frustrating. Help had been there, just across the street, within easy shouting distance, yet so totally inaccessible. The driver had pointed the gun at Amy, who was in the front seat, saying she, then the boy, would die should any effort be made to hail the policeman. Malcolm Anderson had done nothing. The flashing red lights had receded in the distance and, with them, whatever hope they might have represented.

Whatever their abductor's intentions, they had been care-fully planned. First, there was the site in the woods where the car had been waiting, a spot on the edge of town, easily reached yet still quite secluded. Then a quick trip to another wooded location on the edge of town, where they spent the day, waiting. For night apparently. That seemed to be the only flaw in the plan: all that waiting, during which their abductor had to keep them together and under control, all the while running the risk of discovery—although the risk hadn't been too great apparently, as no one had showed up. And if anyone had, what would he have seen? A family on an outing.

Unhappily, Malcolm Anderson realized they were about to find out what the next part of the plan was because the car was stopping behind the mortuary.

His thoughts swirled, his mind unable to find a solution, a plan of attack, some hope of escape. Weakened by the accident, his legs useless, he could not realistically hope to overpower someone who had a gun. Beside him, Mark sat silently, staring straight ahead. Confused, frightened, the boy seemed to be waiting for guidance from his mother and grandfather, leadership neither of them could give—Malcolm Anderson because he had none to offer, Amy because she had all but ceased to function.

He knew about the concept of identification with your abductor, having read about it in newspaper stories that had come out after the fifty-three Americans were taken hostage in Iran. Experts had said a hostage-captor relationship was one of such total dependence on the hostage's part that the captives tended to be grateful for little favors, tended to develop an odd attachment to their captors. That seemed to be what had happened to Amy. That and fear so overpowering her mind had simply withdrawn from it. In any event, Amy would do nothing to help them escape.

And that was unfortunate. Amy was the only able-bodied adult among them, the most physically capable. Without her, they were a force of two: a five-year-old child and a cripple. With no plan.

"All right," the driver said, getting out of the car, "we're going inside. Leave your wallet and purse in the car."

Without waiting for further instructions, Amy got out, leaving her purse on the seat, and hurried to the trunk to get the collapsible wheelchair. Their captor opened the rear door and pulled Mark out, then, holding the gun to the boy's head, led him to the rear of the car. Mark neither cooperated nor resisted; he just went. Malcolm Anderson heard the trunk being opened; then Amy was there, helping him out of the car and into the chair, removing his wallet as she did so and tossing it onto the seat, then wheeling him through the gravel, toward the building. It was dark here, well hidden from the boulevard. Their abductor stood by the door, holding the boy by one arm, waiting.

Releasing Mark, their captor said: "I'm going to open this door. Remember, our friend here in the wheelchair can't get away. If anyone runs, you know who dies."

With that, their abductor produced a nail file, turned to the door, and a few moments later, Malcolm Anderson was wheeled inside, into total darkness. The door closed, and the lights were switched on, revealing a long corridor; then he was moving again, rolling down the hallway.

Why here? Why the mortuary? They couldn't be held in this place more than a few hours because the staff would be here in the morning. Or—and he shuddered at the thought— would people arrive at work to find three bodies waiting for them? A symbolic gesture of some sort—to slay them in a funeral home?

And that thought prompted him to action. He was in front of the others, Amy pushing him down the hallway, Mark and their captor bringing up the rear. His wheelchair had a brake for locking it into position so its occupant wouldn't unexpectedly find himself rolling away at the mercy of gravity. Easing his hand to the lever at the chair's side, he grabbed it and pulled.

The chair came to an abrupt halt, Amy lurching forward onto his back.

"Hey!" their abductor shouted. "What the—"

The sudden stop had thrown everyone off balance. Malcolm Anderson wheeled around and, with all the strength his arms could muster, barreled back into the stumbling people, looking for the one with the gun. Amy had been dumped against the wall, clearing the way. Ahead was a pair of legs, legs in jeans, and Malcolm Anderson slammed into them, the chair bouncing off the target. He heard a yelp of pain and quickly spun the chair around for another attack.

He saw Amy in the background, wide-eyed, frozen, useless. Then he saw the one with the gun, on the floor, the eyes showing pain, confusion. He put all the energy he had left into turning the wheels, the chair seeming heavier now, sluggish. Then he saw the revolver swinging up, turning toward him.

Mark suddenly appeared, flinging his small body at the

kidnapper, his tiny fists pounding the startled face. But the boy was right in the wheelchair's path now, and Malcolm Anderson had to change directions, his momentum carrying him into the wall. He managed to stay in the chair, but just barely.

By the time he turned around, it was over. Mark lay on the floor, crying. Amy, still wide-eyed and immobile, simply stood there, rigid. Their captor, standing now, had backed off a few feet, the gun leveled at Malcolm Anderson.

The eyes into which Janice's father stared displayed a mixture of intense but unidentifiable emotions. Although he didn't see hate or anger or fear in the normal sense, he saw something so overpowering he wanted to turn his head. He felt as if, for a moment, he had stared into the depths of insanity, and what he'd seen there was nearly as frightening as anything else that had happened.

"Move," their abductor said, grabbing Mark's arm and standing him up. "Now." And then Amy was behind the chair, pushing it down the hallway. He shouldn't be too hard on her, he supposed, but had Amy been able to function, had she been something other than a damned automaton, they might have succeeded. Behind him, he heard Mark whimpering. The boy had a bloody nose but seemed unharmed otherwise. The kid was gutsy. And his grandfather was damned proud of him.

"Here. The door on your right."

Amy obeyed unquestioningly, and Malcolm Anderson was rolled into a darkened room. When the lights came on, he saw that it was empty, stripped, the places where equipment had once stood now only discolored spots on the tile floor. And he understood now why this place had been chosen. No one would come here in the morning because no one worked here anymore. The place was vacant, unused. Obviously, Heikkinen had gone out of business, moved, died, something. And he wondered why, at a time like this, his mind sought the logical explanation, why it seemed so frustrating not to know what had happened to the business that had once thrived here. The knowledge would certainly be useless to him.

Taking in the room, he spotted what appeared to be the only thing left behind: the built-in drawers or slabs or whatever they were called, the refrigerated compartments in which the dead had been stored, awaiting embalming or cosmetic work, being prepared for their final public appearance, at which they'd seem at peace, almost pleased to be on their way to the crematorium or the earth. Malcolm Anderson had thought about places like this, thought about them with the morbid fascination of one extremely close to death. He had survived the accident, only to wind up here, in this place of corpses, a year later.

And he saw why their captor had been willing to use the lights. There were no windows. Here was a place people avoided, a place with a stigma about it, and even should someone come around, he would not be able to see the three prisoners within.

Dragging Mark by the arm, their abductor stepped over to the drawers and slid one open. There were two horizontal rows of them; the one that had just been pulled out was in the bottom row, not more than three feet off the floor.

Smiling faintly, their captor studied them a moment, then put the barrel of the gun against Mark's head and said: "Get the old man in here."

There was no movement from Amy, who was still behind the wheelchair. Mark, dried blood on his face from the nose-bleed, stared at his mother and grandfather, although it was doubtful he saw either of them. Incapable of dealing with all this, the five-year-old's mind had simply shut down, ceased to accept any more.

"Get him in there. Now." Their captor pushed harder on the revolver pressed against the side of Mark's head, making the boy wince but having no effect on the dull look in his eyes. "Or do you want to watch the kid die?"

The wheelchair began to move, rolling slowly toward the open drawer. Nearing it, Malcolm Anderson averted his eyes. Although he knew he should study it, look for some means of escape, he could not. For he knew he'd see a corpse there, its body cut and bruised, its legs mangled beyond repair, and its face would be his.

Then Amy was helping him out of the chair and into the drawer. He lay back on the hard surface, and she lifted his legs onto it. For a moment, while she stood above him, their eyes met, hers peering at him through the strands of mussed blond hair that hung limply over her face. He saw confusion, fear, and helplessness in his daughter's blue eyes, and then he heard their captor order the drawer closed, reminding Amy what failure to comply would mean for her son.

"It's okay," Malcolm Anderson told her. "Close it. As long as we're alive, we've got a chance."

Amy stepped back out of his sight, and the drawer began sliding inward on its rollers, Malcolm Anderson's feet, then knees, then midsection gliding into the wall. He had a last glimpse of the ceiling; then the light narrowed to a crack and was gone. The drawer latched with a click, and Malcolm Anderson was in total darkness.

He heard muffled words that he couldn't make out, then silence. Finally, he heard the sound of rollers, another drawer being opened. In a moment, he knew, he would hear the sound again as the drawer closed, to be followed by a third and final series of roller noises. Three drawers, three hostages. Three innocent people for whom the horror had only begun.

Ten

Having left their car in the underground parking area, Janice and Poldoski walked up the stairs to the ground floor. Detective division this time of night would be deserted, the cluttered desks vacant, the door to Captain Bishop's office locked. But when they stepped through the doorway, Janice discovered the room wasn't quite as empty as she'd expected. Mike was sitting at her desk, waiting for her.

"Janice," he said, getting up, "are you okay? Any word on your father and sister?"

"How did you find out?" Janice asked, a little disconcerted.

"It was on the news." He glanced at Poldoski, who stood at her side, then stepped up to Janice, taking her shoulders as if he were going to shake her. Poldoski headed quickly for his desk, where he busied himself with some papers.

Mike looked at her severely. "Why didn't you tell me?" he demanded.

She didn't need this. Not now. She removed his hands from her shoulders. "Because," she said angrily, "I'm working on the case. And I just happened to think that saving the lives of three people—three people who are very close to me—was more important than stopping to tell you what was going on."

Now he looked hurt. "It only would have taken a moment, Janice. What affects you affects me, you know that. I had a right to know."

"No, it wouldn't have taken just a moment, Mike. You'd have been upset, and I'd have had to deal with that at a time when I had more than I could deal with already." She sighed. "But I really wish you'd heard about it from me, rather than on the news. I'm sorry about that, Mike. I really am. You deserve better."

She searched his face. His expression was softening, as no doubt was hers. He reached for her, hesitantly, and she stepped into his arms, resting her head on his shoulder.

"Will you be okay?" he asked gently.

"I'll have to be."

"Do you have any clues at all?"

"We found the van and its driver in two different locations. The driver was drugged, then bound and gagged, but he's okay. So far, we really don't have a hell of a lot to go on, I'm afraid. I'll tell you the rest later. At your place. Over a stiff drink. Okay?"

"You bet." He squeezed her tightly.

Poldoski, who had been on the phone, caught Janice's eye. "Locate's out on Clipp," he said. "Twin Cities as well as here."

"Good." Gently freeing herself from Mike's grasp, she moved to the detective's desk and wrote down Mike's number on the pad. "That's where I'll be if anything comes up. You'd better call it a day, Ron. You look beat."

Poldoski nodded. "I'm going to look in on Ross, and then I'm on my way home."

"Call if there's anything."

"Goes without saying." He smiled. .

"Who's Clipp?" Mike asked, joining them.

She told him, briefly, and as she did, his eyes narrowed.

"Christ!" he exclaimed. "That could be the guy you're looking for!"

"We know he looks good as a possible suspect," Janice said, "but you've got to remember he's nothing more than a name the computers gave us. When you get overly excited about a possible, you have a tendency to ignore the other leads your investigation may have turned up, and if your possible flops you've got alot of catching up to do. You've got to learn to keep things in perspective."

Mike frowned. "Jesus, Janice, you're taking this well. I mean, after all, it's your father and sister and—"

She cut him off. "What the hell would you have me do, Mike? Scream and cry and sit around being distressed? If there was ever a time I needed to have my shit together, this is it. I'm sorry if you find my lack of hysterics in poor taste."

"Janice, I didn't mean . . ." He trailed off, his eyes dropping to Poldoski, who was trying very hard to look busy.

"I'm sorry, Mike. I didn't mean to snap at you. I guess that shows you just how upset I really am." She took his hand. "Come on. Let's go."

As they walked down the hallway, toward the exit, she said: "I have to stop and pick up some of my things, so you can either follow me in your car or wait for me at your place."

"I'll follow you," he replied without hesitation.

The driver stopped the green Chevy on a bridge over a small creek. This was a little-used road; no one was around. Hurrying to the safety rail, the driver tossed a purse and wallet into the darkness below. There was a small splash.

The money, of course, had been removed. The wallet had contained only a few dollars, but the purse had held well over a hundred.

The creek was neither deep nor rapid; the things just tossed into it would soon be found. Their discovery would tell the authorities nothing and just might confuse them.

The next step would be to get rid of the car. That, unfortunately, would mean another long walk back to the motel. All the cars used had to be left in different locations, just in case they were connected to the kidnapping. Perhaps this one should be left in another town, as the orange Pinto had been, followed by a short bus ride back to Dakota Falls.

Returning to the Chevy, the solitary figure climbed in behind the wheel. Wherever the car was abandoned, it would be left as it had been found: with the keys in the ignition.

The destruction of Janice was going just as planned. Soon, the driver thought, soon the years of torment would end. A lifetime of suffering—the constant feeling of being unwanted, the failed marriage, all of it—will be erased. And Janice was the cause of it all—Janice who was everything while I was nothing. When she dies, I'll be whole, wonderfully whole, for the first time in my life.

Starting the car, the solitary figure drove slowly away from the bridge. Before Janice died, of course, she would have to be brought to her knees, to be shown how helpless she was. Her family would die slowly, painfully. Then, when they were dead, Janice would be informed where to find them. The ordeal of their deaths would be obvious, and Janice would see that they had indeed been alive all the time she had been searching for them. And that she had been powerless to help them.

From the moment she and Mike arrived at her father's house, Janice was very glad she would be spending the night somewhere else. There were too many things here she didn't want to see: the wooden wheelchair ramp on the front steps and especially the chair itself, which stood at the far end of the living room, a lonely contraption without its owner, the shot in the sad movie.

Janice hurried to her bedroom, anxious to be out of here and glad Mike was right behind her. It was not a good time to be alone. He stood in the doorway while she quickly threw a few things into an overnight bag. This was no longer the place of happy childhood memories. Those fragile images had been wiped away, replaced by the horrors of the present. Here a pet had been cruelly murdered, the mail opened and read by the murderer. Here an empty wheelchair waited in the living room.

In the bathroom, she grabbed her comb, toothbrush, and other essentials. Then, stepping into the hallway, she hesitated. The door to Amy's room stood open, and on the floor she could see the small suitcase partially filled with Mark's clothes. She walked into the room, picked up the case, and put it on the bed. What did it mean? Why the suitcase sloppily stuffed with the boy's clothes, then abandoned? Hearing a noise behind her, she turned. Mike stood in the doorway.

She flipped through the clothes. Pants and shirts but no socks or underwear. Her eyes wandered across the room, the signs of Amy's presence everywhere: shoes by the bed, clothes in the closet, makeup on the dresser.

She sighed. "Something about this suitcase bothers me. It just doesn't add up."

"Maybe he was going to make Mark take his clothes, but something happened," Mike suggested. "There wasn't time."

"Why just Mark and not the others?"

"Maybe he was only planning on taking the boy."

"I doubt that somehow."

Mike wrinkled his brow. "Well, maybe he had different plans for Mark."

"Maybe," Janice said doubtfully. "On the other hand, this could be unrelated, something Mark was doing for some reason. Kids do all sorts of things that make no sense to adults."

Mike's frown vanished, replaced by a far-away wistful look. "Kids are like that all right. I think we ought to have two, possibly three."

That was enough of a jolt to make her forget everything else for a moment. She stared at him. "Two, possibly three what?" she managed to say.

He looked confused. "Kids, of course. I don't suppose this is the time to talk about things like that, but I thought a pleasant topic might help get your mind off things for a while."

It had worked, even if not the way he'd intended. "There are a lot of things we haven't discussed, Mike. Especially considering that there's the possibility of our getting married."

"Well, I mean, that's what people do when they get married. They have kids. So, I just assumed..."

"You assumed. That was a pretty good assumption, considering that you never once mentioned it to me, and presumably, I'm the one who's supposed to bear all these babies."

Now he really looked flustered. "Janice, I—"

"Mike, it's very common these days for people to elect not to have kids. In fact, studies have shown that childless marriages are often the happier, longer-lasting ones."

"You mean you don't want to raise a family?" he asked in disbelief.

"I didn't say that. What I said is that . . . that you've got a hell of a lot of nerve assuming all by yourself that I'm going to be the mother of two, possibly three kids. What else have you decided? That I'm going to give up my career so I can take care of them? That I'm going to cook and be the good little woman who will help her hubby with his career?" She was getting thoroughly pissed; she couldn't help herself. "What else? You see me as a den mother taking care of Cub Scouts? Come on, Mike, let's hear it all. What else do you have in mind for me?"

She felt tears welling up, and despite her efforts to fight them back, a moment later she was sobbing, letting it all out. Dammit, she thought. Dammit, dammit, dammit.

Mike hurried to her, taking her in his arms. She wanted both to push him away and to be held by him. After a moment's indecision, she put her arms around him, rested her head on his shoulder, and cried.

Apparently uncertain what to say, Mike held her, wisely saying nothing.

There was no light, no sound; the only reality that registered on Malcolm Anderson's senses was pain, the growing soreness in his body caused by lying on the rock-hard surface in his boxlike prison. With effort, he could roll over, giving one sore part a rest, although in time all he would accomplish would be to distribute the pain everywhere, uniformly.

He knew he was suffering from sensory deprivation, because his mind, lacking any external inputs, had begun manufacturing its own. He heard thunks and clunks and whispers while viewing swirling displays of lights. Sounds that covering his ears would not alter. Visions that closing his eyes would not eliminate.

You could lose yourself in these things, forgetting the pain, the fear, reality. In time, he would do so, for the horror would become unbearable, the temptation of escape—even a false escape—overpowering. In those lucid moments he had left, he would have to think.

His most pressing problem, he knew, even more serious

than the possibility of a retreat into insanity from which he might never return, was air. The three of them were in a large, compartmented refrigerator. Eventually, they'd use up its supply of oxygen and suffocate. He had started to use his engineer's knowledge to determine the size of the entire refrigeration unit, then calculate the cubic feet of air. Although he probably could have come up with a reasonable guess at the figure, he'd scrapped the notion when he realized he was missing some critical information. He had no idea how much air the human lungs consumed, and even if he had, the answer he sought would have been in time: how long they had before the oxygen was used up. His watch could not be read in the dark, and without it, he had no way to judge the passage of time. Outside it could be night, dawn, noon. Here in the darkness and silence, an hour was a minute, a minute an hour; seconds, as critical as they were, incalculable.

He forced himself to focus on reality. For the third time, he worked his hands up and felt the interior face of the drawer, finding nothing but a smooth surface. The regular occupants of these containers had no need of an interior latch; the drawers could only be opened from without.

Now he became aware of the other stimuli available for his senses, things he'd noticed before and forgotten. There was the sound of his breathing, although it was best not to concentrate on that because it was rhythmic, which made it hypnotic and brought on the whispers, the swirling lights. Also, there was an odor, a weak chemical smell. Preservatives, disinfectant, something.

And then he heard something else, very faint, very far away, but real. Horribly real. It was the sound of screaming. Highpitched. A woman. Amy.

Janice had dozed, on and off, never quite able to fall into the deep sleep she so desperately needed. Beside her, Mike, who she sensed had been awake most of the night too, lay quietly.

Located on the northern edge of town, his apartment was part of a typical modern complex—overpriced, sterile, paperthin walls, numbered parking spaces. Her place, at least, when she'd lived alone, had been an older building with vines on the walls and other traces of character.

They had had no further discussions concerning their future, a subject that seemed on the verge of becoming taboo, and Janice knew it was only a matter of time before she would have to decide whether two people who were unable to discuss their future were deluding themselves into thinking they had one. She thought about that, worrying, coming to no worthwhile conclusions, but at least she managed to keep her mind off the fate of her family.

Finally, the area around the curtains lightened, and the grayness of dawn began filtering into the room, causing the furniture, the carpet, the designs on the wallpaper to materialize from the shadows. Tuesday morning had arrived.

She rolled over to look at Mike, to study him, to think about what—if anything—the future held for this man and her, and the phone rang. Not caring that it wasn't her phone or what the caller might think if it was for Mike, she leaned across him and snatched the receiver from its cradle, nearly pulling the phone off the bed table.

"Hello?"

"Janice?" It was Poldoski.

"Yeah, Ron."

"We found Clipp. Or rather, he found us. Anyway, he's on his way to the station voluntarily."

"I'll be there in fifteen minutes."

Handing the receiver to Mike, who was sitting up, staring at her, she leaped out of bed. "Clipp came in voluntarily," she said. "I've got to go to the station."

"He surrendered at . . ."—he glanced at the clock on the bed table—"at five in the morning?"

"Not surrendered," Janice explained, fastening her bra. "We don't have a warrant. We just want to talk to him. How he found out or why he decided to get in touch with us at this hour I don't know."

A moment later, fully dressed, she gave him an almost wifely peck on the cheek and dashed out the door, combing her hair as she went.

In the hallway outside the interrogation room, Poldoski quickly filled her in:

"Showed up at his uncle's house about an hour ago saying he needed a place to sleep. They told him we were looking for him and that if he wanted to stay he'd have to call us and get things straightened out first. So he did. Right then. I had a patrol car pick him up. Probably thought he was being real clever, too." He grinned. "Ready?"

Janice nodded, and they stepped into the room. Inside was a small wooden table with four chairs, at one of which sat a young blond man wearing jeans and a wrinkled shirt. The first thing Janice noticed as they sat down facing him was his clean-shaven upper lip.

"We'd like to thank you for coming in," Janice said. "I see you shaved off your moustache."

He looked smug, presumably pleased with himself for getting two police officers in at this hour just to deal with him. He studied Janice a moment, his pale blue eyes lingering on her breasts before moving on. Finally, he looked at Poldoski and, jerking his head toward Janice, said: "Your secretary?"

"This is Detective Anderson," Poldoski said matter-of-factly. "We're aware of your feelings concerning woman officers. Why do you resent them?"

"What women are trying to do these days, it's against nature, against God." He said it flatly, somberly, in absolute sincerity. A fanatic he might be, but apparently not the fiery screaming kind. At least not at the moment.

"No woman," he added, "has the right to arrest a man."

Under the circumstances, Janice decided, it would be best to remain silent, and let Poldoski ask the questions.

"This is important to you, isn't it?" Poldoski asked. "I mean it's something you devote a lot of thought to."

"It's important. A lot of people feel the same way I do, but most of them aren't willing to do anything."

"What are you doing about it now?"

Clipp grinned, making his long thin face seem almost vulturine. "You know I can't tell you that. You'd stop me."

Poldoski didn't push it. "Why'd you shave off your moustache?"

Clipp shrugged. "I was looking in the mirror and decided to shave it off. You know, a spur of the moment thing. Why?"

"Someone fitting your description has been involved in some things."

"Whatever it was, it wasn't me."

"Can you tell me where you were yesterday morning?"

"Sure. Ever since I left my uncle's house I've been with Gracie."

"Gracie who?"

"Gracie Youngstrom." He gave the address.

"And she was with you all yesterday morning?"

"Yeah. Ever since I left my uncle's, she's been with me."

"Neither of you had to go to work or anything like that?"

Clipp shook his head. "Gracie's on welfare. She's got three kids."

"Why'd you go back to your uncle's?"

He laughed. "Another one of her boyfriends showed up, found me in the sack with Gracie, and got mad as hell. He was big and drunk and horny, so I split."

Janice caught Poldoski's eye, and he said: "Will you excuse us a moment, Mr. Clipp?"

"Sure."

"Listen," Janice said after they were in the hall, the door to the interrogation room closed, "I know it's early to be calling anyone, but I think we should get Mrs. Fox down here to take a look at Clipp. Reynolds, too, although he didn't get as good a look at the kidnapper as she did."

Poldoski nodded. "I agree. What do you think of that guy?"

"He scares the hell out of me. He's the calm, cool, collected type that could climb the tower with a sniper rifle."

"Or put a bomb in a nursery school." He grimaced. "You call Reynolds and the Fox woman, and I'll keep him occupied."

Forty-five minutes later, Katherine Fox stood beside Janice, both of them peering through the one-way glass that allowed them to see into the room where Poldoski and Eddie Clipp faced each other across the table.

"He really can't see me?" Katherine Fox asked hesitantly. She wore a flowered hat that belonged to the same era as her furniture.

"To him, it's a mirror," Janice assured her. "All he sees when he looks this way is a reflection of the room he's in."

Katherine Fox stared into the interrogation room a few moments; then a smile appeared on her face. "Wouldn't it be interesting to have a few windows in my house made of this kind of glass! Why I could . . ." She looked at Janice sheepishly. "Well, it's an idea."

"Do you recognize the man with Detective Poldoski?"

She peered through the glass, frowning, then shook her head. "I'm sorry, but I've never seen him before. He's not the man I saw at your house."

"Can you mentally give him a moustache?"

"Well, I'll try." She looked into the next room again, cocking her head first one way, then the other. Finally, she turned to Janice. "It's not him. I'm sure of it. This man is slight like the other one was, but... well, meaner looking. Does that make any sense?"

It didn't to Janice. Clipp's physical appearance was not very threatening. He seemed a meek, harmless type, at least until you spoke with him or looked closely into his somewhat distant eyes. "Could you be more specific?" she prodded.

"Well, that man, the kidnapper, was more effeminate than this one. Like you expect a homosexual to look." She shook her head. "I really can't be more specific, I'm afraid. It's just an impression."

Mrs. Fox's knowledge of homosexuals obviously didn't extend beyond the stereotype. Still, in addition to clearing Clipp, she had provided another element in the description of the abductor. Although effeminate was a hard thing to pin down, it did enable you to eliminate barrel-chested macho types, and every little bit helped.

Janice thanked her for her assistance and for providing it at such an awful hour and sent her on her way. Ten minutes later, Reynolds too said Clipp was not the man he'd seen driving the van yesterday morning, the man who'd jabbed a needle into his arm.

At midmorning, Janice and Poldolski were summoned to Ross's office. The fingerprint man faced them across his desk, looking thoroughly bushed.

"I'm afraid I can't give you much that'll be very helpful," he said. "I've isolated what I'm fairly certain are your sister's prints, a small set that are obviously the boy's, and of course I took your father's prints the day your house was broken into, so they're no problem. After eliminating those, no unaccounted-for prints from the van, the notes, the house, from anywhere match. And none match the partials."

"What about Clipp's prints?" Janice asked. They'd arrived from St. Paul, and she'd sent them to Ross, just in case.

"Clipp's prints don't show up anywhere, and the partials aren't close enough to Clipp's to leave any room for doubt. Completely different patterns." He rubbed his bloodshot eyes. "Sorry I can't give you anything more encouraging. It looks to me like our man wore gloves all the time, except when he left the partials."

Captain Bishop stepped into the office, a clear plastic bag containing an envelope in his hand. His eyes met Janice's; then he held up the bag.

"I think he's communicated with us," the captain said. "This arrived in a taxi a few moments ago. The cabby said he got a call to pick up a package at an address on Woodland Drive. The house was vacant, but he found this pinned to the door along with a ten-dollar bill." He handed it to Ross. "Here. You open it."

The fingerprint man shook the envelope from the bag, then took two letter openers from his desk drawer. With the point of one, he held the envelope in place while he slit it with the other. Janice and the others gathered around the desk to watch. On the front of the envelope in handwritten capital letters were the words:

DELIVER TO DAKOTA FALLS POLICE
ATT: JANICE ANDERSON

Using tweezers, Ross slipped out a single sheet of paper, then unfolded it with the letter openers. The message, too, was in handwritten capitals:

I HAVE YOUR FATHER, SISTER, AND THE
KID. THEY ARE IN A PLACE THEY
CAN NOT ESCAPE FROM. THEY
HAVE NO FOOD OR WATER. SEE
IF YOU CAN FIND THEM BEFORE
THEY STARVE OR DIE OF THIRST.

I'LL GIVE YOU A HINT. THEY'RE
IN AN AIRTIGHT COMPARTMENT.
BUT I WON'T LET THEM SUFFOCATE.
THAT WOULD BE TOO FAST. I'LL
OPEN IT FROM TIME TO TIME AND
LET SOME AIR IN.   YOU BETTER
HOPE NOTHING HAPPENS TO ME
BECAUSE YOU WON'T FIND THEM.
OF COURSE THEY'LL DIE ANYWAY.
EVENTUALLY. AND AFTER THEY'RE
DEAD, I'LL KILL YOU.

Stunned, Janice lowered herself into her chair. What kind of a madman was this? Why did he hate her so much? Why? She forced herself to remain calm; getting emotional would accomplish nothing.

Captain Bishop picked up the phone and dialed three digits. "Ben, this is Bishop. How long can a person live without food or water?" Ben Francis was the police surgeon.

A few moments later, the captain hung up the phone and faced the others. "He says it would depend on the individual, on how healthy he was and things like that. Water's the critical thing. A healthy man can go more than a month without food but only a week without water." He hesitated, his eyes avoiding Janice's. "He says if the body's moisture content is reduced by twenty percent the person will die a very agonizing death."

"And that's how long it takes," Janice said softly, "a week?"

"That's how long. I'm..." Bishop didn't finish the sentence.

Poldolski, who had also returned to his chair, rose and walked to the large framed photo of a fingerprint that hung on the wall. He studied it a moment, then turned to Ross. "I've always meant to ask you. What the hell is this?"

"First case I ever cracked," the fingerprint man said. "Homicide. That print and my testimony got a murder conviction."

Poldoski nodded, then shifted his gaze to Bishop. "Captain, we're at a dead end. Our only suspect didn't pan out. The computers don't have anyone else to offer. Janice's past cases are a big zero. The only prints we have are partials. We'll check out the neighborhood where this note was left, but I don't hold out much hope of learning anything new. The best we can hope for is that someone got a look at the guy, and we've already got witnesses who've seen him, for all the good it's doing us."

He ran a hand through his thick dark hair. "Sure, all cases are like this. Eventually new leads turn up, and you may crack it. But in this case, we've got a time limit. A week, apparently. The way things stand now, we better get lucky. Fast."

"We don't have a week," Janice said. "They were taken yesterday, which means we've got six days." She was still holding herself together, speaking calmly, softly. The others were helping by doing what had to be done, saying what had to be said. By treating her as an officer on an investigation and not the victim of a terrible crime. She was grateful. Her presence had to make this difficult for them.

"Six days," the captain said, "if you believe what's in the note. We've got no choice but to accept it at face value, but you should keep it in the back of your minds somewhere that any or all of it could be made up to suit the purposes of the crazy son of a bitch who wrote it."

"All right," Janice said, "let's consider the note. The only real piece of new information in it is the part about an airtight compartment. Where do they have airtight compartments?"

"Excuse me," Ross said, standing up, "but I think I can be more useful in the next room, dusting this." Picking up the envelope and note with tweezers, he disappeared out the door. Captain Bishop sat down at Ross's desk.

"Meat lockers," Poldoski said. "Grocery stores, meat markets, any place that sells large amounts of food."

"Okay," Bishop said, "where else do they have airtight compartments?"

"Research facilities?" Janice suggested hesitantly.

"Any others?" When no one offered any further suggestions, the captain said: "Places that store food seem to be the best bet. Okay, so let's say it's a walk-in refrigerator. It can't be one down at the neighborhood supermarket because all sorts of people would have access to it. It's got to be an abandoned place."

"Not necessarily," Poldoski said. "Say the guy's a butcher, owns a small shop, a one-man operation. He'd have access to the meat locker, but no one else would, and business would go on as usual."

"Yeah," Janice said, "but the note didn't say anything about it being cold where they are. A working refrigeration unit would be cold, and I can't imagine the note's author leaving out anything that would add to my worries."

The captain shook his head. "Doesn't mean anything. That could have been omitted because it would have told us too much."

"So, what's our next move?" Janice asked.

Bishop wrinkled his brow. "Let's start checking out abandoned places that have freezers or anything else we can think of that would be airtight and large enough to hold three people."

"What about other communities in the area?" Poldoski asked. "There's been plenty of time to get the hostages well away from here."

"Start here and work your way outward. I'll see what kind of help we can get from the other departments in the area. If nothing else, they can let the officers out on the street know what we're looking for. Maybe one of them will spot something."

"Janice and I can handle the vacant buildings," Poldoski said. "But we'll need a couple of people to check out the neighborhood where the note was left for the cabby to pick up. You never know, maybe we'll come up with someone who compulsively writes down license numbers or something."

A faint smile appeared on Bishop's thin lips. "I did meet one once, you know. An invalid. Sat by the window watching the neighborhood and kept a log. Time anyone went in or out, license numbers, you name it." He shrugged. "When the homicide took place, he was at the hospital for his weekly physical therapy session."

Although she didn't let it show, Janice had not needed to hear a story about an invalid at this particular moment.

The captain must have realized that his choice of anecdotes was a poor one, because he suddenly seemed a little embarrassed. Then, his expression becoming serious again, he looked at Janice and said: "One more thing. Just before I left the office, I ran into a reporter looking for you. I don't know whether you've seen the papers"—she hadn't—"but this is a big story. No one in the division is allowed to comment on the case, except me. And any questions from reporters are to be referred to me. Clear?"

Both Janice and Poldoski said it was.

Forty-five minutes later, Ross reported finding one set of prints on the envelope, most likely the cabby's, and none on the note itself.

Eleven

The first problem Janice and Poldoski encountered in locating vacant buildings was that no one kept a list of them. The city kept track of any that had been condemned, real estate agents of most that were for sale. But not all. A few, of course, were being sold privately, by the owner, and no one kept a list of those. Nor did anyone keep track of buildings that were not in use but not for sale either.

On the patchwork list they were able to make up, they found only four places in Dakota Falls that might have airtight compartments: two meat markets, one neighborhood grocery store, and a building that had once housed a fur storage operation. By midafternoon, they had permission to enter the fur storage place and one of the vacant meat markets.

* * *

Amy was beginning to awaken, and for some reason, in that hazy state between sleep and consciousness, her mind was briefly rational. The first sensation to pour in on her was heat. She was sticky, sweating. And thirsty, very thirsty. She reasoned that it was afternoon, the hottest part of the day, and that it would be late night before the heat in the building diminished.

Then, as she came closer to being fully awake, she thought of how hard she'd tried to please, to make friends with their captor. And she had pleased; she was sure of it. She had only been put in here so it wouldn't appear to the others that she was the favorite. That was it. Oh, yes. Soon, the drawer would open, and she'd be freed, rewarded for her loyalty. Oh, yes. Soon. Very soon.

And she wasn't abandoning the others. No, no, no. She would never do that. Once she was free, she'd go for help. It would be a disloyal thing to do when their captor had trusted her enough to free her, but she would have to. She couldn't let her little boy and her father stay here. But she'd still be loyal. She'd never reveal the name; she wouldn't even think it.

Amy was awake now, her mind having risen out of the darkness and silence of slumber. But when she opened her eyes, seeing only more blackness, her ears hearing only more silence, and when she blinked and couldn't tell she had except for the movement of her lids, she screamed. A long, pitiful wail that began somewhere in the back of her throat, rising in pitch, continuing until she ran out of breath, choking, gasping for air.

A solitary figure standing near the drawers heard the muffled scream, and it answered two important questions. They were still here, in their prison; no one had come here, found them. And they were still alive; the supply of air had not been used up.

Very well. It was time to open some of the drawers and let in some air. But not those in which they lay. No, no. There was no point in disturbing them, and since this appeared to be one big refrigerator with many doors, opening any of the compartments would do. Although it would be simpler to leave them open, that was impossible. Should someone come here, it would be a thing out of order, a thing that might be noticed. And the people within could more easily hear the footsteps of the intruder, would know when to cry for help. And with the drawers open, those cries would most likely be heard.

No, that wouldn't do at all. This place would have to be visited two or three times a day so the drawers could be opened. The hostages could not be allowed to die too quickly.

Things were going quite well indeed. The green Chevy, Malcolm Anderson's collapsible wheelchair in its trunk, had been left in a Minneapolis neighborhood crowded with old apartment buildings. Blending in with all the cars parked on the street by the apartment dwellers, the Chevy would go unnoticed. At least until someone spotted the keys hanging from the ignition, when it would quite likely be stolen again. Before the car had been abandoned, the two used syringes had been dropped into a Minneapolis storm sewer. And all this had been accomplished in time to catch the last bus back to Dakota Falls.

And best of all, Janice had received her note this morning. She would be badly shaken now; her destruction was going nicely.

Mark had always been afraid of the dark and small places. Since the funny man had made his mother put him in here, he'd found there were only two things that would keep him from being so scared he'd begin shaking. First, if he lay real still, keeping his hands at his sides, he couldn't touch the sides or top of the dark box, so he didn't know how small it was. Second, if he kept his eyes closed, then it was okay if it was dark, because that's how it was supposed to be with your eyes closed.

But sometimes he couldn't stand to lie still or keep his eyes closed any longer, and then he'd start shaking again. Once, he wet his pants. He was so ashamed of that that he almost hoped no one came to let him out until his damp pants had dried. No, he didn't really hope that. He wanted out of here so bad that wet pants didn't matter.

He heard a noise, a sound like one of the funny big drawers being opened. It wasn't real, though. He'd heard lots of noises since being put in here. Mommy had whispered to him, and once even Daddy. But Daddy was dead. He couldn't whisper anymore. Mommy had explained all about what had happened to Daddy, and Daddy couldn't see them or talk to them anymore. Or whisper. Mommy had also told him once that in the dark, sometimes you heard noises that weren't really there. And that's what most of the noises were. Noises that weren't really there.

But then he heard the sound again. And he could feel it, sort of. Mark thought about that a moment. He'd never felt the make-believe noises; he'd only heard them. So this must be a real noise. And he had to let the person out there know he was in here.

Raising his legs, he began kicking the roof of the compartment as hard and rapidly as he could. But it didn't make much noise. Sort of like kicking a mattress. Near panic now, afraid the person out there would go away without finding him, he scooted down to rear of the dark box and began kicking its back wall with both feet.

Again and again, he kicked. Something was loose there, and it made lots of noise. Nearly out of breath now, his legs tired, he couldn't stop. He kicked, lifted both feet, and kicked again. Over and over.

Then he heard a click, felt movement, and suddenly there was light, bright light that hurt his eyes. And in the next instant, out of the light, something had his neck, choking him, and he heard a voice, the voice of the funny-looking man who had made Mommy put him in the dark box.

"Stop it, you little shit! If you make noise like that again, I'll come back and choke you again, until you die. Do you understand?"

The hands went away, and Mark was gasping, trying to breathe again.

"Do you understand? Any more noises and I'll choke you until you die."

Mark tried to say he understood, but when he moved his lips, no words came out.

Then he was moving again, and the light was changing, shrinking. There was a click, and it was dark once more, except for the funny lights that seemed to float in front of his eyes no matter where he looked.

He lay completely still, trembling, only dimly aware that his pants were sopping wet again.

* * *

Accompanied by a real estate agent, Janice and Poldoski stepped into the now vacant building that had once held a fur storage company. Janice felt the hot, musty air close in around her, seeming to stick to her. Beads of perspiration had already begun to form on her forehead.

They were standing in an empty room with a tile floor. No traces remained of the business that had once operated here. On the edge of downtown Dakota Falls, the building was brick, neither new nor old, a place that was likely to stay vacant, a victim of the shopping malls.

"This way," the agent said. She was a gray-haired woman in her fifties, efficient, businesslike.

Following her through the empty room and through a door at its rear, they found themselves in another vacant room with a tile floor.

"This is it," the agent said.

"This is where the furs were stored?" Janice asked, surprised.

"Right here."

"But I thought they were kept in cold storage."

"They were. This room was dustproof and had a special cooling system at one time. All that's been stripped out, and the room's been restored to its previous condition. It was required by the lease."

"Oh. I wish you'd told us."

The older woman sighed. "It's an old line, but you didn't ask."

Janice let out a sigh of her own. She hadn't asked. She'd assumed there was still an airtight room here. Valuable time had been wasted. The day was more than half spent, which meant she had to assume three members of her family had only five and a half days to live. At least that was the time the police surgeon had given a healthy man. But only one of the three was a man, and he was far from healthy.

And as perspiration trickled down her face, she realized there was another factor that could shorten the time even further. If they were in a vacant building, it would be sweltering inside. They'd perspire, their bodies using up precious fluids in an effort to remain cool, causing them to dehydrate even more rapidly.

The thought made her thirsty, and the knowledge that she could quench her thirst without difficulty made her feel guilty.

Having thanked the agent for her time, Janice and Poldoski headed for the vacant meat market several blocks away.

Carl Olson, the grounds keeper at Heikkinen's Funeral Home, straightened up, trying to work the kinks from his sixty-four-year-old back and surveying the roses he'd just fertilized. They ran along the front of the building, a dazzling display of reds and whites. It seemed a shame that all the flowers, all his work, all his loving care would be ruthlessly ripped apart by the bulldozers, beauty replaced by concrete. Hell, soon enough there wouldn't be any gasoline to run cars on anyway, so why did they keep building freeways?

These thoughts saddened him, and he pushed them aside. He had a thing to do that he'd been putting off. Mr. Heikkinen had told him to go inside and check out the building at least once a day. Just give it a once-over, he'd said. Make sure there's no pipes leaking or anything like that.

Until the place had closed down, Carl Olson ordinarily had gone inside only to pick up his paycheck. The outside was his place, out here with the flowers and grass and trees. Inside were the dead and those who wept for the dead. He chuckled. Some of them wept not for the dead, but because they'd found out what Heikkinen planned to charge them. In any case, it was an unhappy place on the inside, and being there gave him the willies.

Well, no point putting it off. Pulling out the key ring at the end of a chain fastened to his belt, he strolled over to the glass door and let himself into the building.

After quickly looking through the waiting area and the rooms where the dead had been viewed, he switched on the lights and headed down the long hallway leading into the depths of the building. He didn't like it here at all, because this was where they took the bodies to work on them. Given his choice, he wouldn't come here or anywhere like it until he was a real paying customer. Only the dead belonged here. And anyone crazy enough to become a mortician. He quickened his pace as he went from room to room. I'm just passing through, he communicated mentally to no one in particular. I'm not ready to stay yet.

Then, sticking his head into one doorway, he froze. Some of the drawers, the damned sliding coffins where they kept the bodies, were open. Someone had been in here. He took a cautious step into the room and stopped, his eyes darting around. No one was here now anyway.

Then he heard a noise, a muffled groan. No, no, he thought, nothing in there's alive. Nothing in there at all, and when there was, it sure as hell never groaned.

He should go over and check, he supposed, but something about all this was making him feel damned uneasy. The thing to do would be to report this to Heikkinen, and let him come take a look if he wanted to.

The decision made, he turned to leave the room, and as he did so, he saw movement in the doorway. Then he saw the knife.

Standing over the grounds keeper's body, the figure in jeans folded the knife's long sharp blade back into its handle and pocketed it. This presented a new problem because people would come looking for the old man, and this was where they'd check first. Turning away from the grounds keeper's body, his murderer paced the length of the room and back again. What to do? What?

Soon, in a couple of hours or so, the old man should be on his way home. Shortly thereafter, he'd be missed. There was time, but a plan had to be formulated, executed. A way had to be found to make it appear the old man had been killed elsewhere.

The jeans-clad figure continued pacing, thinking, ignoring the body sprawled near the doorway. It was an unfortunate complication, nothing more. It could be handled.

"Sorry I'm late," the real estate agent said, climbing out of his car. He was about thirty-five—fluffy, styled hair, and an expensive, trendy suit. Janice and Poldoski had been waiting outside the building for over half an hour. More valuable time wasted.

The agent introduced himself, then pulled the keys from his pocket and unlocked the door of what had been Pat's Meat Market. A small brick building on the corner, the place was one of those little neighborhood businesses that struggled along for years, then suddenly went belly-up. A lot of them had been doing it lately, Janice reflected. Even gas stations, and a few years ago who would have predicted that?

Inside, the refrigerated glass display counter was still in place, empty now, although Janice could almost smell the meaty odor of the steaks and sausages and chops that had once filled it.

In the rear of the shop, they found two large metal doors. Behind both, they found shelves, meat hooks hanging from the ceiling, sawdust on the floors, and that was all.

A few moments later, they were on their way back to the station, a terrifying image persisting in Janice's mind. She saw herself opening one of the big metal doors and finding her father, sister, and nephew, each hanging from a separate meat hook, their eyes bulging, glassy, staring at her, their bodies swaying as if in a breeze. With all her willpower, she shoved the picture back into the unconscious part of her brain and slammed the door on it, hoping it would never escape again.

Sergeant Ed Mullins sucked on his cigar and looked down at the body of Carl Olson, formerly the grounds keeper at Heikkinen's Funeral Home. The old man had the day off or maybe sneaked off to do some fishing, and someone had mugged the poor son of a bitch.

He studied the scene a moment, looking for anything that was inconsistent with that explanation. The small lake was right on the edge of town, only a mile or two from where Olson had worked. The dead man's rod and tackle box lay beside him, his car no more than twenty feet away under a tree. No blood in the car, keys in the ignition. And between the victim and the car was the dead man's wallet, whatever cash it had held missing.

No signs of a struggle. His attacker apparently sneaked up behind him. Mullins mulled that over a moment. Could have been someone he knew, too. The wallet left to make it look like a robbery. No, didn't seem likely. Who would want to kill a sixty-four-year-old grounds keeper?

He turned to the nervous teen-age boy who'd discovered the body. "What time was it when you found him?"

"Uh, maybe five-thirty. I was at a friend's house, and this

is a shortcut I use to get home." He was about sixteen, tall and thin, with a bad case of pimples.

Mullins grunted. "See anyone in the area? Any cars or anything?"

The boy shook his head.

Watson, who'd been on the radio, climbed out of the unmarked car and joined them. "ME's on his way," he said. "Also a lab guy. Kline."

Mullins scratched his head. Was anything out of order here—anything at all? "You a fisherman?" he asked the boy.

"No, sir. I hate fish."

"How about you, Will?"

"I get my fish from the grocery store," Watson said, running a hand over his thick wavy hair. He and Poldoski were the ladies' men of the division, although even Watson hadn't been able to score with Janice. And Poldoski, for some reason, hadn't tried.

And why was he thinking about pussy when he had a homicide to deal with? He spat out the remains of his cigar. He wasn't a fisherman either—bowling was his sport—so, if there was anything wrong with that part of what he saw here, he'd never know it. Anyway, it looked normal enough. The line was even baited with one of those fancy imitation bugs, whatever you called them.

Yup, the old guy had gone fishing and got himself mugged. Christ, the scumbugs were even in the woods these days. No place was safe anymore.

"When you were on the radio just now," he said to Watson, "you hear anything more about the kidnapping?"

"Nothing new."

Both he and Watson were following the case closely, as were all the officers in the department. It didn't matter that neither of them approved of women on the force. This was family business. And the son of a bitch that would go after a cop's family—any cop's—was one scumbug Mullins would really like to get his hands on.

Janice spent the remainder of the afternoon at her desk, trying to track down the owners of vacant buildings, both in Dakota Falls and neighboring communities. It was a long shot, she knew, but what else did they have to do?

Collins and Reynolds, the latter having made it through the shift in great shape for a man who'd been drugged the previous day, had checked out the area where the note had been left for the cabby, finding no one who had seen anything.

It was after six, and the room was empty now, except for Janice and Poldoski. The door to Captain Bishop's office was closed; Mullins and Watson were out on a homicide; and the rest had gone for the day, although any or all of them were on call should they be needed in the investigation of the kidnapping. It wasn't because the division was going about business as usual that so little effort had been put into the kidnapping; it was because there was nowhere to put any additional effort, no useful task to which it could be applied. Janice knew that if anything broke—anything—she and Poldoski could have virtually every officer in the department.

The captain had been wise in putting her on the case. This way she wouldn't be sitting on the sidelines, worrying that not enough was being done. Because she was in on everything, she knew firsthand there was nothing that could be done other than what they were doing: playing the long shots and hoping like hell for a lucky break.

There was one thing that had been bothering her, one of those details she'd been trained to look for, a thing that was odd, not quite as it should be. Mark's partially packed suitcase.

She swiveled her chair around to face Poldoski, whose desk was across the aisle from hers. She started to speak, then hesitated. Engrossed in the papers spread out in front of him, he was unaware of her stare. He had a handsome profile, its outline ruggedly masculine, his features showing both strength and kindness. His thick dark hair was mussed and hung loosely over his forehead in that natural, casual way many men strived for but never attained.

Then, apparently sensing her gaze, he turned his head, and she was looking into his intelligent brown eyes. Whatever unspoken message would have passed between them at that instant was left uncommunicated, though, because Janice's phone rang, shattering the moment.

"Anderson."

"Hi, it's me, Mike. When are you coming home?"

His apartment was not her home, not yet anyway, but she

let it pass. "I've got some things to do yet."

"How's it looking? I heard on the news that the kidnapper had communicated with you, but the content of the message wasn't released."

"Nothing to report yet, Mike. Things are still about like they were. I'll tell you about the message later. It'll take another stiff drink, I'm afraid."

"That bad, huh?"

"That bad. I'll tell you later. I don't want to go into it now."

"Okay," he said with artificial cheeriness. "What time should I expect you?"

"I don't know yet. Expect me when you see me."

"Janice...." Whatever it was, he left it unsaid. She was sure he felt cut off from her, wanting to help yet unable to, but there wasn't much she could do about it.

"I'll see you when I can," she said gently. "I've got to run now."

She hung up, feeling somewhat guilty, in part because she had to cut him off from this, but also because of what had nearly passed between her and Poldoski. Or was she just imagining things?

"Ron," she said, looking at him but not quite meeting his eyes, "I want to have another look at the house, specifically at that suitcase."

"Want some company?"

"Sure. Maybe you'll notice something I won't."

"Got anything specific in mind?"

"No, it's just one of those things that doesn't fit. And let's face it, we're not doing a hell of a lot of good here."

Janice tried not to react to the empty wheelchair and the other reminders of her father. She was a police officer, and these were the things at the scene of a crime, facts to be investigated.

"What do you see?" she asked Poldoski, who stood beside her in the center of Amy's room.

"A room where people were staying temporarily, visitors, a woman and a boy. Nothing out of the ordinary except the suitcase."

Janice frowned, her eyes exploring the room. "That's all I see, too."

"What do you want to do?"

"Let's start with the dresser the clothes in the suitcase came out of."

Janice stepped over to it, her eyes taking it in. Made of dark wood, it had five drawers. On its top were a number of Amy's things—makeup, hairbrushes, and a small wooden jewelry box, which Janice opened. Inside were a handful of small but expensive pieces, tasteful, not gaudy. She closed the box. Beside a jar of face cream was the only thing on the dresser that appeared out of place. At least it would have been, had it not been for the fact that a five-year-old boy had shared this room.

"What do you suppose this is?" she asked, picking up the Y-shaped stick.

"You weren't ever a boy, were you?" He took it from her.

"Ron, I can truly say no one has ever asked me that before."

He chuckled. "Watch." He held the stick out in front of him with one hand, stretching imaginary rubber bands back with the other.

"Of course," Janice said, feeling foolish. "A slingshot. Don't shoot it in the house, Ron. You'll have to play with it outside."

Grinning, he handed it back to her, and she put it back where she'd found it, turning her attention to the drawers. The top three contained Amy's things, the bottom two Mark's. The bottom drawer itself had not been touched; everything that had been put in the suitcase had come from the drawer above it. She poked through it. The clothes it contained weren't mussed, so the things in the suitcase must simply have been lifted off the top. Again, why?

The bottom drawer was full of underwear and socks, and poking through these, she discovered two more things that didn't seem to belong. She handed them to Poldoski.

"Okay, Ron, seeing as you have all the answers, what use would a boy have for a rusty spring and a big nail?"

He shrugged. "Who knows? When I was a kid, I used to collect things like rocks and even nutshells. They had some significance at the time, but I've long since forgotten what."

"Nutshells? What on earth good were nutshells?"

"Don't ask. All little boys are part pack rat."

"I think you were part squirrel."

He laughed and handed the items back to Janice, who returned them to the drawer. "All I can tell you," he said, "is that these things were important. That's why they were so carefully hidden away."

She sighed, turning to face the bed, on which lay the open suitcase. Why was it here, half packed?

"Where'd the boy sleep?" Poldoski asked. "There's only one bed?"

"On a cot. It's in the closet there." She motioned in the appropriate direction. "Amy made him fold it up and put it away each morning."

Moving to the bed, he studied the suitcase. "Shall we open it?"

Janice hesitated, knowing that, once they did so, there would be nothing left to do but leave, having accomplished nothing. Somehow, she felt that if the suitcase was there, still waiting for them, she could maintain a little longer the hope of finding something useful here.

When she didn't answer, Poldoski looked up, their eyes meeting. Caught totally off guard, Janice felt that unspoken communication pass between them, uninterrupted this time by the phone. She moved forward, reaching more or less in the direction of the suitcase, yet uncertain just what she was looking for, and stepped into Poldoski's arms. His lips brushed hers, tentatively, questioningly, and then there was no question about it as each responded to the other.

Gently, his hands were beginning to find all the right buttons, touching them, stroking them, and she pushed away while she still could.

"No, Ron, not now. Not on my missing sister's bed, not with my father's empty wheelchair in the next room."

He looked at her apologetically, embarrassed. "Janice, I wasn't trying to take advantage of the situation. It just happened, and I couldn't seem to stop it."

"Under different circumstances, Ron..." She let the sentence trail off unfinished.

"Let's see about the suitcase," he said, pulling the bag over in front of them.

It was a sloppy packing job, as if the clothes had been dumped in hastily. Janice began removing the garments one by one, examining each and setting it aside. When she'd emptied the suitcase, she had a pile of clothes containing five small pairs of pants and two shirts.

"It still makes no sense," she said. "Why so many pants and only two shirts?"

But Poldoski wasn't listening; he was trying to work something from the lining of the suitcase. The object resisted a moment, then poped out of a slit in the lining.

"A poker chip?" Janice asked.

"Not exactly." He handed the red disk to her. On one side was a gold numeral ten. On the other side, also in gold, were the words ELK RIDGE STATE HOSPITAL.

"What the hell is it?" she asked.

"I don't know. But more importantly, how did it get in the suitcase?"

She sat down on the bed, turning the coin over and over in her hand. Something was hanging in the back of her mind, one of those memories whose presence you could sense but which darted away whenever you tried to focus on it. Poker chip, poker chip. Where, just recently, had she heard something about a poker chip?

Then she had it. Her father by the window, watching Mark snoop around outside. He'd reported seeing the boy unearth a poker chip from under the lilac bush. And the bush was near the window that had been forced open the day her tormentor killed Sam. Excitedly, she explained all this to Poldoski.

"Come on," he said. "Let's go back to the station and get on the phone. We've finally got a lead that may take us somewhere."

As they hurried to the car, Janice realized that, although she'd been right in assuming the suitcase might hold a clue, she'd thought so for all the wrong reasons. It seemed the partially packed bag had been nothing more than a hiding place for one of a little boy's treasures. She recalled the words of one of her instructors at the police academy. He'd told his students they had to learn to think like a criminal. He'd said nothing about learning to think like a little boy.

Twelve

Malcolm Anderson had heard the drawers being opened, had felt the slight breeze as fresh air entered his prison. He'd been on the verge of calling out, but something had told him not to, not yet. Then he'd heard kicking, a drawer open, their captor's voice. Helplessly, he'd lain in the dark, listening while their captor had threatened Mark, choked him, then returned him to the stale blackness of their horrible prison. There had been no more kicking, although as far as he could tell the boy had only been warned, not . . . not seriously harmed.

The opening of the drawers, he had to assume, had been solely for the purpose of letting in some badly needed fresh air. For whatever reasons, their abductor apparently didn't plan to let them suffocate, although he was unable to draw much comfort from that conclusion. Their deaths were being postponed, nothing more.

He moved slightly, and pain shot through his body, forcing him to ease himself back into his original position. If he lay still, the suffering parts of his body would eventually stop troubling him, the agony becoming merely a dull ache. He should move, he knew, and not allow any one part of him to remain in contact with the slab too long, but doing so hurt so much.

It was unbearably hot. In the summer, a refrigerator with its plug pulled became an oven. Although his clothes were

149

soaked, his throat was so dry he doubted he could speak, and sometimes, when his mind played tricks on him, he'd see water, even hear it gushing around rocks and tumbling over falls. A desert mirage, except these hallucinations came out of the blackness rather than shimmering in the burning sun.

Again, he thought of their captor's visit. There had been other sounds before the drawers had been closed, the supply of fresh air once more cut off. He'd heard a gasp, and something had fallen. Next there had been some unidentifiable noises, followed by something scraping along the floor, as if it were being dragged. For a few moments, he tried to invent scenarios to go with the sounds, but then his mind began to wander.

Suddenly, he was in a rubber raft, shooting the rapids of some unidentified mountain river. He felt afraid; yet the fear itself was exhilarating as he struggled to keep the raft away from the jagged rocks protruding through the surface; water, cold and invigorating, splashing into the air, rainbows forming in its spray.

Janice and Poldoski, sitting at their respective desks, were both on the line with Dr. Ivan King, the man in charge at Elk Ridge State Hospital north of Duluth. The doctor was at home.

"The coins," he said, "are a kind of money that can only be used at the institution. We have what we call the canteen, although it's actually more like a PX. The patients are given the coins as a reward for . . . well, for all sorts of things. It depends on the patient. Some are in such a bad way that they're rewarded simply for using the bathroom . . . for not soiling themselves. It's an attitudinal thing really. The harder they try, the more they cooperate with us, the more coins they get, and the coins are the only way they can get things like cigarettes and candy bars. There are other kinds of rewards, too. Special trips and things like that.

"Doctor, are the coins accounted for in any way?" Janice asked.

"No, not once they've been given to the patients."

"Would any patient be likely to have the coins in his possession?"

"Oh, certainly. They all get rewarded for something at one time or another. Some patients value them so highly they take them with them when they leave us, even though they're of absolutely no value in the outside world."

"Have there been any escapes from Elk Ridge lately?" Poldoski asked.

"Oh, no. Our security's very good. We have walkaways from time to time, but those are patients who aren't dangerous, and the tight security isn't necessary in their case. The last time a maximum-security patient escaped was over four years ago."

"Doctor," Janice said, "we'll need a list of everyone released from Elk Ridge in the past six months."

"When do you need it?"

"Immediately. Three lives are at stake."

"Oh, dear. I can have the list Teletyped to you first thing in the morning. You want to tell me what this is all about?"

Janice told him.

"Oh, my goodness," the doctor said. "That's terrible. I do hope your father and sister and the little boy are all right."

"Thank you, Doctor. Now I need to know which one of your former patients might be apt to do something like this. The description should help you narrow it down quite a bit."

"None, I hope," he said a little nervously. "Not if we've released them."

"The coin seems to indicate one of them is involved," Janice said.

He sighed. "So it would seem. I'll have to call the staff doctors together first thing in the morning. There are hundreds of patients at Elk Ridge, and I'm not familiar with all of them."

"Could it be done sooner, Doctor?" Poldoski asked. "There are three lives at stake here."

"I'm sorry, but I don't see how. They've all long since gone for the day, and I doubt I could even reach all of them."

After ending the conversation with Dr. King, Janice and Poldoski hung up their phones, turning to face each other across the seven or eight feet of floor tiles separating their desks.

"Well," he said, "we might as well go home."

She nodded. "We might as well."

"Too bad the guy we're looking for wasn't on that bus that crashed. None of this would ever have happened."

"What bus?" Janice rarely read the papers or watched the evening news.

"Up north a while back. A bus from Elk Ridge. Everyone

on board was killed. Twenty-some-odd people. One of those special trips the doctor mentioned, I guess."

"You don't suppose they let the dangerous ones go on those trips, do you?"

He shrugged. "Who knows?"

Yes, Janice thought, it was definitely too bad the kidnapper hadn't been on that bus. But that was only pointless wishing. In the real world, events did not arrange themselves to suit the needs of Janice Anderson.

At least they were making progress now. Although she tried not to let her hopes rise too high, she knew it was likely they would have the name of the kidnapper tomorrow morning. And there would still be five days left to find his captives. Five days before hope of finding them alive began evaporating.

In room eighteen at the Falls Motel, a solitary figure lay on the bed, watching a sitcom on the black and white TV set chained to the wall.

The surprise appearance of the grounds keeper had been handled well. The worn plastic body bag had been ideal. The only thing in the storeroom, it had been discarded, left behind. Dragging the bundle to the car had not been easy, and getting it in the trunk had been exhausting, but both had been accomplished. And the solution, the way to make it appear the old man had died elsewhere, had been right there in the car, waiting. A trunk full of fishing gear. If the authorities checked, they would undoubtedly discover the old man had been an avid fisherman.

A quick drive to the closest likely fishing spot, one within walking distance of town, then the body had been pulled from the trunk, rolled down the incline, and removed from the bag. No blood in the car because of the bag, no marks on the ground because of the thick accumulation of old leaves, no fingerprints because gloves had been worn. Then walk away, the body bag folded and stuffed in a grocery sack that had previously held some of the old man's fishing equipment.

The sack rested on the floor now, beneath the TV set. Its contents would be returned to the mortuary later tonight, when fresh air would again be allowed into the cabinet for corpses.

When to see to that? After this TV show ended? After the news? No, after the late movie. There was no rush.

* * *

"Hey, that's good news," Mike said enthusiastically when Janice had finished relating the latest developments. They sat on the couch while, across Mike's living room, a sitcom played on the color TV set, canned laughter periodically erupting from the speaker.

It made Janice think of how her father hated television, how she'd always expected him to throw out the set as soon as both his TV-watching daughters had left home. When she'd asked him why he hadn't, he'd replied: "Got to have it for election nights." He had to be the only person in America who only watched television once every two years. But these were not good things to be thinking about at the moment.

She addressed herself to Mike's statement. "It's not all good news I'm afraid. I haven't told you yet what was in the note from the kidnapper."

As she related its contents, Mike's expression became worried. When she'd finished, he said: "Christ, Janice, it doesn't make any sense.".

"The only one it makes sense to is apparently a former mental patient."

"Yeah, I guess." He hesitated, frowning, as if what he was about to say would be difficult. "Janice, are the other detectives you work with competent? Can they handle a case like this?"

She certainly hadn't expected him to ask that. "Sure they are. For a town this size, Dakota Falls has a very good police force—well staffed, well trained, well equipped."

Again, he paused, apparently feeling his way cautiously. "Who's the best detective you've got?"

"Mike, why are you asking me all this?"

"Just wondering. Who's the best?"

"Hell, I don't know, Mike. They're all fairly good. I wouldn't single out anyone as being especially good or especially poor. There are a few whose methods I don't like—Mullins for instance—but they get the job done."

"So the investigation wouldn't suffer if any particular officer wasn't on it."

"No, it wouldn't. Now why are you asking me all this?" She had no idea where this was leading. Unless . . . unless he had noticed something about her relationship with Poldoski. She'd been feeling somewhat guilty about what had happened—or almost happened—in Amy's bedroom. Was he going to tell her he didn't want her working with Ron anymore? He'd damn well better not, she decided. He had no right.

"Janice," he said, taking her hand, "I think you should consider stepping back from this, letting the others handle it. Not because you're not doing a good job," he added hastily, "but because . . . well, dammit, you're in danger, and I'd feel a lot better if you were here with me. Besides, you're too close to this thing, too personally involved." His eyes stared into hers, pleading.

Janice was stunned, speechless. When she finally found her voice, she said: "You want me to stay here so you can protect me?"

"Well, yes, dammit, I do. You're very important to me, Janice. I love you." Still, his eyes pleaded for understanding.

Why she didn't explode, she didn't know. Perhaps it was that look in his eyes, the genuine concern she saw there. "Mike," she said slowly, "I'm a trained police officer, and I don't need protecting."

He looked dejected. "Janice, why is it you never listen to me?"

There it was, the problem in their relationship that refused to go away, that sooner or later would have to be dealt with. But why did it have to come up now? "Mike, do *you* ever listen to *me?*"

He looked surprised; apparently the failure to listen had all been on her part. "Of course, I do. You know I do."

"Oh, you hear the words, Mike, but do you ever respect my decisions? Or do you just go along with me to avoid an argument?"

"Janice, I do respect your decisions. It's just . . . just that I don't always understand them."

"No, Mike, what you don't understand is me. You see me as the little woman, someone to be protected. I'm not that, Mike. I can never be that. For your sake as well as mine, please don't expect me to be."

"But, dammit, Janice, when you love someone, you want to protect them. It's natural."

She sighed. "Okay, Mike, but why is the protecting always on your part—even though I'm trained in firearms and self-defense and you're not?"

For several seconds, he stared in silence at the shag carpet. Finally, he said: "I'm sorry. I'll try harder to understand in the future."

If they had a future. But that was too emotional, too draining to be dealt with now. It would have to wait. She squeezed his hand. She did love him, and he obviously loved her. Whatever the future held for them, at the moment she was simply glad to have someone who cared and who wasn't connected to her work.

"This isn't a good time," she said, kissing him on the cheek. "We know now we've got a problem to deal with, but let's handle it later, when there aren't so many other things to worry about."

"Sounds good to me. You eaten?"

"Not since lunch."

"Well, come with me to the kitchen, and I'll show you my collection of TV dinners."

She accompanied him to the refrigerator in the apartment's tiny kitchen, relieved the tense conversation was behind them, even if the problem was not. Staring into the freezer, trying to decide between a roast beef and a turkey frozen dinner, she suddenly lowered her eyes. While she stood before a refrigerator full of food, her father, sister, and nephew had nothing to eat, nothing at all.

Turning away from the refrigerator, she said: "I'm sorry, but I'm really not very hungry right now."

"Can I get you something to drink then?"

Oh, God, she thought. Why did he have to say that?

Amy had been talking to her mother. Even though she'd been only nine when her mother had died, there was no doubt in her mind about the identity of the person who had come to visit. They'd discussed general things: the best makeup to use, the latest fashions. Then, suddenly, Mom had said she had to go, and Amy was once more alone in the blackness.

It had been a nice visit. Not only was Mom's voice so soft and soothing, but her face had been visible in its own gentle light. Now Amy tried to recall that face, but the image had gone from her memory as completely as it had gone from her presence. Why couldn't she remember what Mom looked like? It had only been a few moments ago that she'd left.

"Mom," she whispered. "Please come back. Please."

When there was no answer, she tried again. "Please," she whimpered. "Please come back, Mom. It's so lonely here."

And then there was a presence with her. She could feel it. "Mom?"

The presence was stronger now. Someone was here! "Mom, is that you? Please answer me!"

Something touched her, and she tried to draw away, but there was no room to move.

"Mom! Please!" —

Then something else touched her . . . and something else. Things were touching her all over. Wriggling and kicking, she tried to shake them off, for she suddenly knew what they were.

Caterpillars. The fuzzy bluish caterpillars with the black and white markings that swarmed over trees, turning whole forests into collections of leafless stalks. Thousands of them. All over her.

Frantically, she rolled from side to side, trying to brush them off with her hands. Oh, God. Oh. God. They were on her face, and she couldn't wipe them off. They were all over, above her, below her, dropping on her, crawling on her.

And then she felt wet strands, tightening, restricting her movements. Nooooooo! They were wrapping her into a huge cocoon!

She tried to scream, but the silken strands had been wound around her jaw, sealing her mouth.

"Pleash," she gasped through her teeth. "Pleash, Mawm. Pleash shelp meh."

Neither hearing the sound of drawers being rolled out nor feeling the gentle stirring of the air, Amy was unaware that she had been spared once more from suffocation. She knew only that the cocoon was rapidly enclosing her.

And that the caterpillars were working from within, sealing themselves inside. With her.

Thirteen

Sherrill Roberts trotted into the wooded area near her apartment, on the last leg of her customary early-morning jog. The trail was wide and free of tree roots, and she put on a final burst of speed, her blue jogging suit flowing with the movement of her lithe form, her long dark hair stretching out behind her. Ahead was the footbridge over South Creek, after which the path veered to the right, and left the woods.

It was a pleasantly cool Wednesday morning, the light mist in the air caressing her face as she ran. Soon the sun would burn the mist away, and the day would turn hot and muggy.

An assembly-line worker in a Minneapolis plant manufacturing circuit boards, she got no exercise at all during the day, so she ran in the mornings to keep in shape. Though a twenty-two-year-old with an eye-catching figure, she gained weight easily and was hopelessly addicted to sweets. So far, anyway, the running had done its job. Her husband, who woke up groggy and grouchy, thought she was crazy for expending so much energy so early in the day, but then Burt hated sweets and wouldn't gain weight no matter what he did.

She could see the bridge now through the trees. It was a crude wooden structure of logs and planking with no handrails. Six or seven feet below it, the creek splashed its way over and around the rocks in its bottom, heading, she supposed, for the Mississippi, where the clear water would be lost in the river's

157

mud as it began its long journey to the Gulf of Mexico. This was the only spot where the creek had any current to speak of; in most other locations, it moved leisurely, almost reluctantly along.

She slowed as she stepped onto the bridge, as its damp, moldy planking was usually quite slippery. She had already reached the other bank when something below caught her eye and she stopped. A woman's purse lay near the bank in a shallow pool of water that was unaffected by the current.

Leaving the bridge, Sherrill climbed down the grassy bank, slipping in the moist earth. She managed to reach the water without sliding into it and, leaning precariously forward, grabbed the purse. She scrambled up the bank before examining her discovery.

It was an expensive bag, thick leather, well made. Poking through its soggy contents, she located a wallet. First, she checked to see whether it contained any money. It was, after all, someone else's property, and if there was cash involved, she ought to find out how much. But the change and bill compartments were empty.

Next, she looked for some identification, finding a California driver's license bearing the name Amy Anderson Withers.

Stuffing the wallet back into the purse, she headed for home, where she'd phone the police and report her discovery.

As promised, the list of patients released from Elk Ridge State Hospital during the past six months came in over the Teletype shortly after 8:30. Poldoski had immediately taken it to the computer room, where the names of the former patients were fed into the machine. When he returned, a computer printout in his hand, Janice could tell by the look on his face that the machine had failed to find what they were looking for.

"Only one hit," he said, standing beside her desk. "Mary Truscott. Remember her?"

Janice nodded. While her husband was out of town on business, Mary Truscott had murdered their two young children and buried the bodies at night in a backyard garden. Janice had assisted on the case. "How could they release *her*?"

"That's what I was wondering until I checked. The good doctors decided she's now competent to stand trial, and the

DA's office sent someone to pick her up. She's in the county jail."

"And that's it? Not a single, solitary soul who got out of the nut house in the last six months has any connection to me at all?"

"Not to any of your cases, no. But there might be other connections, things the computer wouldn't know about." He laid a sheet of Teletype paper on her desk. "There's only about thirty names on the list. See if any of them ring a bell."

She scanned it quickly. "I've never heard of any of these people, Ron. Except for Mary Truscott." She studied the list more carefully. "She's also the only one here from Dakota Falls." She looked up at Poldoski. "Are you sure she's in jail?"

"Positive. Besides, we're looking for a man."

Janice sighed. The disappointment she'd been holding back was slowly sinking in. "A friend or a relative of hers maybe?"

He shook his head. "Her parents are both dead, no brothers or sisters. Her husband, poor bastard, quit his job and moved to New Mexico. Besides, let's face it, Janice, your role in that case was pretty limited. If someone was seeking revenge, they'd go after Mullins or Greene. They were the investigating officers."

She couldn't deny that. All she'd done was run errands. In fact, she'd never even seen Mary Truscott, except for the photo in the newspaper, and she hadn't been called to testify at the hearing to determine whether the woman was competent to stand trial.

She pushed the list of names away from her. Unless the doctors came up with someone, the case was right back where it had started. And time was running out.

But then how did the coin get under the bush outside the house? Who had dropped it there? And when?

"Ron, when Dr. King calls, I'm going to ask him to send down the fingerprints of every person on this list so Ross can compare them with the partials."

"Good idea."

The call from Elk Ridge came through half an hour later. Janice signaled Poldoski, who was back at his own desk, and he got on the line.

"I'm sorry to report that we can't help you," Dr. King said. "I met with the staff doctors this morning as I promised, but neither they nor I could think of a former patient who'd be likely to do what's being done to you, Miss Anderson."

"None that were even borderline?" Janice asked in desperation.

"No, I would have told you in that case."

"Doctor, this is Detective Poldoski. Can you tell us what kind of person might do something like this?"

"Well . . . it's difficult to talk about such things in generalities, but I'll tell you what I can. There are two basic possibilities. First, that this is someone who has a real grudge against Miss Anderson, someone who's been badly wounded by something she's done. The second possibility is that this person sees Miss Anderson as a symbol of something. The logic here is sometimes very distorted because of the type mind you're dealing with. Say someone, for whatever distorted reasons, despises authoritative women or beautiful women or tall women or whatever category Miss Anderson might fit in to. This person can decide that Miss Anderson symbolizes the entire class in question, and that by destroying her he can destroy all women like her, at least symbolically.

"Of course, in a way, these two possibilities I gave you are actually opposite ends of a continuum. There are all sorts of possibilities between the two. It could be someone Miss Anderson knows, but to whom she's done nothing she's aware of, not knowing she's become a symbol to this person. On the other hand, it could be a complete stranger, someone who saw her quite by accident, and something in her appearance or in her behavior triggered something in this person's mind.

"I had a case very much along these lines recently. The patient had always wanted to be like one of her former friends, a girl she called Shirley. But it wasn't in her to be like Shirley, and she couldn't tolerate the thought of being anything less. Given the chance, she would do everything possible to destroy Shirley because only by doing so could she escape from Shirley's shadow. Shirley, of course, probably knew nothing about any of this. In fact, I gather the two were just casual friends who never developed a real close, lasting relationship. Did that help you at all?"

"Believe me, Doctor, every little bit helps," Poldoski said. "What became of this patient you were talking about?"

"She's dead. One of those on that bus, I'm afraid. Terrible

thing. Everyone on board killed. Twenty-eight people."

Janice thanked the doctor for his help and requested the fingerprints of those named on the list of former patients. He said he'd have copies made and have them sent air express from Duluth.

As soon as they ended the conversation, Poldoski came over to Janice and put his hand on her shoulder. "Well, this didn't do us much good, did it?"

Sighing, Janice shook her head. Five days left and their best lead had just fallen flat on its face. Oh, God, Janice thought, are they going to die a horrible death while we stumble blindly along, accomplishing nothing? All because I'm a symbol to some crazy son of a bitch I never even met?

"I'm afraid I got my hopes up, too," Poldoski said softly.

Again, she sighed. "Well, we both should have known better. The best-looking lead is often the first one to fizzle out, and we both know it. Well, what do we do now?"

"We go back to checking out abandoned buildings, I guess. Next one on the list is in Bloomington."

Something tugged at Janice's memory, something Dr. King had said. Like an afterimage, it vanished whenever you tried to focus on it. "Ron, why did you ask what happened to Dr. King's patient? My name's not Shirley, and our kidnapper, as you pointed out, is male."

He shrugged. "Just curious. He was speaking about her in the past tense, and I wondered why."

"Oh. I was hoping you were onto something."

"If I was, you wouldn't have to ask."

She nodded. He stood there a moment, looking down at her, then turned and went back to his own desk.

Janice let her eyes wander around the room. As usual, the office was in a constant state of flux, nearly every desk occupied one moment, the place practically deserted the next. A detective's paperwork was endless, and it seemed every time you had an hour or so you could use to catch up, the phone would ring and out you'd go again, creating still more paperwork that would have to be done sometime. Preferably sometime before the captain asked you where the hell your report was.

At this particular moment, the only people at their desks besides her and Poldoski were Mullins and Ted Reynolds.

Every last one of them, she knew, had gone to the captain

and volunteered to work on the kidnapping, even those who disapproved of her. In a way, she was grateful, although she knew it wasn't because of any feelings toward her that they were volunteering. It was because they took it personally, because they knew what could happen to her could happen to them.

Her thoughts were interrupted by the captain, who had just entered the room from the hallway, carrying a brown paper bag.

"Ron, Janice," he said, and they followed him into his office. As soon as they were seated, Bishop dumped the contents of the sack on his desk. It was a familiar-looking brown leather purse.

"It's Amy's," Janice said excitedly. "Where was it found?"

"In South Creek," the captain answered. "A jogger discovered it this morning. No money in it, but your sister's ID was there. Ross has already dusted it. Nothing."

Nothing, Janice thought. It was always nothing. And what did finding the purse in South Creek mean? The stream wound its way along the southern edge of town, passing through some very lightly populated spots. A convenient place to toss something away. Then a new thought struck her.

"Captain, I don't know how much, but I do know Amy was carrying quite a bit of cash in that purse. Any chance the person who found it removed the cash before reporting it?"

Bishop frowned. "Not from what I can gather, although you never know. Hell, someone else could have found the bag before the jogger did and wiped off his or her prints. Why are you concerned about the money?"

"It's just that it fits the pattern. The merchant patrolman was attacked for his gun and money, and now my sister's money has been taken. There's a good chance that whoever we're dealing with has to steal to survive."

"We touched on that before, Janice. What are you getting at?"

"Well, it just doesn't seem likely a person like that would be living out there in some white frame house with flowers in the front yard. Sure, it happens. You find common burglars living in hundred-thousand-dollar houses, but not many. I think we should have Katherine Fox get together with Jacobs and get a composite made. Then we can use it to check out the hotels and motels in the area. We might get lucky."

Bishop nodded. "All right. I was going to have a composite made anyway, so I could give it to the papers and TV stations. I'd have done it sooner, but hell, most average citizens could be sitting right next to the guy we're looking for and never recognize him from a composite."

They were pretty iffy, all right. Still, it was worth a try. Hell, anything was worth a try at this point.

"Captain," Poldoski said. "I think we should have some people checking out the area along the creek. I know it's another long shot, but somebody might have seen something. It might help if they had the composite to take with them."

"Also," Janice put in, "we're getting too bogged down on this abandoned building thing. We spend all our time on the telephone, trying to find out who the owners are and get permission to go inside. We could use some help there, too."

"We can do the checking," Poldoski said. "What we need is someone to do the phoning."

"We can do the motels, too," Janice added. "We're only getting into the buildings at the rate of two or three a day, and it only takes a few moments to see whether there's anyone inside."

"Good enough," Bishop said. "Reynolds can do the phone work, and I'll put Mullins and Watson on South Creek. Now, what has Elk Ridge come up with?"

Poldoski sighed. "A big zero. We ran the names of all the patients released over the past six months through the computer and came up with nothing. None of the names mean a damn thing to Janice. And the only likely candidate the shrinks came up with is the wrong sex and dead. We've asked for the prints of all the people on our list of former patients, and we'll have Ross compare them to the partials."

Bishop looked thoughtful. "I don't know of anything to do except what we're doing. We can have just about every officer in the whole damned force if we need them, but until we get something to go on, there'd be nothing for them to do."

"If we don't have anything by tomorrow," Janice said, "I'm going to call Elk Ridge back and have them send us the names of all the patients released during the last two years. It's always possible we didn't go back far enough, although I find it hard to believe anyone would carry around a completely useless coin for any great length of time, especially when it came from a place he'd have no reason to remember fondly."

"Yeah, but you're not crazy," Poldoski said.

"That's one of the things that makes a case like this so difficult," the captain said. "We're not crazy, so the only way we can look at things is with more-or-less conventional logic, and the guy we're looking for doesn't think that way at all." He shook his head. "Not at all."

Janice was still grateful for the way Bishop and the others were treating her. No punches were being pulled, and only rarely was bad news accompanied by sympathetic looks or hesitating voices. No sugarcoating. It wouldn't have been this way when she first joined the division. Had she showed what she was made of, gained some measure of acceptance? Or . . . or was this, in some twisted way, a method of showing her she didn't belong? She recalled the times when, as a patrol officer, she'd pointedly been shown the bloody remains of accident victims while the other cops watched from the corners of their eyes, ready to snicker should she turn away in horror.

Stop it! she told herself. She had enough problems without adding paranoia.

Picking up Amy's still-damp purse, she examined it, turning it over in her hands. Amy would have selected it, as she chose everything, with great care. A purse was a truly personal thing, its contents perhaps the most revealing thing about a woman other than the place she lived. And like her home, the inside of a woman's bag was private, a place where the real you could hide undetected. Without opening it, she put the bag back on the desk. Although she knew the captain would ask her to examine the purse's contents, she wanted to put it off for at least a few moments.

Realizing her mind was drifting in a dangerous direction, she abruptly shifted her thoughts. If her theory was right about the kidnapper's needing to steel to survive, then what had happened to her father's wallet? Had it, too, been tossed into the creek? Much smaller than the purse, it might never turn up at all if that was the case. And why relieve Amy of her bag? Why not just take the money, then give it back? On the other hand, why give it back? So many questions. So few answers.

And so little time.

*   *   *

In the hot, muggy blackness, Amy slept, her mind having sought escape in slumber. She would sleep a long time, for when she awoke she would still be encased in the cocoon with thousands of fuzzy caterpillars. Hungry caterpillars that had nothing to eat. Nothing except . . .

Though still asleep, she screamed, her dry throat restricting the noise to a gasp, her fingers clawing at the sticky white fibers imprisoning her.

She was unaware that only a few feet away, just outside the confines of her prison, a gray-haired man in a dark suit stood motionless, his eyes taking in the room. Nor had she been aware of the sudden jerk of his head at the instant she had cried out in her sleep.

Fourteen

James Heikkinen had been shocked by the death of his grounds keeper. A nice old guy who'd probably never offended anyone in his life, Carl Olson certainly hadn't deserved to die at the hand of some thug. And it was not at all like him to slip away from work to go fishing. Though definitely an avid fisherman, Carl simply didn't sneak off like that; he was just too dependable and trustworthy to do such a thing. Still, the facts spoke for themselves, and James Heikkinen was not a flawlessly accurate judge of character.

These thoughts were on his mind as James Heikkinen stepped into the room he and his assistants had referred to among themselves as the meat locker. All the somberness usually associated with morticians, of course, vanished when they weren't dealing with clients. The living ones. Many a crude joke had been told while dealing with the other variety.

He had come here to the now vacant Dakota Falls mortuary to make sure everything was in order. If Carl had been taking surreptitious fishing breaks, it was possible he had been neglecting his duties, although the grounds had certainly shown no sign of it. Nor, so far, had the building.

A tall man in his fifties with a full head of gray hair and deeply set blue eyes, Heikkinen had become a funeral director simply because his father had been one, which had provided him with a ready-made job. He had no regrets about his occupation; the Dakota Falls funeral home had been exceedingly lucrative, and he expected the new one in Bloomington to be even more so.

He stood for a moment in the "meat locker," looking at the built-in refrigeration unit with its rows of compartments. It had been a shame to leave such an expensive piece of equipment behind, but removing it from the wall and reassembling it in Bloomington would have cost more than the new unit he'd purchased. For that reason, he had been unable to sell it, and the highway department had refused to pay him for it. He was threatening to sue.

As he was turning to leave the room, he heard something that made his head snap around, his eyes sweeping the refrigeration unit. He listened intently, hearing nothing, although he could have sworn he'd heard a noise come from the unit. A gasp or a groan.

Feeling rather uneasy, he stepped up to the unit and rolled out one of the slabs. God knew how many bodies had lain here over the years, awaiting burial or cremation. But at the moment, nothing was here, living or otherwise. He rolled out another slab, then another, finding only empty compartments. After a moment's hesitation, he pushed them back into the wall.

Disgusted with himself, he sighed. Good grief. Perhaps the uninitiated heard spooky noises in places like this, but certainly not a seasoned career mortician. The next thing you know, he thought, I'll be whistling in graveyards—and for a funeral director, that could be disastrous.

The building had been securely locked and nothing within

had been disturbed. There was no way anyone could be in the refrigeration unit. Before his mind could play any more tricks on him, he left the room and resumed his inspection.

A few minutes later, satisfied everything was in order, he left the building. He started his black Cadillac and, taking the back way out of the grounds, drove slowly along the hedge-lined road that led to Roosevelt Avenue. He had nearly reached the street when, rounding a curve, he came upon a young woman walking toward him. The car was very quiet, and its sudden appearance had startled her. Pulling up beside her, he stopped.

"Can I help you?" he asked.

"Help me?" She was blond, wearing blue jeans, rather plain-looking. She seemed confused, nervous.

"Are you looking for something?"

"No," she replied, her intense blue eyes watching him war-ily. "I'm just here to enjoy the park."

This had happened before, and it always irritated him. "This is *not* a park. This is private property. Didn't you see the sign?"

"Sign? No, I must have missed it."

They always said that, probably knowing he wouldn't be-lieve it but couldn't disprove it. "Well, this is a funeral home, not a public park."

"Oh."

They stared at each other a moment; then she turned and began walking in the opposite direction. Heikkinen watched her go. She was average height for a woman but too thin, practically shapeless. Even so, a little makeup, some better clothes, and the judicious use of a curling iron would do won-ders for her appearance, he decided.

There had been a look in her eyes he'd seen often in his clients'. They heard him, acknowledged his words, but their minds were elsewhere, dealing with their grief. Although this young woman had not seemed to be grieving, her mind had indeed been elsewhere. Behind those blue eyes, her brain had been struggling with powerful emotions.

Strange, he thought, how that so often manifested itself in an outward calm. Though nervous at first, presumably from the start he'd given her, the young woman had been quite cool by the time their brief conversation had ended.

He waited until she was out of sight, then continued on his

way. When he pulled onto Roosevelt Avenue, she was nowhere to be seen. Dismissing her from his thoughts, he headed toward Bloomington.

Mark had been scared when he heard the drawers being opened, afraid the funny man would choke him again. He'd lain perfectly still, not making a sound, hoping the funny man would go away. It had been especially scary because each time he heard a drawer being opened, it had been closer to him. The third one the funny man had opened had been right next to him, and he'd been sure the man would open his next and choke him again, maybe choke him until he couldn't breathe anymore.

But then the funny man had closed the drawers and gone away. At least Mark thought he went away. He couldn't be sure because he couldn't see him.

He still kept his eyes closed and his hands at his sides, although every now and then he had to lift his lids a little to make sure the blackness was still there. It always was, and it was scary. But not as scary as the funny man.

He wished he could have a drink of water. His mouth felt funny, like it was full of sand. Even his eyes felt that way a little. Usually he didn't like water very much. He liked Coke or Kool-Aid. But now, he just wanted water. A lot more than he'd ever wanted Pepsi or Kool-Aid or orange pop.

He hurt, too. The thing he was lying on was too hard. He wondered if the funny man would ever let them out. He didn't understand why the funny man didn't like him or Mommy or Granddad. He thought maybe they were being punished, but he didn't understand why. He wondered what they'd done to make the funny man want to hurt them.

And he wondered about the voices that sometimes whispered to him . . . if maybe they weren't just pretend voices like he'd thought, if maybe they were really there.

He had no answers for any of these questions, and he began to cry, very quietly so the funny man wouldn't hear him and get mad and choke him again. He failed to realize that, although his body shook with sobs, his eyes, having no moisture to make tears, were dry.

* * *

Dr. Andrew Eklund sat at his desk, staring at the walls of his small office in the basement of the St. Louis County Medical Center in Duluth.

Before him was a stack of twenty-seven file folders, each representing a bus-crash victim whose remains had been identified to his satisfaction. The folders had names now, instead of just numbers. It had seemed an impossible task, but he'd accomplished it. With one expection.

Another folder, which bore the name of the twenty-eighth victim, lay beside the others. By simple process of elimination, the one remaining body had to go with the one remaining name. That was easy enough. All he had to do was fill out a couple of forms, make a phone call to the medical examiner, and everyone would be off his back, case closed, back to the normal everyday business of his department.

More than once, he'd picked up a pen and started to do just that, and each time, he'd stopped short of completing the act through which he could rid himself of the whole tiresome business. But, dammit, the remains were simply not those of a five-foot-five-inch twenty-eight-year-old, and no amount of wishing or paper shuffling would make it so. Something somewhere was wrong.

He'd checked with Elk Ridge and had been informed there was no error; the people said to have been on the bus had indeed been on it. Patients and staff alike were checked off a list as they boarded. No patients or staff members were unaccounted for, so there could have been no unauthorized switching of job assignments or shuffling of patients. It was all very carefully supervised. The list provided was beyond question.

Reluctantly, he picked up the phone and called Walter Mitchell, the security chief at Elk Ridge.

As soon as Eklund had identified himself, Mitchell said: "Hey, are you ready to release those bodies yet? Christ, I've got the relatives of damn near every last one of them screaming at me."

"So have I. But I've still got the same problem with—"

"I know who with. The name's burned permanently into my memory. I've told you everything I can tell you. One of those bodies has to match up with that name. There's no other way."

"You'll have a hard time convincing me of that unless you can find some way to stretch a person five inches and make them ten years younger."

The security man sighed. "All I can do is repeat myself. There's no way any unauthorized person could have been on that bus."

"It wouldn't pick up a passenger, would it?"

"You've got to be kidding!"

He had to admit it was a dumb question. "All right, how about this? Someone sees the crash and tries to help, only to get caught in the explosion and fire."

"Then you'd have twenty-nine victims instead of twenty-eight."

At least he had an answer for that. "Not if one of the patients escaped."

The security man sighed again. "Look, Doctor, you're reaching for something that isn't there."

"Dammit," the pathologist said angrily, "so are you if you think I can change a five-foot-ten-inch teen-age body into one that's almost thirty and nowhere near that tall."

"How can you be so sure when so many of the bodies were burned beyond recognition?"

"We've been over this before. According to the data your people provided, *no one* on the bus matched that description. Admittedly, the bodies were badly burned, but not so badly that I couldn't determine the height, sex, and approximate age of the victims."

"Well," the security man said, sounding resigned, "what do you suggest we do?"

"Could we ask the state police to reinvestigate the accident?"

"Forget the *we*. I've got to work with those guys. *You* ask them."

"What I want to know is: Would it do any good?"

"I don't see how it could. All the evidence has been removed. There's nothing to investigate. They've already gone over the bus. They found it had a ruptured fuel tank, which was responsible for the fire."

"Is smoking allowed on the bus?"

"Absolutely not."

"Then what ignited the gasoline?"

"Heat from the engine or sparks thrown off as the metal slid over a rock. How the hell should I know? Sometimes cars get hit in the rear end and go boom. Why not a fire caused by a bus crash?"

Eklund could find no fault with that argument. "I'll get back to you about the identification," he said.

"When?"

"As soon as I can."

After hanging up the phone, the pathologist reached for the form that would put his problems to rest. He filled in the first few blanks, then wadded up the paper and threw it away.

Charles Nordin lay in his hospital bed, thinking. Again and again, he'd forced himself to recall the blurry face hovering above him. It hung there, menacing only because of the circumstances, not really a threatening image by itself. *An angel of the night.*

Damn, he thought. What the hell does that mean?

And then he nearly had the answer. It had something to do with his misconception of that face, something he'd assumed incorrectly. He tried to relax his mind, to let it come, but in the next instant the answer was gone, no closer than it had been before. He muttered to himself, frustrated.

It was something totally obvious, something he'd concluded without really thinking about it. An angel, an angel. Trying to picture one, he came up with an image of someone in a white robe, floating on a cloud and holding a harp. The person who'd attacked him sure as hell hadn't stabbed him with a harp.

It was like trying to remember the name of someone or the title of a song. You knew the damn thing, but the harder you tried to recall it, the farther away it seemed to get. It seemed to be closest when you were thinking about something else. But sooner or later, you'd get it.

Just as he'd get this. Eventually.

Janice was at her desk when Jacobs returned from Katherine Fox's house with the composite of the kidnapper. A short, bald man in his late forties, Jacobs was one of the trio that worked in the department's lab. Unlike Ross and Kline, who were police officers, Jacobs was an employee, a lab technician who handled the microscope and test-tube work. How he became the department's specialist at working up composites no one seemed to know. It was just taken for granted that when you wanted one you saw Jacobs.

He stopped at Janice's desk and said: "I was so sorry to hear about your father and sister and the little boy. I hope they're all right."

"Thank you," she replied, thinking how empty those words sounded, even when they were spoken with sincerity.

"We've got a good bunch of people here," Jacobs said. "We'll find them." With that, he turned, taking two quick strides to Poldoski's desk. "Anything new on the kidnapping, Ron?"

"Nothing promising. That the composite?"

Jacobs handed him the manila envelope he was carrying. "We worked on it for over an hour, and she says that's as close as she can get."

Janice joined them as Poldoski slipped the single sheet of paper from the envelope, a copy of the face Jacobs and Katherine Fox had assembled using transparent overlays bearing the various features. Like most composites, it was really no one, for real people didn't have number one noses or number two eyebrows that could be fitted together as if assembling a picture puzzle. Yet, as she stared at the expressionless face, its features outlined in black and white, it nudged in her memory. Had she seen that face before?

It was a plain face, average in most respects, small nose, thin lips, a moustache, the hair somewhat long for a man's but not unfashionably so. Its overall quality, if it had one, was that it seemed the sort of face you'd never pick out of a crowd, an unmemorable face. And vaguely, she sensed what Katherine Fox had described as effeminate. It was a hard feeling to pin down, but except for the moustache, the face seemed to have few masculine qualities.

Again, she felt something in her memory being gently prodded. Do I know you? she thought. Have I seen you somewhere, done something to you? Or am I nothing but a symbol, something your deranged mind has decided must be destroyed to satisfy some need understood only by you?

"Anyone you know?" Poldoski asked, studying her face.

"No. But there's something . . . something vaguely familiar about it."

"You think you might have seen him before?"

"I don't know."

"At best," Jacobs said, "a composite is a close resemblance. Don't look at it as if it were a photograph. Try to let your imagination change the things that don't seem quite right."

Janice tried, but nothing happened. Did she want so badly to recognize that face that she was forcing herself to think it was familiar? Poldoski and Jacobs were looking at her expectantly. She shook her head. "The longer I look at it, the less familiar it seems."

Handing the composite back to Jacobs, Poldoski said: "I'll need about a hundred copies." Then, when Jacobs had departed, he said to Janice: "On this vacant building thing, I've discovered there are some places we didn't know anything about, buildings that are going to be torn down to make room for a new freeway. None of those were on the list we got from the city because they were condemned by the state. We have to get that list from the highway department."

"Are we going to check out that place in Bloomington?"

"Reynolds hasn't been able to locate anyone who can give us permission to enter. Let's start on the motels, and if Reynolds has any luck on this list, he can either let us know or handle it himself."

A few minutes later, Jacobs came in with the copies of the composite. Janice got her purse from the bottom drawer of her desk.

There weren't that many motels in the area, and by midafternoon, they'd checked most of them. Having just left a place called the Suburban Manor Motor Lodge, they were heading west on Pennington, Poldoski driving their unmarked car.

It was another hot, muggy day, and although Janice tried not to think about it, she knew conditions for anyone locked in an airtight compartment would be unbearable. Deprived of water and forced to breathe hot, stale air, an invalid, a woman, and a little boy were being slowly and very cruelly murdered.

Suddenly, the scenery changed, the homes and businesses replaced by a block-long expanse of trees and grass and flowers. Heikkinen's Funeral Home. Janice looked away. Despite the peaceful beauty of its parklike grounds, the last thing she wanted to see right now was a mortuary.

And then, in spite of her efforts to block the thought from

her consciousness, she wondered whether this was where she'd have to go to make the arrangements if she had three bodies to bury. Except for Mark's family on his father's side, about which she knew practically nothing, she was the only close relative for any of the three. Should it be necessary, the arrangements would be her responsibility. The only way she could pay for it would be by selling the house.

She shuddered.

How could she think about such things? What was wrong with her that she allowed herself to consider funeral expenses while three members of her family were suffering at the hands of a madman? They were still alive. They would be rescued. They would, dammit, they would!

Ahead was another motel. A seedy-looking place, the one-story structure formed a U around a graveled parking area in which clumps of weeds were growing. Poldoski pulled up to the office. The sign out front, in white letters on a faded blue background, said FALLS MOTEL.

Inside, they were greeted by a paunchy man with thick, furry arms and a tangle of chest hairs poking out at the top of his shirt.

"Afternoon," he said. "What can I do for you?"

Flashing their shields, they introduced themselves. His eyes taking in every inch of Janice, the man behind the counter identified himself as Nick Quiller, the motel's owner. Through an open door behind him, Janice could see a portion of what she assumed to be Quiller's quarters. A beer can stood on the arm of a shabby chair.

"If it's about the broad that was selling it in fourteen," he said, "I pitched her out last week." He grinned. "Right after I noticed this car hanging around. Looked a lot like the one you drove up in just now. Had the same little antenna on the trunk lid."

"Wasn't one of ours," Poldoski said. "We didn't know anything about a prostitute in room fourteen."

"That right? Well, it doesn't matter. I've got nothing against whores, but I don't run a cathouse. I can put up with anything from one-night stands to nymphomaniacs, but I don't care to be a pimp."

Janice handed him a copy of the composite. "Any of your guests look like this?"

Laying it on the counter, he studied it thoughtfully. "No," he said slowly, "never seen this guy."

"You can keep that picture." She pulled a card from her purse. "Here. If anyone should show up who looks like that, we'd appreciate a call."

"Sure," he said, examining the card. "What's this guy done?"

"Kidnapped three people."

His eyes widened. "You mean the kidnapping I heard about on TV? The guy who grabbed a cop's family?"

"My family," Janice said icily.

"Oh. Hey, I'm sorry if I . . . I'll sure call you if he shows up here."

A few moments later, Janice and Poldoski were back in the car, again heading west on Pennington.

After the cops had gone, Nick Quiller remained at the counter, studying the picture of the kidnapper. Suddenly, he chuckled. By God, he did recognize that face—not that it would help the dicks any. Take off the moustache and it would look a hell of a lot like the broad in eighteen. Arol Adkins. Now wasn't that a laugh?

Weird chick, that one. Never said anything to anyone. Weird name, too, as if her folks had named her Carol and the C got torn off the birth certificate or something. Wasn't much to look at, but he wasn't fussy. He could show her the picture, show her how much it looked like her with a moustache. It would be an excuse to get together with her and see if she wanted to fool around a little bit. Sometimes the plain, skinny ones were dynamite in the sack.

And thinking about the sack, man, would he like to bed that lady cop. That, Nick old buddy, was some of the finest stuff you've seen in a long, long while. Eatin' stuff, pure and simple.

He sighed. Best thing that ever happened to him was when his wife had run off with that welder. Left him free to enjoy the better things in life. She was still back in Kansas, he supposed. When his aunt had died, leaving him the motel, he'd left Wichita without even bothering to find out whether she was still in town. Probably a good thing, too. If she'd known he'd inherited something, she'd have wanted a legal divorce so she could get a piece of it. Aw, to hell with her, he decided.

Again, he turned his thoughts to Arol Adkins. The more he thought about it, the more convinced he was she would be good in bed. Damn good experiences he'd had with those plain, skinny ones. Damn good. Probably should have tried her before now. It was that cold, weird look in her eyes that had put him off, he supposed.

Yup, later on he'd pay her a visit and take the picture with him.

Fifteen

It was early evening when Nick Quiller, his thick black hair carefully combed, his favorite cologne having been liberally applied, rapped lightly on the door of room eighteen.

There were two parts of his theory of how you scored with women. The first was that they preferred men who were clean and smelled nice. The second was not to give up too easily, not to take no for an answer until you were sure they meant it. They all wanted it, he knew that. The problem was that some of them felt they had to say no and then pretend to let you talk them out of it.

"Who's there?" Arol's voice said from behind the door.

"It's me, honey. Nick Quiller."

"Who?"

"The manager."

"What do you want?"

"Let me in and I'll tell you."

"I'm busy right now."

"I've got something to show you," he teased. "You've got to let me in if you want to see it."

"What?"

"The police brought it today. They were looking for you." He chuckled to himself. "Really, honey. I'm not making it up. They left me something to show to you."

From the other side of the door came nothing but silence.

"Arol?"

After another few moments of silence, the door swung open. She stood there in a thin white robe, her hair dripping wet. "Let me see it," she demanded.

"Not out here." He smiled.

She hesitated, her expression confused. And then he noticed her eyes. They were wide, frightened. Jesus, he thought; was it possible she was really wanted for something? He must have scared the hell out of her. Her usually pale face was damn near as white as her robe.

"Come in," she said, stepping back from the doorway.

Once inside, he plopped down on the bed, grinning at her. "It's nothing to get upset about, honey. Nick's here, and he'll take care of you."

She stared at him, her thin fingers nervously pulling at the ends of her wet hair. "What do you want to show me?"

"In a minute, honey. You get your hair taken care of and come back when you're presentable."

Her eyes narrowed. "Show it to me."

"This?" He slipped the folded picture from his shirt pocket and held the white square of paper in the air. When she came forward and grabbed for it, he stood, holding it above her reach, then slipped his free arm around her, pulling her against him. As he'd expected, she was all skin and bone.

"Now you go make yourself presentable, honey. Then I'll show it to you." He gently pushed her away.

Again, she stared at him, but now there was hostility in her eyes, the fear and confusion replaced by anger. And he saw something else in those blue eyes, something he couldn't quite put his finger on, something fierce and determined.

"Go on," he said. "Go pretty yourself up, and then I'll show it to you." He returned the picture to his shirt pocket.

She remained where she was a moment or two, apparently

sizing him up, then turned and walked into the bathroom, closing the door behind her.

Letting his eyes wander around the room, he decided she kept the place neat enough. For his kitchenettes, he provided only weekly maid service, so most of the cleaning and straightening was up to the occupants. There were no dirty dishes piled in the tiny sink; the bed on which he was sitting had been made; the blue jeans and shirt draped over the back of a chair were the only clothes that had been left out. Couldn't tell much about her from the room.

Usually, when he'd got this far, he had a pretty good idea whether he'd score. But with this one, you just couldn't tell. Broad was weird. Really weird.

His eyes still sweeping the room, he suddenly realized there was something wrong here. For a closet, the room had an alcove with a bar running across it for hanging clothes. On that bar were a few hangers, and that was all. No clothes. And there were no suitcases anywhere to be seen. She really might be on the run from the law.

Getting off the bed, he went to the dresser and opened the top drawer. It contained a pair of panties, three pairs of socks, and a lot of unused space. He noted the absence of bras, but then she was so flat-chested she'd probably never worn one in her life.

The middle of the dresser's three drawers was empty. He pushed it closed and opened the bottom one. Well, now, he thought, studying its contents. What is all this? The drawer contained two scarves, a ball of string, a notepad, pens and pencils, a box of crayons, and a roll of clothesline from which a sizable length had been removed. He picked up one of the scarves to see whether there was anything underneath it, and something fell out that started his mind churning furiously. There, in the bottom of the drawer, was a fake moustache that looked very much like the one in the police drawing. Jee-sus! he thought. Could it be? Could this weird, skinny broad be the one who'd grabbed the lady cop's family?

Stuffing the moustache in his shirt pocket, he closed the drawer and went to the clothes on the chair. In the pockets of the pants, he found a nail file, a wad of bills and some change, and a wicked-looking knife. A switchblade. He pressed the release, and a long, sharp blade snapped into place. A knife like this was good for one thing: hurting somebody. He folded the blade back into the handle, putting the knife and the other things he'd found in the pants on the dresser.

His thoughts racing, he tried to recall the details of the kidnapping as he'd heard them on the news. Scarves. The driver of the van had been gagged and blindfolded with scarves. And tied up. With clothesline? He either couldn't remember or the reporter on the news hadn't said—or maybe it was one of those things cops didn't reveal, so they could trip up people who liked to confess to things they didn't do. And there was something else, something that had just come out, something he'd heard on the radio just before coming over here. There'd been a stabbing, that was it. Some night watchman or something. And the cops thought it might have been done by the same guy. Guy? Hell, it wasn't any guy. The broad had fooled them completely. Cops would look like a pack of dip-shits when they found out.

Hearing a noise behind him, he turned. She was standing beside the bed, her hands behind her back, watching him. She was dressed now—clean jeans and a fresh shirt—and her hair, though still damp, had been combed out.

"I'm really surprised at you, honey," he said, grinning. Taking the picture from his pocket, he unfolded it and held it up. With his other hand he held up the moustache, his eyes darting between the young woman's face and the objects in his hands.

She watched him calmly, saying nothing.

"How'd a skinny broad like you ever manage to do all that?" When she didn't answer, he said: "At least tell me this. Why'd you do it?"

She smiled faintly. "Why am I destroying Janice, do you mean?"

"Yeah, whatever her name is."

"So I can survive. So I can become whole for the first time in my life."

Oh, oh. This crap about being whole was coming from somewhere out in left field. This one was headed for the loony bin. "That don't make no sense at all, babe."

"It makes perfect sense."

"Yeah, well, you'll get a chance to tell it to the shrinks. You and me are going over to the office and wait for the cops to get here."

"NO!" she screamed. "No police! I have a right to be whole!"

"Now calm down, honey. Just accept it. You and me have to go over to the office and call the cops. There's no use in your getting all upset about it."

Suddenly, she was calm again, her blue eyes fixed on his face. "You haven't called them yet."

"Hell, honey, I just now figured out it's you they're looking for. Came as quite a shock, too." He shook his head. "A skinny broad like you. Amazing."

This was the point, he figured, where she'd start unbuttoning her blouse, offering him a little fun if he'd just forget about the cops. And he'd have to decide whether to screw her first or just take her over to the office. No, he decided, couldn't screw her. This whole thing would be damn complicated, and balling her would just make it worse. Oh, well, there was always the broad in nine. A little chubby, but then sometimes the chubby ones appreciated it more.

"Come on, honey. Give me your hand. I won't hurt you, but I can't take the chance that you might run for it when we get outside."

Apparently, she wasn't going to resist, because she removed one of her hands from behind her back, reaching toward him with it. But as he started toward her, the other hand came out from behind her, and it was holding a gun. Before he could react, both hands were gripping the revolver, aiming it at him, and behind the barrel, which looked enormous at that moment, he saw her eyes, and they were intense and cold and merciless. They were killer's eyes.

The gun fired.

Janice sat beside Mike on his couch, trying to lose herself in the inanities of the sitcom playing on the TV set. She and Poldoski had finished the rounds of the motels and checked two vacant buildings in Bloomington, all to no avail. Mullins and Watson had learned nothing by checking with the residents of the South Creek area. The fingerprints of the former patients had arrived from Elk Ridge, and none of those prints had matched the partials.

Beside her, Mike stared at the TV screen, a slight frown on his face. They had spoken little that evening. Both realized there was something wrong with their relationship and that any serious discussion of it was being held in abeyance until the present crisis was over. Now it seemed their relationship was being held in abeyance as well.

If all this hadn't happened, would she have agreed to marry him, to go to Seattle with him? One time she would answer that question yes and the next time no. The problems they were having had always been there, and they'd have come out sooner or later. She was difficult, she knew, and it would take a special man to be compatible with her. But in so many ways, Mike was special. Very special. Yet...

She leaned her head against his shoulder. "What am I going to do with you?" she murmured.

"That's easy. Marry me."

Well, at least *he* wasn't having second thoughts on the matter. "Ummmm," she replied.

"Was that a yes or a no?"

"That was an ummmm."

"Oh."

They fell silent again. The sitcom had been replaced by a a commercial that was nearly as entertaining and probably less asinine than the show. Why did she watch this crap instead of reading like her father?

But he wasn't reading now, was he? He was locked away somewhere without books or food or water. Or even air, except when provided at the option of some madman.

Stop it, she thought. Stop it, stop it, stop it. And then the phone rang, snapping her out of her thoughts.

Mike snatched the Trimline phone form its spot on the end table, putting the whole unit in his lap. "Hello." He listened a moment, then handed the receiver to Janice. "For you."

"Anderson."

"This is Myra in dispatch. A Charles Nordin's been trying to get in touch with you. He said you'd know who he was and where to reach him, and that he wants to see you right away. He says it's urgent."

"Thanks, Myra. I'll be at Brookwood Hospital if anything comes up."

"Ten-four."

She handed the receiver back to Mike, who was looking at her expectantly. "The merchant patrolman who was mugged in the alley says he needs to see me right away."

"Want me to come with you?" he asked hopefully.

"It's official business, Mike. You know that."

He shrugged, looking resigned and a little sad. Janice hurried to the closet where she kept her purse.

The explosion of the gun still ringing in her ears, the thin blond woman in room eighteen looked down at the man she'd just shot. He was on his back, his arms flopped out to the sides, the growing red stain on the front of his shirt marking the spot where the bullet had slammed into his upper chest. He appeared to be dead.

The shot would have been heard; people would come to see what had happened. She had to run, to get away. On the verge of panicking, she looked wildly around the room, uncertain what to do. She had to calm herself. A few seconds used wisely now could save her a lot of grief later. Her fingerprints were all over the room, but there was nothing she could do about that. Besides, they were the fingerprints of a dead person.

She stuffed the gun in her belt, then hurriedly collected the fake moustache, which lay on the floor by the dead man, and the other things that might tell the authorities too much. Quickly, she wrapped the clothesline and scarves with the shirt and jeans that had been on the chair, tying the bundle with string. Then she hastily pocketed the money, the nail file, and her knife. The revolver she left in her belt, hidden beneath her shirt, just in case she needed quick access to it.

Time was up now. She had done as much as she could; every additional second spent here was an unacceptable risk. The bundle under her arm, she opened the door, seeing no one approaching. But then, in a place like this people would stay inside, lock their doors. They wouldn't want to get involved.

She hurried through the gravel parking area, then crossed Pennington and headed for an alley that ran behind a cluster of businesses. She didn't have far to go, only a few blocks. For the next few days, until this was over, she would join her prisoners in the place of the dead. No one would look for her there.

Just a few more days. That's all she needed. Just a few

more days and she'd be whole for the first time in her life. Then she could get away from here, go somewhere no one knew her, live a normal, fulfilling life, just like all the other whole people in the world.

Charles Nordin had improved dramatically since Janice had last seen him. He was sitting up in bed, his eyes bright, the color back in his face.

"I've got it," he said, grinning.

"It?"

"An angel of the night."

Janice pulled over a chair and sat down beside the bed. "I can tell you're just itching to tell me, so tell me."

"It was a woman."

"A woman..." But Reynolds and Katherine Fox had identified the kidnapper as a man. "Are you sure?"

"I'm sure. I finally made the image of what I saw that night come out right. You see, I figured if I was mugged, it would be a man that did it to me. I never questioned it, just took it for granted. So, whenever I tried to see that face, I was trying to see a man's face, and it wouldn't work. I got nothing. Well, I can see it plain as day now, and it was a woman."

"Describe her," Janice said, trying to unscramble her thoughts. She took out her notebook.

"Well, you've got to remember that all I saw was her face. I can't give you anything about her height or weight or anything like that. But her face I can give you. It was thin, very pale. Blue eyes. Blond hair, not too long; and straight, no curl. How's that?"

"That's pretty good. How old would you say she was?"

Nordin frowned. "Hard so say. I'll take a guess and say mid-twenties."

Janice looked at what she'd written down in her notebook, then let her eyes return to Nordin. "You're sure of this now."

"I'm sure all right. I'll even tell you how I figured it out. A nurse here told me a little story, a puzzle sort of. A father and a son are riding in a car, and they have an accident. The father is killed. Now, when the boy arrives at the emergency room, he's unconscious. And when the doctor looks down at the boy, the doctor says, 'My God, that's my son!' What was the relationship between the doctor and the boy? Well, I thought about that and thought about that. If the boy's father was killed, how the hell could he be a doctor at a hospital? I finally gave up. You want to know what that nurse told me?"

"It was his mother."

He looked disappointed. "Guess you heard it before, huh? Anyway, she told me the purpose of this story was to point out the attitude toward women. That got me thinking, and all this business with an angel of the night fell right into place."

If it was true, if the kidnapper was a woman, Janice was just as guilty of sexist assumptions as any of the men in the division. But, dammit, witnesses had said it was a man. On impulse, she pulled one of the composites from her purse and handed it to Nordin.

"Damn!" he said. "Take that moustache off of there and you've got it. That's the angel of the night right there."

Christ, Janice thought. What idiots we've been. All the clues were there. The driver of the van had said he'd seen a hand like a child's. A woman's hand would be small, smooth, hairless. And Katherine Fox had described the kidnapper's face as effeminate. There had probably been other, less obvious hints, all of which had been overlooked on the assumption it had to be a man. Like Nordin, they had imposed their own preconceptions on reality, muddling it hopelessly.

"Mr. Nordin, have you ever thought of becoming a feminist?"

He frowned. "Hell, girl, at my age I'm not thinking of becoming anything . . . except something besides a patient in this damn place."

"Well, let me tell you something, Mr. Nordin. What you just told me may go a hell of a long way toward saving the lives of three people who are very close to me." She rose and, leaning over, gave him a kiss on the forehead.

He grinned. "Give me a little while, and I might just think of something else."

Watson was already on the scene when Mullins arrived at the Falls Motel. He met the sergeant at the door to room eighteen.

"Shot once at close range," Watson said. "Woman did it apparently. Arol Adkins. Some of the other guests heard the shot, then saw her hurry away on foot. Patrol's got units looking for her."

Mullins took a last puff on his cigar, then tossed it into the parking lot. It was a typical crime scene outside. Curious on-lookers crowding around, uniformed men keeping them away, police cars everywhere. Following Watson into the room, he found the medical examiner bending over the body of a heavy-set man.

"How you doing, Alex?" Mullins inquired.

"Not bad. You, Ed?"

"Getting by."

Alexander Melovidov was in his thirties, curly brown hair, athletic-looking. He straightened up, closing his bag. "He's all yours, Ed. Looks like it went through his heart. Probably a thirty-eight. I'll send you the report."

"Good enough." He watched Melovidov leave, then turned to Watson. "What's the ID on this guy?"

"Nick Quiller, age thirty-nine. He's the owner of this place. No wife or family that we know about. Lived here alone in the quarters adjacent to the office."

"And the chick—this Arrow whatever her name was?"

"Not Arrow. Arol. *A-R-O-L.* Arol Adkins. At least that's how she's registered. Blond, thin, five-five. This is her room. Nobody seems to know much about her. Never spoke to any-body apparently. No car as far as we can tell. None of the vehicle information asked for on the motel registration card was filled in."

"Been through the room?"

Watson nodded. "Didn't find anything real interesting. Ross is on his way to dust the place so we can get her prints."

"Run her through NCIC?"

"Not yet, but I'm going to. Even without social security and a DOB, we might get something back with a name that unusual."

"Yeah. That's what I was thinking."

Watson frowned. "You know what's strange about this place? There's nothing here. No clothes or anything, no suitcases. All she had with her when she took off was a small bundle, maybe a couple of things."

"You run into all kinds. You going to shoot the photos?"

Watson shrugged. "Why not? I'm at least as bad a photographer as you are." He left the room, returning a few moments later with a camera, and began shooting the usual gory photos.

Being careful not to disturb too many fingerprints, Mullins gave the place the once-over, discovering that Watson had been right about the general lack of possessions. The dresser was empty except for a handful of socks and a single pair of panties in the top drawer and some paper, pens, crayons, and string in the bottom one. The only other clothing to be found was a robe left in the bathroom, in which he also discovered a toothbrush, toothpaste, and a comb. Nowhere was there any perfume or makeup or the like, all those little bottles and jars women usually surrounded themselves with. Arol Adkins had kept almost no food in the tiny refrigerator beneath the three-burner electric stove, and her utensils consisted of the barest minimum. A single plate, one saucepan, one knife, one fork, so on. Under the bed he found a blue baseball cap.

"I think I got enough photos," Watson said. "Meat wagon's outside. Shall I send them in?"

"Yeah. Just warn them not to touch anything."

Watson stepped outside, and a moment later two ambulance attendants came in, carrying their collapsible gurney. Without a word, they laid it beside the body, moved to opposite ends of the dead man, and lifted him onto it. When they picked up the gurney, its legs fell into place, and they wheeled Nick Quiller out the door.

Mullins' eyes swung back to the spot where Quiller had lain, and there, lying on the floor, apparently having been concealed by the body, was a sheet of paper. On the upside anyway, it was blank. Pulling a pen from his shirt pocket, he flipped the paper over.

"Well, I'll be damned," he muttered. "Hey, Will," he called. "Come here and look at this."

"Whatcha got?" Watson asked, stepping into the room.

"Look what was underneath the guy."

Watson bent over for a closer look. "Hey, that's one of the composites of the guy who kidnapped Janice's family." He straightened, frowning. "You figure there's any connection?"

"Beats the hell out of me, but I figure we better notify Poldoski or the captain."

Sixteen

It was after ten when they met in the conference room down the hall from the chief's office. Captain Bishop stood at one end of the long table at which Janice, Poldoski, Mullins, Watson, and Ross were seated.

"First," the captain said, holding up a handful of papers, "here are the new composites. It's the same one we've been using but with the moustache removed. Ed, you've been to the motel with one of these. What did you find out?"

"Most of the people I showed it to seemed to think it was a pretty good likeness of the Adkins woman," Mullins replied.

Bishop handed the composites to Ross, who was closest to him, and the fingerprint man took one and passed them on. When Janice received hers, the first of the revised pictures she'd seen, she again felt a tug at her memory, stronger now. The plain, thin face that stared blankly at her from the paper was someone she had encountered. Sometime. Somewhere. But any more than that was locked away in her memory, inaccessible.

"I've seen this face before," Janice said. "I don't know where. I don't know when." With the moustache removed, the picture, at first glance, clearly showed a woman. Yet, on closer inspection, the feminine characteristics seemed to disappear, the face becoming that of a frail young adult of indeterminable sex.

"And the name Arol Adkins?" Bishop prompted. He already knew the answer. He was asking her to repeat it for the sake of the others.

"It means nothing to me," she said.

"Ron, what did the computer say?"

"It found no one named Arol Adkins connected with any of Janice's cases. The name Arol Adkins is a big zero. There's no such person as far as the machine is concerned."

"Will, what did NCIC have to say?"

"The same," Watson answered. "No such person as Arol Adkins."

"Frank."

"The prints we found in her motel room match the partials," Ross said. "Arol Adkins is the kidnapper all right. I've Wirephotoed a complete set of her prints to the FBI, but it'll probably be a week or two before we get anything back."

"All right. We've narrowed it down to one person, and we're sure that person did it. Besides her description, what do we know about her?" He turned to the blackboard behind him and picked up the chalk. "First, we know that she calls herself Arol Adkins." He wrote it at the top of the board. "But there's a good chance it's an assumed name." He put a question mark after it. "What else do we know about this person calling herself Arol Adkins?"

"She's somehow connected to Janice," Poldoski offered. "But the link might not be clear. If you believe the head shrink at Elk Ridge, it could be a symbolic thing, something that wouldn't make any sense at all to the rest of us."

The captain wrote LINK TO JANICE under the name. "What else?"

"We're dealing with a psycho," Mullins said.

"I think that's safe to assume." He wrote that, too, on the board. And beside it: KILLER.

"We know she had to steal to survive," Janice said. "She's probably unemployed."

"Also," Watson said, "she was staying in a cheap motel, and she didn't bring anything with her. No clothes or anything. That must tell us something. She moved in there a couple of weeks ago."

Bishop wrote UNEMPLOYED, NO POSSESSIONS, and below that TWO WEEKS on the board. "Nobody has nothing.

If she didn't bring it with her, where'd she leave it?"

There were a few moments of silence; then Mullins spoke up. "Maybe her old man kicked her out of the house."

Bishop's brow wrinkled. "Ummm, I don't know. She had to come from somewhere though. Where else could she have come from?"

"She sounds like an escapee from somewhere," Poldoski offered. "We found that Elk Ridge coin at Janice's place, but that's been a dead end. Tomorrow, we're going to ask for the names and prints of everybody released from there over the past two years. So far, we've only gone back six months." He frowned. "Of course, anyone who'd been out for very long wouldn't have shown up at the motel with no possessions."

On the board, the captain wrote ELK RIDGE CONNECTION? "All right, we know she showed up recently, has no legitimate means of support, no possessions, and probably uses an assumed name. That's going to give us plenty to think about all by itself. But here's something else. Where has she gone? We'll have alerted every motel and police force in the area by morning. Where *can* she go?"

"A rescue mission," Watson suggested.

"We'll alert them, too."

"She could make the rounds of a few bars," Mullins said. "Get herself picked up and spend the night with some guy."

"Or some woman," Watson put in.

"Those are possibilities," Janice said, "but it seems to me there's only one place she's likely to go. The same place she's holding the hostages."

On the board, Bishop added: WHERE IS SHE NOW? "I think Janice is right. That's the safest place to go with everybody looking for her. It hasn't been discovered yet, so it's fairly secure. It's where I'd go if I were her."

"We're still checking the vacant buildings that might have airtight compartments," Poldoski said. "It's still a mess though because of the problems we're having locating the owners and getting permission to enter. And we keep discovering places we've missed. The highway department has condemned a whole bunch of buildings for a new freeway, and we don't even have that list yet."

"Stay on it, and use whoever you need. The whole damned department's at your disposal."

"One thing bothers me here," Mullins said. "We keep talking like this chick was in this all by herself. Well, she's five-five and skinny as a rail. How the hell is one little chick like that going to pull all this off without help?"

The captain shrugged. "There's nothing to indicate an accomplice. The people at the motel say she was a loner, never spoke to anyone or had any visitors. All I can tell you is that, if you run into this particular five-foot-five-inch woman, don't underestimate her. And don't take any chances."

Mullins said nothing. He stuck a cigar in his mouth and began chewing on the end. He didn't light it.

"Where does Quiller figure into all this?" Poldoski asked. "What was he doing in her room if she didn't have any visitors?"

Watson answered him. "From what I can gather, he liked to try to put the make on all the female guests. Fancied himself a cocksmith."

"What about the copy of the composite he had with him? Janice and I left it with him earlier today, and he said he didn't recognize it. I watched him when he first looked at it, and he gave no signs of recognition at all."

Watson shrugged. "Maybe after a while he noticed the similarity and took it with him. Who knows? Maybe he wanted to compare the face to the picture. Or maybe he wanted to use it to blackmail her into putting out for him. Or maybe none of the above. It doesn't seem that Quiller was involved though. It's the first time he'd been seen with her. My guess is that he was there to see if he could get laid and somehow got killed instead."

"All right," Bishop said, tapping the blackboard with the chalk. "I want everybody to put some thought into this. Dream about it tonight—if and when you get to bed, that is. We've got hotels and motels and rescue missions to notify, and I want these new composites distributed by morning. And I want to make sure the papers and TV stations all have a copy and use the damn thing."

He held up one of the composites. "I want this face all over this part of the state by morning. And I want the word out on the streets. Anybody knows anything and lets us hear about it gets an IOU from the department. We've got a break now; let's use it. If there's too much for you to do by yourselves, get Reynolds or Greene or anybody else that seems to be getting too much sleep out of bed and have them hustle their asses down here. If you want to see home again, bring me a kidnapper and three hostages."

With that, he turned and strode from the room.

For Malcolm Anderson, everything had become a dreamlike blur. The pain in his body had become a dull ache that only registered somewhere on the periphery of his consciousness. His craving for water, too, had diminished, the need no longer constant but now an intermittent thing.

The drawers opened; the drawers closed. He paid little attention to that now, for it was a sound from another world, another reality. His reality now consisted of the dreamlike things he saw and heard and sometimes even smelled. That these things were fantasies, products of sensory deprivation, no longer seemed to matter. They were the only sensations he had, and he clung to them.

At moments, he would wonder about the well-being of the daughter and grandchild imprisoned nearby, but that was something he couldn't know, and speculation seemed useless. About his own well-being he did know something though, even though he was only partially aware of it. Changes were taking place within his body; a biological sequence had been set in motion, a slow process that would lead inevitably to his death. Although it had only begun and there was probably still ample time to reverse it, he was starting to die.

And he could feel hints of other goings-on in his body, things that told him he would not just fade away into dreamland when the time came. Death would be slow and excruciating.

In St. Paul the next morning, Linda Lomar sat at the breakfast table in her tiny apartment, a cup of coffee and the morning paper before her on the red Formica surface. The paper was still rolled and tied; she'd get to it after a few more swallows of coffee. There was no hurry. Reading the help-wanted ads always depressed her.

Once, she'd been the head woman's fashion buyer for a major department store chain headquartered in the Twin Cities. A tall, attractive woman in her forties, she'd been on her way up the corporate ladder. The next vice-presidency to open up could have well been hers. Even without a promotion, she'd had her own secretary, a large, modern office. Dressed conservatively yet fashionably, her striking salt-and-pepper hair groomed weekly at an exclusive salon, she had sat in that office, making decisions that involved hundreds of thousands of dollars and that could have an impact on the entire fashion industry.

Once.

Before her nervous breakdown.

Before she walked uninvited into a meeting of the board of directors, babbling happily about some scene or another from *Alice in Wonderland*. The strain had been too much, and she'd cracked. It had been as simple as that. But she'd been totally unprepared for it.

She had, of course, lost her job, the president of the company politely suggesting she check herself into a mental hospital. All well and good, except that her insurance didn't cover that sort of sickness. Her mother and father were dead, and she had never married; there was no one to help pay for a private hospital, which she couldn't afford because she'd somehow managed to end up having almost nothing in the way of savings. She had made a lot of money, but she had spent a lot of money. The new cars every year. The trips to Europe. The luxury apartment in an exclusive high rise.

So she had voluntarily committed herself to the only place she could go: the state hospital at Elk Ridge.

And now she read the want ads each day, hoping some firm somewhere would want a down-and-out middle-aged executive who'd spent eight months at the funny farm. Surprise, surprise, no one did.

Taking a sizable gulp of coffee, she picked up the paper, slipped off the string, and unrolled it. Before tackling the want ads, she would read about the kidnapping, which she'd been following closely, probably because it reminded her that there were others whose situation was far worse than hers. At least no one was holding *her* hostage.

As usual, the story was on the front page. The headline read: KIDNAPPER IDENTIFIED AS WOMAN. Well, now, that was a new twist. She started to plunge into the story, but then her eyes were drawn to the accompanying photo, one of those police composites. She knew that face! Someone at Elk Ridge. Yes, another patient. The name, the name. Yes, Corrine

MacDougall, a thin young woman who kept to herself.

She studied the picture more closely. Well, it was rather crude; she couldn't be absolutely certain. Still, she should call the police and tell them what she thought. Besides, what else did she have to do, other than read the want ads?

Janice stared bleary-eyed at the surface of her desk. She'd managed to get two hours sleep last night at Mike's, and that was all. It was better this way, though, because now she was doing something, accomplishing something, not just guessing, hoping. Every damn place in the metropolitan area where someone might try to hole up now had a copy of the composite, and the picture had appeared in the morning papers. For Arol Adkins, it was damn hot out there right now.

Calls had been coming in all morning, people who thought they recognized the composite. Each tip would have to be checked out. Fortunately, the earlier version, the one with the moustache, had never made the papers, sparing her and the others from having to check out all the erroneous leads that would have followed its publication.

Poldoski hurried over to her desk, a piece of note paper in his hand. "This might be of interest. One of our callers claiming to recognize the composite has identified the kidnapper as a Corrine MacDougall. Says they were in Elk Ridge together."

Janice jotted down the name, and a moment later, she was on the phone with Dr. King at Elk Ridge. Skipping the pleasantries, she got right to the point. "Doctor, what can you tell me about a patient named Corrine MacDougall?"

"But I already told you about Corrine MacDougall."

Janice was confused. "What do you mean you already told me about her?"

"The former patient who thought all her failings were the fault of someone named Shirley."

"Wait a minute now. Is there any chance that Shirley wasn't the other person's real name?"

"You're very perceptive, Miss Anderson. I've always suspected that Shirley was a name she used to avoid using the woman's correct name. I didn't push her on it because Shirley's identity was of no real importance. She was strictly a symbol."

"Describe Corrine MacDougall for me."

"Oh, let's see. Late twenties, thin, blond."

Janice felt her heart begin beating faster. "Where is she now, Doctor?"

"But, I already told you. She was killed in the bus crash."

"She's . . ." Then she remembered. He had indeed told her that. In her excitement, she'd forgotten. "Are you sure she was killed in the crash?"

"Mrs. MacDougall and twenty-seven others got on that bus, Miss Anderson. After the crash, they found twenty-eight bodies."

Well, so much for that. Besides, she was fairly certain that when she heard the name that went with that face, she'd recognize it. And she had never heard of Corrine MacDougall.

She asked the doctor for the names and prints of any patients released over the past two years, excluding of course those he'd already supplied. The doctor said he'd get them to her right away.

Corrine MacDougall sat on the carpeted floor, her legs folded beneath her. She was in a small plush room that had apparently been used for displaying the bodies—viewing the departed or whatever it was called. It was cozy and comfortable here, and the carpet was soft enough for sleeping. For the next few days, it would do. The building still had electricity and running water; all she'd have to do would be to stock up on food, and she had money enough for that.

And perhaps they'd die sooner than she'd expected. The last few times she'd opened the drawers, she'd heard no sounds coming from within the wall. Unless she'd inadvertently allowed them to die of suffocation, they should still be alive, but the next time she gave them air, she'd check anyway, just to make sure. And once they were dead, she'd tell Janice where to find them.

Then Janice, too, would have to die. As yet, Corrine MacDougall had no plan for that, no precise notion of how to handle the grand finale, the event that would set her free, allow her to become whole. Janice's death would have to be something special, not just a simple pulling of a trigger or thrusting of a knife. Her death would have to be prolonged, and at least as unpleasant as those of her father, sister, and nephew.

Corrine had not planned it because the chances of capturing

Janice would be few and would depend on circumstances that could not be predicted. Also, Janice would be an armed, dangerous adversary, not easily taken.

Well, there was still time to figure out a course of action. If necessary, she supposed, she could always simply pull the trigger, though killing Janice in such a manner seemed so unsatisfactory. Still, Janice would be dead; Corrine Mac-Dougall would be whole.

But these decisions did not have to be made yet. First, Janice would have to suffer some more, and for that Corrine did have a plan. All she needed was a tape recorder, which she had; she'd bought it yesterday and hidden it in one of the drawers for corpses, there being no need to take it back to the motel. With it were the stamps and envelopes she'd also purchased. She could make the recording at her leisure because mailing it would have to wait until it was safe to go out, as would getting the groceries. Enough time would have to pass to allow things outside to cool off. Right now, following the incident at the motel, the police would be frantically hunting her.

Pushing these thoughts aside, Corrine MacDougall considered her name. It had an alien sound to it, as if it were someone else. MacDougall, of course, was her married name, and she'd never called herself Corrine until the doctors started addressing her that way, unaware that she had never used her legal first name, that she had always been known by her middle name.

When she was away from here, when she was finally whole, she'd have to have a new name. What should it be? Lynne? Anne? Jill? And then she had it. April. April was a fresh, new sort of month, the spring thaw, a new beginning. April was perfect.

And for a last name? The next month, of course. April May. People would think she'd had parents with a sense of humor. The real meaning would be her secret, and she'd always liked keeping secrets.

Or had she kept them only because she'd so rarely had anyone to share them with? No matter. Once she was whole, she wouldn't have that problem anymore.

James Heikkinen that Thursday morning was sitting behind the polished-wood desk in his appropriately sedate yet plushly furnished office in his new Bloomington funeral home, a steaming cup of coffee in front of him.

Lighting a cigarette, he reached for the morning paper, which his secretary folded and placed in his in-basket each morning. He should check the help-wanted ad he was running for a new grounds keeper. For Carl, whom he'd always liked, he was providing all funeral and burial services without charge, as the late grounds keeper's elderly widow would be hard put to pay for any funeral, much less one arranged here. It seemed the least he could do.

Before he had the chance to unfold the paper, his phone rang. "Yes," he said.

"Mr. and Mrs. Carpenter are here," his receptionist informed him.

The Carpenters were a well-off couple whose only son had died in an auto accident. "Show them in, please."

Stubbing out his cigarette, he tossed the paper back into the in-basket.

Seventeen

It was Friday morning, twenty-four hours after the composite had first appeared in the papers, before Captain Bishop had a chance to even think about anything other than the kidnapping. In front of him, a stack of reports awaited his approval. He took the top one and flipped open the folder. Mullins' report on the murder of Carl Olson.

Through his open office door, he could see the activity in

the next room, detectives answering phones, making calls, hurrying in and out. They were still checking out calls from people who claimed to recognize the kidnapper. It was time-consuming; each possible had to be interviewed, investigated, alibis established. It was one of the things he hated about composites; they looked like no one, and yet they reminded you of people. Still, as composites went, this one had certainly been more valuable than most.

So far, though, checking out the calls had turned up no good suspects, no one who might be Arol Adkins. Nor had the continuing search of vacant buildings turned up any trace of the three hostages. Nor had Arol Adkins tried to spend the night at any of the places that had been alerted to keep an eye out for anyone matching her description, although they had managed to scare the hell out of one young woman who'd checked into a motel on the west side of town. She was blond, thin, and about the right height. She was also a sales representative for a cosmetics firm, and she had been in Milwaukee until last night. When she'd opened the door and found a hallway full of police officers with deadly-serious expressions on their faces, she'd nearly panicked.

The additional fingerprints requested from Elk Ridge had arrived yesterday afternoon and had immediately been checked by Ross. None had matched those of Arol Adkins. Greene was checking with the state prison to see whether anyone matching her description had been released or escaped recently.

They were making progress, but not fast enough. If what the note from the kidnapper said was true, it would only be a couple of days—maybe less considering that none of the hostages were healthy adult males—before the situation became critical.

Well, all that could be done was being done. If they didn't find them in time, it certainly wouldn't be because they hadn't tried. His one regret was the sluggishness with which the investigation had gotten started. But all investigations were like that. Before you could do much, you had to have something to work with, and getting those first usable bits of information didn't require manpower nearly as much as it required time. Time, unfortunately, was the one thing they didn't have.

He'd been flipping through Mullins' report, giving it a cursory inspection, and was on the verge of approving it when he realized something was wrong. He began going back through the pages, studying them more closely this time. After a few moments, he looked up to see whether the sergeant was in and spotted him filling his cup at the coffee urn.

"Ed, see you a minute?"

"Sure." He came in and sat down, taking a sip from the steaming cup.

"You know anything about fishing?"

"Uh-uh."

"I guess that was obvious."

"What are you talking about?"

"In your report here, on the Carl Olson murder, you say the victim had apparently been mugged while fishing in Griffith Lake."

"Yeah, that's right. The guy loved to fish. I checked. He went every chance he got."

"No way, Ed. Not in Griffith Lake."

Mullins frowned. "Why not?"

"This guy was an avid fisherman. He'd have had more sense."

"Come on, Captain. What the hell are you talking about?"

"There are no fish in Griffith Lake. I don't know whether it was pesticides or acid rain or what, but the last time a fish was pulled out of Griffith Lake was more than five years ago."

"Well, I'll be damned."

"Looks to me as if the fishing gear was a cover-up for something else."

Mullins sipped his coffee thoughtfully. "I don't know what. There was no blood in the car, no signs that the body had been dragged there, no signs of a struggle. Looked like he heard someone and started to turn, and that's when he got it. I suppose he could have gone out there to meet somebody for some reason or another. But, hell, what reason would anybody have to kill a grounds keeper? The guy had no money. He was a nobody."

"I wonder if the Adkins woman was involved in this."

"Why would she be?"

"I'm probably reaching, but there are similarities between this and the mugging of that merchant patrolman. Both were older men. Both were robbed. Both were stabbed by someone who came up behind them."

"Pretty damned flimsy if you ask me, Captain."

"Mention it to Poldoski anyway. Just in case."

"Sure."

The captain handed him the report. "Hang on to this. Once this kidnapping is taken care of, it looks like you'll have some more work to do on the Olson case."

A few moments later, the report tucked under his arm, Mullins stepped out of the captain's office, looking for Poldoski. Ron's desk was piled high with papers, but the detective himself was nowhere to be seen. Mullins tossed the report on his own desk and started to sit down.

"Hold it," Watson said, grabbing his arm. "Don't even think of letting your ass touch that cushion."

"Why not?"

"We've got to check out a housewife. Somebody out there says she's the spitting image of Arol Adkins."

As they walked down the hallway, heading for the stairs that led to the underground parking area, the men's room door opened and Poldoski emerged with an electric razor in his hand. Mullins was in the car before he realized he should have said something to Ron about the Griffith Lake murder. Well, he'd try to remember to tell him later. Probably didn't mean anything anyway.

Phones were ringing all over the room, and it took Detective Ted Reynolds a few moments to realize his was one of them. He grabbed the receiver.

"Reynolds."

"Uh, yes, this is James Heikkinen at Heikkinen's Funeral Home in Bloomington. I was told that I should speak to someone in the detective division about this."

"Yes, sir."

"I'd have called you sooner, but I never looked at the paper yesterday, and I didn't see the picture until this morning. I think I've seen her, the woman, the kidnapper. She was on the grounds of my Dakota Falls funeral home, and I asked her what she was doing there. She said she thought it was a public park. I corrected her and sent her on her way."

"When was this, sir?"

"Uh, a couple of days ago. It was at Heikkinen's Funeral Home on Pennington."

Reynolds, who had been writing all this down, got the man's address, phone number, the correct spelling of his name, and thanked him for calling. He then tore the sheet from his pad and took it to Poldoski, who was in charge of the investigation. His desk was cluttered with papers; he looked swamped.

"Here's another one, Ron."

"A name or a sighting?"

"Sighting."

"Current?"

"Couple of days ago."

"Thanks." He took the sheet of paper and, without looking at it, added it to a stack on the left side of his desk. "I'm arranging these things in categories," he said. "Names go in one pile, current sightings in another, and old sightings in another. The names get investigated. The current sightings I phone in to dispatch so a patrol unit can be sent to the scene. The old sightings—where someone thinks he may have seen her somewhere a few days ago or whatever—I'll look at when I get the chance."

"May I?" Reynolds asked, indicating the old-sightings pile.

"Sure."

In addition to the mortuary sighting, people had reported seeing Arol Adkins at a coin-operated laundry, a grocery store, a bar, in an elevator. . . . The list went on and on. He put the pile of papers back on Poldoski's desk and returned to his own.

Corrine MacDougall strolled across the asphalt parking lot, heading toward the supermarket. The small shopping center was only a few blocks from the mortuary, a short walk.

Although she hadn't dared go out yesterday, so soon after the incident at the motel, now she was too hungry to put it off any longer. Her last meal had been at the motel, the day before yesterday. She'd stock up on canned goods, enough to hold her for a couple of days, when it should all be over. All but Janice's death.

Her captives, she'd discovered, were still alive, though so confused and disoriented they had seemed unaware that she was poking them, holding the small tape recorder close to their lips. And they smelled terrible, especially Amy and the boy. From soiling themselves, she supposed. And from the look of them, they weren't even aware of it.

She had dropped the envelope containing the tape into a mailbox near the funeral home; it would arrive at the police station tomorrow. She was anxious for Janice to hear it, especially Amy's part, for which holding the recorder near the captive's lips had been totally unnecessary.

Corrine was about to enter the grocery store when the newspaper rack on the sidewalk caught her eye, and she froze.

"Excuse me, please." It was the shopper who'd been following her into the store. A plump, middle-aged woman with gray hair.

Corrine hurriedly moved aside, her eyes still fixed on the newspaper. The headline read: POLICE STILL HUNT THIS WOMAN, and beside it was one of those weird pictures cops put together. Her picture. Not exactly, but close. Very close. Fumbling in her pocket, she found some change, slipped it in the slot, and got a paper. She quickly scanned the story. They were calling her Arol Adkins, which meant they were still unaware of her real name. But they knew she was the kidnapper and that she'd robbed the merchant patrol guy, who, she was mildly surprised to learn, was not dead. She needed a radio or a TV set so she could keep track of the news without leaving the mortuary.

The headline said the authorities were *still* looking for *this* woman. Had the picture been published yesterday as well? It looked too much like her. She could be spotted, recognized. This one necessary trip to get food was far more dangerous than she had figured it would be. Anyone—a checker, another customer—anyone could recognize her, call the police.

Then something made her look up, look toward the entrance to the grocery store. The woman who'd been behind her was standing there, staring at her, frowning. Before their eyes could meet, the woman looked away.

Suddenly, Corrine MacDougall felt exposed, vulnerable. She'd been recognized! The police were already on their way. They had to be. She had to get away before it was too late.

She turned, ready to run as fast as she could, and at that moment, she noticed the young woman whose groceries had just been loaded into a light blue station wagon by one of the carry-out boys. The boy was wheeling the cart away, the woman taking her keys from her purse, unlocking the door. The woman was no more than thirty feet away, her station wagon parked directly in front of a drug store.

Dropping the newspaper, Corrine MacDougall started to run. The woman was tall, with long dark hair. She had the door open now; she was starting to get inside. Then Corrine was at the car, grabbing the woman by the hair, pulling her out of the station wagon, the woman screaming as she was thrown to the pavement. The keys fell on the asphalt, and Corrine grabbed them, throwing herself into the station wagon. She heard screams coming from the supermarket. It had to be the other woman, the one who'd spotted her.

As she struggled to find the right key and get it into the ignition, she saw the woman she'd pulled from the car scramble away, yelling, waving her arms. The carry-out boy was running toward the station wagon. Corrine locked the door.

Finding the right key, she turned the ignition, and the engine started instantly. The carry-out boy was beside the car now, pounding on the window. She pulled the shift lever to reverse and slammed the gas pedal to the floor, the station wagon shooting backward with a loud squeal of tires and smashing into a car behind it. There were more shouts now. Corrine shifted to drive and again pushed the accelerator to the floor, spinning the wheel as the station wagon lunged forward. The carry-out boy was in front of her, waving his arms. He leaped out of the way, and she roared past him, bouncing off the rear end of a car that was backing out of a parking space. The station wagon swayed, but she retained control of it, and then she was out of the parking lot and on the street, speeding away, toward safety.

She had to calm down, to think. She couldn't keep the car too long; the police would be looking for it. She needed a place to leave it that was close enough to the mortuary for her to get there on foot, yet not so close that it would point to her hiding place. And she didn't want to part with the groceries. She had to have something to eat, and coming out again would be too dangerous.

Had she been stupid? Had she panicked? But worrying about that was pointless. All that mattered now was dealing with the situation in the best way possible. In the distance, she heard sirens.

She had driven a few blocks, staying away from the main thoroughfares, when she noticed an unpaved alley running through a residential section. Pulling into it, she began looking for a spot to hide the car. She could not keep it any longer. Partway down the alley, she spotted a garage, separate from the house, concealed from the neighbors by high bushes.

She stopped the car and ran over to the garage. Through the small windows in the door, she could see that it was empty. She tried to raise the door, but it was locked. Slipping around the corner of the small white structure, she found a side window. She tried it; it was unlocked and pushed up easily. She climbed over the sill.

Inside was the usual collection of things: tools, a lawn mower, a wheelbarrow, garden hoses. She stepped around the greasy area in the center of the concrete floor and went to the door. When she pulled on the handle, nothing happened.

Stepping back, she studied the door, looking for another handle or lock. Then she noticed the mechanism above her head, and the electric motor. Her eyes followed the wires that led to the wall, then down it to a button. Quickly, she pushed it, and the motor hummed; the door began rolling up on its metal tracks, opening onto the alley.

She ran to the station wagon.

"I recognized her right away," the woman said. "From the picture in the paper. So I went inside and told the checker to call the police; then I went back to the door to watch her. She was looking at the paper, but then she looked up and saw me watching her, and . . . and that's when everything happened."

Janice nodded. The plump, middle-aged woman's name was Adele Haldorsen, a housewife. They were standing outside the supermarket. A few feet away, the carry-out boy, a thin, dark-haired teen-ager, was standing off to the side while Mullins talked to the woman who had been pulled from her car. Ross was dusting the newspaper rack's plastic cover.

"Was it her?" Adele Haldorsen asked. "Was she the one?"

"There's a good chance of it," Janice replied. She moved over to where Mullins was talking with the young woman.

"I just didn't know what was happening," she was saying. "Suddenly, the door was yanked open, and I was being dragged out of the car." She was in her early twenties, tall, thin, and attractive. She looked bewildered.

Mullins chewed on the end of his cigar. "She say anything?"

"No, not that I can remember."

"You resist at all? Try to fight back?"

"I-I never had the chance. It all happened too fast."

Mullins flipped back through his notes. "You're Bonnie Snelling, two-twenty-seven East Fourteenth Street, and you're a part-time student at the technical school, is that right?"

"Yes. In data processing."

He turned to Ross, who was squatting beside the newspaper rack, holding two cards side by side, studying them. On one were squares of transparent tape bearing the prints he'd just lifted; on the other were the prints of Arol Atkins. "Got anything, Frank?" Mullins asked.

"I've got one print that looks like a match. I'd say it was her all right. What do you hear from the units looking for the blue wagon?"

"Not a trace of the goddamned thing."

Every second that went by, Janice knew, reduced the chances of finding the wagon with Arol Adkins still inside it. It was beginning to look as if she'd made a clean getaway. Janice resisted the implse to find something and slam her fist against it.

Obviously, Arol Adkins was holed up somewhere, and she'd risked coming out because she needed food. Had she come here because it was close to her hiding place? Were the hostages with her? In this general area, the orange Pinto had been stolen, and Charles Nordin had been attacked. The Falls Motel wasn't far away either. Nor was her father's house.

She scanned the neighborhood, seeing homes and small businesses, all so innocent-looking. Were her father, sister, and nephew imprisoned in one of those ordinary-looking structures, locked in an airtight compartment, dying?

She turned to Mullins. "You mind getting a ride back with Frank? I want to drive around the area."

He looked at her a moment, frowning, then spat out his cigar and said: "Sure. Go ahead."

The supermarket was on Manhattan Avenue, a thoroughfare running parallel to Pennington four or five blocks away. The car was the unmarked beige Ford Mullins used whenever it was available. She drove slowly, studying the buildings, looking for any that might contain airtight compartments. At Roosevelt Avenue, she cut over to Pennington, passing Heikkinen's Funeral Home. She refused to look at it. She didn't want to think about that place and the role it or one like it might soon be playing in her life.

She followed a route that took her past the spot where the orange Pinto had been stolen, past the alley where Charles Nordin had been mugged by an angel of the night, past the Falls Motel, seeing nothing but suburbia, a nice place to raise a family away from the confusion and congestion of the city. Then she visited all those spots again, taking different streets. And then again, using still other streets. And each time she passed the mortuary, she looked away.

As she drove, the traffic coming over the car's two-way radio kept her informed about the search for the light blue station wagon. Arol Adkins had got away.

Finally, she gave up and returned to the station, where she found a group of detectives gathered around Captain Bishop, who was taping a map to the wall outside his office. Janice joined them.

"Here," Bishop said, tapping the map, "is where the Pinto was stolen. Here the merchant patrolman was mugged. The motel is here and the Anderson house here. And here's the supermarket." With felt-tip, he drew a circle that enclosed the points he'd mentioned, along with a good-sized chunk of southwest Dakota Falls. "I've got a bunch of patrol guys waiting down in the squad room. Watson's going to organize them into groups, and they're going to knock on every damn door within this circle I just drew. If she's hiding in there anywhere, somebody must have seen her." He paused, then said: "That's all I wanted to tell you. Everybody back to work."

As the others headed for their desks, the captain caught Janice's eye. "I gather you had the same idea."

She sighed. "Yeah, but I didn't find anything except lawns and gardens and kids and dogs."

He put his hand on her shoulder. "We're close, Janice. Just keep hanging in there."

"Time's running out, Captain. I just hope we're close enough." It was afternoon now. Friday. The fifth day.

He stood there a moment, as if trying to think of something

else to say, then, giving her a small reassuring smile, turned and disappeared into his office.

Janice noticed Poldoski sorting through the stacks of papers on his desk and joined him. "How's it going, Ron?"

"Coordinating all this is a bitch, but it has to be a one-man job. Otherwise, I'd know part of what was going on, and someone else would know the other part. It just wouldn't work."

"In that case, I won't offer to help you."

"Don't. If you get a chance, you might check with Reynolds and see if he's got that list from the highway department yet. I don't know what the holdup is, but if it's not there, tell him I said to scream and yell. On second thought, we'll have the captain scream and yell. He's better at it."

Leaving Poldoski to his work, she moved to Reynolds' desk. The young detective was on the phone, and she waited until he hung up. "Ted, Ron wants to know whether you have the list from the highway department yet."

He shook his head. "They say their computer's broken down and, as soon as it's fixed, they'll get the list over to us by special messenger. Probably tomorrow sometime."

Tomorrow. Would her father, sister, and nephew still be ... She deliberately let the thought go unfinished. "Holler if it doesn't arrive," she said wearily.

"It will," he said confidently. "Tomorrow's Saturday, and they're keeping the people fixing the computer there on overtime. They know it's important."

As she turned to head for her own desk, she found Mullins blocking her path. "Come on," he said. "We've got another Arol Adkins look-alike to check out."

Janice had been out on some of the other calls involving young women thought by someone—often an anonymous voice on the phone—to resemble the composite, and as far as she was concerned, very few of them had looked anything like it. But Gloria Smith, a receptionist at a dental clinic, turned out to be a dead ringer. However, one dentist, another receptionist, and a bookkeeper all swore she was at work when the kidnapping occurred.

Janice and Mullins were back at the station within an hour.

It was midafternoon when Corrine MacDougall left the garage and walked casually down the alley, carrying a grocery sack. By now the police would have decided she'd got away and would have stopped scouring the area for her. In the bag, she had all the usable, nonperishable foods she'd found among the groceries in the station wagon. Fresh fruit and canned goods mostly. It was heavy.

In the glove compartment, she'd found a can opener—of the church key variety—which she'd also taken.

While waiting, she'd helped herself to some of the other items in the grocery sacks. The contents of the bags had included bread, lunch meat, and lettuce, from which she'd made a sandwich. She'd washed it down with several gulps from a carton of milk. Very nice of that woman to provide all that food.

On her head was the old, sweat-stained baseball cap she'd found in the garage. Although it was too big for her, she'd managed to tuck her hair up underneath it and make it stay there. After checking out the arrangement in the car's rearview mirror, she'd decided she could pass for a teen-age boy.

Her hasty retreat from the supermarket had taken her away from the funeral home. It would be a long way to carry a bag full of heavy cans. Still, she *was* within walking distance, and the spot she'd abandoned the station wagon would offer no clues to her hiding place.

The alley ended after two blocks, forcing her to head for the parallel residential street half a block away. She had preferred the alley; this was more open, more public, and she felt exposed. As she reached the corner and started down the tree-lined street, she saw the police car.

It was ahead of her, in the middle of the block, two cops talking to someone at the front door of a white house. She couldn't afford to risk calling attention to herself by turning around or suddenly crossing the street. She had to bluff it out. Her heart pounding, she walked as casually as she could down the sidewalk.

Officer J. D. Tomlinson and his partner Steve Hakkala remained outside on the stoop while a gray-haired man of about seventy stood in the doorway, examining the composite.

"Saw this in the paper," he said. "But I haven't seen anyone around here who looks like that."

"If you should see anyone who does, we'd appreciate it if

you'd call us," Tomlinson said. He and his partner were both large men in their late twenties. Both were career policemen, and both wanted very much to get a piece of anyone who'd go after a cop's family. Ordinarily, Tomlinson wouldn't treat a woman the same way he'd treat a man, but this one, the one they were after, had forfeited the protection of her sex. If he found her, he'd hurt her. There were always ways to hurt them and get away with it if you really wanted to. And nobody could be allowed to go after a cop's family. Nobody.

The old man said he'd certainly call if he saw anyone resembling the composite and closed the door. Tomlinson and his partner cut across the lawn to the next house and rang the bell.

"Yes?" a middle-aged woman in a housedress said, opening the door.

Tomlinson introduced himself and Hakkala, then handed her the composite and began repeating the words he'd been uttering on doorsteps all afternoon. He hardly noticed the teen-age boy in jeans and a baseball cap who strolled casually by on the sidewalk, a sack of groceries in his arms.

"I'd just come home from work. I came down the alley and hit the automatic opener like I always do, and there it was, sitting in my garage." His name was Goodman. He was about forty-five, thin, going bald. He worked as an electrician.

"You live here alone?" Janice asked. She, Ted Reynolds, and Goodman stood beside the now somewhat battered blue station wagon in the electrician's garage.

"I've got a wife and a boy, but they're in South Dakota right now, visiting my wife's mother. She's in the hospital."

Closing her notebook, Janice returned it to her purse, then walked around the station wagon. It had a long, deep dent and some missing chrome on the right side; the rear bumper was bent, and a taillight was missing. In the back seat were several grocery bags that had been thoroughly rifled, their contents scattered on the seat and floor. She opened the rear door on the driver's side and climbed in, unconcerned about how many fingerprints she might disturb. There was no doubt as to the identity of the car thief.

Checking the groceries, she noted the absence of canned goods, fresh fruits, things that would keep. And some of the perishable things had obviously been consumed on the spot. Lunch meat, bread, and milk had been opened; leaves had been stripped from a head of lettuce. Apparently Arol Adkins had had a sandwich and milk for lunch.

Climbing out of the car, Janice said: "She took all the stuff that will keep."

"She's holed up somewhere," Reynolds said, stating the obvious. "Unless she had a car stashed somewhere nearby, she had to be on foot, which means she can't be too far from here—especially considering that she took some of the groceries with her. Those bags get heavy if you carry them very far."

"Especially when they're full of cans," Janice added. Although Reynolds had a good point, he'd missed the one she was trying to make. "There's no refrigeration where she is, Ted. Otherwise, why leave the perishable stuff?"

The young detective thought about that a moment, then said: "So the vacant building theory might be right on the money."

And, she thought dismally, the conditions for the hostages would be every bit as bad as she'd imagined them. Time had reached the critical stage now; there could be little doubt of that. Patrol officers were still knocking on doors all over this part of town, but so far, they'd found nothing. Where was her family? Across the street? Two blocks away? A mile away? Had the patrol officers walked right past the spot without knowing it?

"Hey," Goodman said. "About this car here. How long will it have to stay in my garage?"

Janice glared at him; she couldn't help herself. The lives of three people were at stake, and all this jerk cared about was an unauthorized car in his garage.

Goodman looked a little flustered. "I, uh, I was just wondering," he said.

"As soon as a lab guy gets here and takes a look at it, we'll call a wrecker and have it towed away," she replied, her anger gone now. It wasn't his fault. He had a right to be concerned about his garage.

She turned to Reynolds. "Ted, why don't you call in and make sure the lab's on the way?"

He nodded and headed for the car.

Feeling a little shaky, she leaned against the station wagon, and then she had to fight hard to hold back the tears that wanted so desperately to come. Goodman was staring at her.

Corrine MacDougall sat on the soft carpet in the room she'd chosen as her living quarters, her back against the wall, empty cans and a paperback novel beside her. Besides the can opener, the book was the only nonedible thing she'd taken from the car. She'd found it in one of the grocery bags.

Although she'd been exhausted when she finally reached the mortuary, her arms aching from carrying the grocery bag, now she felt quite content. She had made it; she had food; she even had something to read. Things had worked out well enough.

For supper, she'd have a can of stew and a can of peaches. Though her opener was the church key type, she'd discovered that, if you kept making holes around the top of the can, pretty soon you'd have it open. She had no silverware, which meant she had to sort of drink her stew and peaches, but that had been no real problem. The thicker parts of the stew had been coaxed out with her knife. Some of the other things, like the canned hash, would be more difficult but still no real problem. The bag of groceries was across the room from her. There was an apple in there she planned to have later for a snack.

In her explorations around the building, she'd found what had once been a lunchroom with a stove and refrigerator. Unfortunately, all that remained of the appliances was a hole in the counter where the built-in range had been and an outline on the floor where the refrigerator had stood. Not that it really mattered. Soon this would be over, and she could have all the hot meals she wanted. Soon she would be whole.

She hadn't checked on her prisoners lately. Perhaps the time would come sooner than she thought.

Stretching, she adjusted her position against the wall, then picked up the book. A novel of romantic suspense. A middle-class housewife in New Jersey gets recruited by spies and falls madly in love with a handsome secret agent. At least that's what she gleaned from the hype on the cover. She opened the book and began to read. In a few moments, she was totally engrossed in the story.

Eighteen

Janice awoke confused, uncertain where she was or what had awakened her. Then she realized she had fallen asleep at her desk and the phone was ringing. Around the room, other detectives were at their desks, looking bleary-eyed and drowsy. Poldoski's head rested on a stack of papers. She glanced at the clock on the wall; it was after eight in the morning.

She, Poldoski, and some of the others had been here all night, running down any leads that came in, no matter how slim. They'd checked out any prowler reports coming from the southwestern part of the city and even a barroom brawl in which a young blond woman had been involved. The most interesting call had come in around three o'clock. A passing motorist had spotted someone—a woman, he thought—trying to break into a house. It turned out to be a teen-age girl who'd sneaked out to be with her boyfriend. The motorist had happened by just as she was climbing in through her bedroom window.

The phone was still ringing. Janice answered it. "Anderson."

"Uh, Miss Anderson, this is Dr. King at Elk Ridge."

Janice was suddenly wide awake. "Have you got something for us?"

"Well, I might. Uh, there seems to be some confusion as to whether Corrine MacDougall is really dead. A Dr. Eklund just called me. He's the pathologist in charge of identifying the bodies from the bus crash. It seems he wasn't getting any satisfaction from my head of security, so he decided to call me. Luckily, I was here this morning. I don't usually come in on Saturdays."

Stunned, Janice said nothing, waiting for him to continue.

"Anyway, Dr. Eklund says he's identified twenty-seven of the twenty-eight bodies, but the one that should belong to Corrine MacDougall is actually that of a teen-age girl. There were no teen-age girls on the bus, and how she came to be there I have no idea. In any event, I can not account for Corrine MacDougall's body, so it's entirely possible she's alive."

"Doctor, we need her prints, photo, and any background information you have right away."

"All right. I don't know if we can get copies made and get them to Duluth in time for the midmorning flight, but there's one early this afternoon, and—"

"That's not soon enough. Have the prints and picture taken to the Duluth police, and they'll Wirephoto them to us."

"All right. I'll get someone on it right now."

"Oh, and Doctor, after you've done that, call me back. I have to know everything you can tell me about Corrine MacDougall."

When the doctor called back half an hour later, Janice, Poldoski, and the captain were waiting in Bishop's office. The captain put the call on the speaker so the three of them could hear and be heard.

"Miss Anderson?"

"Yes, Doctor, I'm here." It seemed strange talking over the phone and not having a receiver in her hand. "Detective Poldoski and Captain Bishop are here with me. We have you on speaker."

"Oh. Well, the things you wanted are on their way to the Duluth Police Department. Now, you wanted to know about Corrine MacDougall. I have her file here in front of me."

"Tell us about her, Doctor," Janice said.

"Yes, all right. Well, she'd been a patient here for more than two years. She came to us after the breakup of her marriage, which only lasted five months. Her husband, as I recall, moved to Florida right after that. She lived in Duluth and had for several years. She moved there with her family from the Twin Cities area."

"Where in the metro area?" the captain asked.

"To whom am I speaking, please?"

"Captain Bishop."

"Oh. Just a moment. I'll have to check." The rattling of papers came over the speaker. "Up here, you know, we don't make the same fine distinctions between suburbs you do down there. It's all sort of one big city to us. Ah, here it is." There was a moment of silence; then he said. "Dakota Falls."

Janice, Poldoski, and the captain exchanged looks.

"Please continue, Doctor," the captain said.

"Well, her father died shortly after they moved to Duluth, and her mother moved to the West Coast. Corrine had a job as a secretary, and she decided to stay in Minnesota. She really hadn't been that close to her parents. In fact, she'd never really been close to anyone—even in her marriage. She'd always had a fear of personal relationships. She was afraid she wasn't worthy, that she'd be rejected. This, of course, made her quite reserved, and the whole thing became self-fulfilling.

"Her marriage was the first bright spot in her social life. A young man where she worked took a liking to her and stayed with it long enough to get her to respond, which most people didn't. By this time, she was a confirmed loner, almost totally friendless. She was already a very disturbed young woman. She accepted the young man's marriage proposal because she knew she was miserable and thought marriage might be the answer. But she had no real idea of what marriage meant. She was incapable of a close personal relationship. The young man, though, had been infatuated with her. His dream girl, apparently, had been someone who was extremely quiet and shy and would love him madly—someone he could possess totally, I suppose. Corrine was quiet and shy all right, but he didn't realize she could never love anyone madly. She didn't know how. As for possessing her, he might as well have possessed a piece of furniture. She was there, but quite lifeless in any emotional sense."

He cleared his throat. "So the marriage failed, confirming what Corrine had always known about herself: that she was somehow incomplete, unacceptable to society. She became so miserable that it began to affect her work and she was fired, again proving her unworthiness. At this point, there was very little left of Corrine's rational mind.

"Her divorce settlement had included no alimony or anything like that, so she was penniless. The bank, of course, started bouncing her checks. She decided the bank was stealing her money, and went in to demand an explanation. When the teller tried to explain that Corrine was overdrawn, she grabbed the woman's hair and started screaming that she'd kill the woman if she didn't hand over Corrine's money. That's how she came to the attention of the courts. After psychiatric examination, the attempted bank robbery charge was dropped, but Corrine was committed to Elk Ridge."

The three people in Captain Bishop's office listened to King's words intently. Janice doodled absently on a note pad. Poldoski stared at his hands. The captain pursed his lips.

"Somewhere along the line," Dr. King went on, "she decided her failings had begun when she was a teen-ager. Although she had no real friends, she hung around with another girl and the girl's older sister. The relationship began when the girls were in their pre-teens and lasted through high school. She was a hanger-on, so to speak, and although the girls weren't too fond of her, they were too polite to send her away. But Corrine knew she was simply being tolerated."

Janice had stopped doodling; she was staring at the speaker on the captain's desk, her mind racing.

"The girl, of course, was this Shirley I mentioned before. Corrine called the older sister Lynne, although that might or might not have been her real name, just as the name Shirley is questionable. Both these girls, the sisters, were attractive and quite popular, just the opposite of Corrine. The older sister was probably the most popular of the two, but Corrine identified with the younger one because they were the same age and in the same grade in school. I know that Lynne, the older one, was the head cheerleader. That should give you an idea."

"Amy," Janice blurted.

"What's that? I'm sorry, I couldn't hear you."

"Never mind," the captain said. "Go on with what you were saying."

"Very well. Uh, to Corrine, Shirley had become a symbol of everything she wanted to be and never was. She felt that, had she been like Shirley as a teen-ager, the rest of her life would have been fine. It was only a short jump from there to it was all Shirley's fault. Finally, Shirley became the one thing that stood in her way. The only way she could ever be a complete person would be to destroy Shirley."

Poldoski leaned forward, frowning. "Did she ever make any moves against this Shirley at all?"

"No, no. She was still deteriorating when she came to us, and she developed most of these notions while she was here. We were unable to check her deterioration. It just kept getting worse for the first year. Then she bottomed out, I suppose you could say, and a few months after that, she began responding to treatment."

"How did she come to be on the bus?" the captain asked.

"For that very reason. She was responding to treatment, and the outing in the woods was a reward, reinforcement. It's the same thing with the coins we give them. Rather than drugging or confining problem patients or punishing undesirable behavior in some way, we try to encourage desirable behavior through reinforcement."

"I see," the captain said, but the look on his face said he didn't. "Tell me, Doctor, do you use knockout drugs there?"

"Yes. In throwaway syringes. For subduing violent patients. Your next question, I believe, will be whether the staff members assigned to the bus had them. The answer is yes, they did."

Memories of her high school days were tumbling furiously through Janice's mind. There was little doubt that she was Shirley and Amy was Lynne, although she still wasn't certain who Corrine was. "Doctor," she said, "was MacDougall her married or maiden name?"

"Her married name. She never bothered to change it back. Let's see, her maiden name was . . . Ah, here it is. Lindgren."

That registered. "Doctor," she said excitedly, "did she have a nickname or another first name?"

"The name on her records is Corrine Lindgren MacDougall. But she told me once her initials had been *CLL*. I remember because she made an awkward rhyme out of it: '*CLL*, a double *L* just like in hell.' For her, it summed up her life."

And for Janice, the *L* had been enough. "Lora!"

"Yes, I believe it was Lora, come to think of it. And you,

Miss Anderson, are Shirley, I take it."

"Yes," Janice said softly, "I'm Shirley."

"What's that? I'm sorry, I didn't hear you."

Janice didn't respond. She was recalling thin, quiet Lora Lindgren, the girl who used to tag along when she and Amy went to the Saturday morning kiddie shows, almost unnoticed. The plain, blond girl who had always seemed to be around, never really a part of things, yet always there. How many years had Lora Lindgren been on the periphery of her life, a stranger looking in, wanting acceptance but never finding it? And how were she and Amy, their own traumas of growing up to contend with, supposed to know they were planting the seeds of destruction in this shy, brooding girl whose presence had been tolerated but never sought?

But they weren't to blame. They had been no different than any other youngsters, probably kinder than most. If they had been cruel to Lora Lindgren, it had been unintentional, a thing done because they lacked the wisdom to know they were doing it. Certainly nothing Janice could have done to Lora could justify what Lora was doing to her.

Things were falling into place now. She had failed to recognize the composite because it had shown an adult's face, a woman nearly thirty, and Janice had not seen Lora since they were teen-agers. The spot in the woods where the van had been abandoned had also triggered something in Janice's memory, something too deeply buried to recall. It was near that spot— or perhaps that very place—where Lora had been taken by a boy on what was quite likely the only date she'd had in high school. The boy, whose name Janice could not recall, had asked Lora out, apparently thinking she'd be easy. He'd taken her to a movie and immediately afterward to the woods. But when he made his move, Lora had jumped out of the car and run. All the way home.

Janice thought of the time they'd wasted digging up names from her past cases. When she'd last seen Lora, becoming a cop had been the farthest thing from Janice's mind. The pretty blond girl everyone expected to marry a doctor or a lawyer had remained single, joined the police department, worked her way up to detective. The plain blond girl, for whom most of her classmates would have predicted absolutely nothing because they were unaware of her existence, had changed, too. She had become a monster.

Janice searched herself for some feeling of sympathy for what Lora must have suffered and found very little. What Lora had done was too horrible, too personal. The monster had to be stopped and contained. Or destroyed.

While Captain Bishop was getting the address and phone number of Lora's mother from Dr. King, Poldoski leaned over and showed her a pad of paper on which two names were written, one above the other. Arol and Lora. She looked at him quizzically.

"Don't you see it?" he asked.

She looked again, and this time she did see it. "Arol is Lora spelled backwards."

Dr. King had just said he knew of no other relatives besides Corrine MacDougall's mother.

"Doctor," the captain said, "this MacDougall woman is holding three people hostage. Is there anything you can tell us that might give us some clue as to where?"

The speaker on the desk was silent for a moment; then Dr. King said: "No, I'm sorry. If she had any favorite hiding places or anything like that, she never discussed them."

Bishop thanked the doctor for his help and hung up. "How about you, Janice? Apparently you knew her better than just about anyone."

"I really didn't know her, Captain. She hardly ever said anything. As far as I know, when she wasn't with us, she was at home. She used to spend a lot of time in her room, reading."

"All right," Bishop said, "let's see what her mother can tell us." He picked up the phone and dialed.

"The number you have reached is no longer in service," the recorded voice said over the speaker. "If you need assistance, please—" Bishop broke the connection and dialed again.

"Directory assistance for what city, please?"

"Portland, Oregon."

"Go ahead, sir."

"I need the number for a Helen Lindgren." He spelled it. "The last address I have for her is one-two-one-eight Peaceful Valley Court."

"That number is five-five-five-six-eight-one-one."

"Operator, I already called that number. I get an intercept."

"Just a moment. I'll check new listings." A few silent seconds passed; then she said: "I'm sorry, but I have no new listing for anyone by that name."

"Operator, this is the police department in Dakota Falls, Minnesota. If she's moved from that address, it's very important that we find out where she went."

"I'm sorry, sir, but I have no other information. If she's moved, it's possible she left a forwarding address with our billing department. You can call them during normal business hours."

He sighed. "All right. Thank you, operator." He hung up. "Well," he said to Janice and Poldoski, "now that we know the name of the kidnapper, are we any better off than we were before? We can't check with her friends because she didn't have any. The only relative we know about is a mother in Oregon whose phone has been disconnected. Just what the hell do we do with this new information?"

"Something Janice said struck me," Poldoski said. "That this girl spent a lot of time at home. It might not hurt to check out the house she lived in when she was here." He looked at Janice. "You know where it is?"

"I can find it."

"Go ahead and check the place out," Bishop said. "In the meantime, I'll call Portland PD and see if they can tell me what happened to Helen Lindgren. And I'll get Duluth PD to send me what they have on Corrine MacDougall's arrest. It's not likely to tell us much, but we might as well have it."

Janice and Poldoski started for the door; then Janice stopped, turning to face Bishop. "Captain," she said softly, "this is the sixth day."

Bishop's eyes met hers, and he said: "I know. I've been counting, too." As she turned to go, he said: "It's actually only the fifth day."

"What do you mean?" she asked, again facing him.

"It's the sixth day of the kidnapping, but if you take Monday morning as the point when they began going without water, they've been without it five days now, not six. I'm not saying the situation isn't critical, but we're not out of time yet."

She nodded. He was right about the days. But either way you counted it, the week was nearly up.

*   *   *

Accompanied by Poldoski, Janice checked out the house where Lora had lived, discovering that the people who lived there now had bought the place from the Jensens and had never heard of the Lindgrens. When they returned to the station, Janice and Poldoski were immediately summoned to Captain Bishop's office.

As soon as they were seated, the captain said: "As you know, I've alerted the mail room to be on the lookout for anything that might be a message from the kidnapper. Well, this arrived while you were out." He held up a tape cassette, his tired eyes finding Janice's. "It was addressed to you."

"Have you played it?" she asked.

Bishop added. "Her prints aren't on it. She's still being careful." He took a portable tape recorder out of his desk, set it in front of him, and inserted the cassette. "There was no note or anything, just the tape."

The captain stared at the tape recorder for a moment; then he looked up, his eyes again finding Janice's. "Before I play this, I'd better tell you what's on it. There's no message or anything. Just sounds. The sounds of people suffering."

"Go ahead, Captain," Janice said. "Play it." Her voice sounded tinny, distant, as if it weren't really hers.

Bishop nodded, then pressed the play button. For a few seconds, the tape ran silently; then a soft moan came from the recorder's speaker. The sound had a masculine quality to it; Janice was fairly certain it had been made by a man. Was it her father? She couldn't be certain. The tape was silent again; then there was a groan, followed by a grunt, then a whimpering sound. These noises had clearly been made by a child, but it was impossible to say whether it was a boy or a girl, although Janice had no doubt she was listening to Mark. And the first sound, the moan, had to have been her father.

She steeled herself. There was nothing here she hadn't already known. Their strength sapped by lack of water, the hostages would have to be semiconscious, incapable of carrying on a normal conversation. But it was something she hadn't wanted to contemplate. To force herself to stop thinking about the suffering the sounds on the tape represented, she turned her thoughts to Lora. My God, she thought, what kind of a monster could do something like this?

The tape was still running, Janice and Poldoski staring intently at the machine, waiting for whatever would come next. And when it came, Janice flinched. It was a woman's loud, piercing scream.

"The caterpillars! They're eating me! They're eating me!" The screamed words were followed by a shriek of pure terror; then the tape recorder was silent, and Captain Bishop punched the stop button.

"That's all," he said.

Janice closed her eyes, the screams still lingering in her ears. A wave of dizziness swept over her. Something in her mind seemed to be telling her that if she simply collapsed they'd have to send her home and then she wouldn't have to think about what she'd just heard. She could take a sleeping pill, withdraw into slumber, let Mike take care of her.

But then the feeling passed, and she opened her eyes.

Leaning forward in his chair, Poldoski had her arm. "Are you all right, Janice?"

She nodded. He looked worried, and the captain was staring at her anxiously.

"I can't be sure about the first two," she said, "but the last one was definitely Amy."

"It was mailed yesterday here in town," Bishop said. "What does this tell us that can help us? Are there any clues here?"

Poldoski asked the obvious question. "What about the caterpillars?"

The captain sighed. "I don't know. Up north, they're having a caterpillar infestation right now. They strip whole forests, there are so many of them. But they don't eat people, and they'd have no way of getting into an airtight compartment— if the hostages are really in one."

"Unless," Poldoski said slowly, "they were put inside intentionally."

Janice shuddered at the thought. "I'm not sure it means anything. Amy has always been extremely frightened of bugs. Right after she arrived, Mark came in with a caterpillar he'd found in the yard, and Amy nearly fainted. The incident could have touched off something in her mind. She could be hallucinating."

"Still," Bishop said, "I'm going to put out an urgent bulletin. Special attention of the law-enforcement agencies in any area where there's a caterpillar infestation. Is there anything else on the tape that can help us?"

"I only noticed one other thing," Poldoski said. "After the screams there was an echo. I'd say the recording was made in a fairly large room and probably an empty one, with no furniture or anything to absorb the noise. And it would have to be a room with mostly hard surfaces, to bounce the sound back. The floor probably wouldn't be carpeted or anything like that."

Bishop frowned. "Would a walk-in refrigerator be too small, do you think?"

"I don't think you could get an echo like that in one." He shrugged. "On the other hand, an echo isn't enough to allow us to rule anything out either."

"Does the tape tell us anything else?" the captain asked. When neither Janice nor Poldoski offered any further ideas, he said: "Okay, let's get back to work."

As she rose to leave the office, Janice pushed the horrible tape recording out of her mind. She could not afford to dwell on it. She'd be unable to function if she did.

The day wore on.

The Wirephotos from Dr. King came down from Duluth, and to no one's surprise, the prints of Arol Adkins matched those of Corrine Lora MacDougall, nee Lindgren. The photo was copied and distributed to the media. Poldoski continued his paperwork, while Janice and Mullins ran down the last of the leads generated by the publication of the composite, none of which put them any closer to Lora. Watson was still coordinating the door-to-door check by patrol officers, who were now using the photograph rather than the composite. The effort, though massive, had generated nothing useful. Reynolds succeeded in locating the owner of a vacant building at home and got permission to enter. Collins and Greene checked it out. The bankrupt restaurant in Minnetonka held no surprises.

The highway department reported its computers were not yet repaired, but they would be by late afternoon. The list of condemned buildings should be delivered by six at the latest. At 9:30 that evening it had still not arrived.

Janice sat at her desk. Although her mind was nearly too exhausted to function, her body still flowed with the nervous energy that had kept it going these past few days. Around her, most of the desks were vacant now, the room quiet. Poldoski was at his, trying to concentrate on what looked like a map, his head nodding as he hovered on the edge of sleep. Leaning back in his chair, Mullins *was* asleep, an ashtray full of cigar butts in front of him. The light coming from the captain's office showed that Bishop was still in. The others had gone home to get a few hours of much-needed sleep.

There was no reason for all of them to be here now; there was nothing for them to do. What could be done had been done. The only thing to do now was wait, hope for some unexpected break, something to move on, and that could be done as well at home as anywhere else.

She'd called Mike earlier to let him know they'd learned the identity of the kidnapper. He hadn't understood about Lora, but then Janice didn't understand it herself. Even Dr. King only comprehended it professionally, as a scientist comprehends a molecule. Only to Lora did it make sense, and Lora was insane.

"Janice. . . ." Captain Bishop was standing beside her desk. His eyes were bloodshot, and he looked exhausted. Like her, he'd had about two hours' sleep Thursday night and hadn't gone home at all last night.

"Have you got something, Captain?" She knew he didn't. When he had things to tell people, he was brisk, businesslike, never hesitant.

He shook his head. "No, I was just wondering if you were staying in the house—your father's house."

"No, I'm staying with a friend."

"Oh. If you were there all alone—at the house—I was going to offer you the use of my guest room." He shrugged.

The question of whether he'd have made the same offer to a male officer flickered briefly in her thoughts. But at the moment, it hardly seemed to matter. He was being kind, and she was too sensitive. "Thank you anyway, Captain. For the offer."

"Sure. In any case, I think you should get out of here and get some rest. You're not doing any good here at the moment, and if something comes up, you'll be notified immediately."

"Not just yet, Captain. I'm going to hang in here a while longer. Just in case."

"It's up to you, but you can't help your family by collapsing from exhaustion."

She nodded. He gave her a stern look and headed for his office. Picking up the phone, she called Mike.

"Anything yet?" he asked anxiously.

"No."

"Are you okay?"

"Unless you count exhaustion."

"You're not planning to stay there all night again, are you?" By the way he asked, she could tell that he was resigning himself to the likelihood that she would.

"No," she said. "I'm leaving now." The captain was right. She was accomplishing nothing by staying here. "I'll be there in fifteen minutes or so."

"Good," he replied, sounding relieved. "I'll have some sandwiches ready."

Hanging up the phone, she glanced around the room. Both Poldoski and Mullins were asleep at their desks now. Having told the captain she was leaving, she went to the basement parking area and took an unmarked AMC. Her Datson had no two-way radio, and she had no intention of being out of touch with the department, even during the fifteen-minute drive to Mike's.

As she pulled onto the street, she grabbed the microphone. "One-thirty-three, PD."

"Go ahead, one-thirty-three."

"Log me ten-eight."

"Ten-four."

Though nearly ten o'clock, it had just barely become dark, and even now the last hints of gray lingered in the sky. The light was red at the first intersection she reached. When it turned green, instead of turning right, toward Mike's place, she turned left, toward the Falls Motel, the alley in which Charles Nordin had been mugged, the supermarket where Lora had attacked a woman and taken her car. Lora had to be there, somewhere in that part of town.

She made the rounds, going from each spot to the next, looking for anything that might give her a clue to Lora's hiding place, blanking her mind each time she was forced to pass the lighted grounds of the mortuary. After forty-five minutes of driving, she had found nothing.

It was then, as she was driving west on Pennington, that an urge hit her, a desire she hadn't experienced in years: the desperate need for a cigarette. It would pass, she knew. She'd experienced these urges with diminishing frequency the first year or two after kicking the habit. Yet, instead of driving on, toward the Falls Motel, she turned the car around and headed for the Seven-Eleven store she'd passed a few blocks back.

"Help you?" the thin young man behind the cash register said, smiling a very friendly smile as he tried not to be too obvious about giving her the once-over. She was the only customer in the place.

Janice stared at the array of cigarettes behind the counter. There were so many new brands now she didn't know which one to choose. Then she noticed the sign taped to the wall by the cigarettes:

NOTICE TO OUR CUSTOMERS: WE WILL BE
CLOSING PERMANENTLY ON JULY 1st.

"Business that bad?" she asked, indicating the sign.

"No, no. It's a little slow at the moment, but this isn't a bad spot, really. We have to clear out because of the freeway that'll be coming through. There's places all through here that'll have to close. Down there where the funeral home is now, there's going to be an interchange, so I understand, and most of the businesses between here and there will be gone." He shrugged. "I was getting tired of this job anyway."

Christ, Janice thought, instead of waiting days for a list from the highway department, why didn't they just call the clerk at the Seven-Eleven?

"Can I get you something?" he asked.

"Yeah, a pack of . . ." It wasn't indecision that stopped her; she'd just realized the significance of what the clerk had said. "The funeral home, is it vacant?"

The clerk shrugged. "Some people have moved out and some haven't. They don't all have the same deadline."

Cigarettes forgotten, Janice abruptly turned and left the store, leaving the clerk staring after her bewilderedly. It was a long shot, but every time she drove this area, it seemed she was constantly passing the mortuary. The size of the place could account for that, she supposed; it was hard to miss something that took up an entire square block. And she wasn't even sure it was vacant. Still, it wouldn't hurt to take a look at the place.

Back on Pennington, she drove toward the funeral home. Did such places have airtight compartments? They had to, she realized, some sort of a refrigerator for keeping the bodies. She refused to consider what it might be like to be held prisoner in one.

She was way overdue at Mike's. If she saw a pay phone, she'd stop and call him. But she hadn't seen one by the time she reached the grounds of Heikkinen's Funeral Home. First, she'd check out the mortuary; then she'd call Mike.

The grounds were so well lighted she almost didn't need the car's headlights. And the place had been carefully maintained. The asphalt drive curved gently around trees and flowering shrubs separated by immaculate stretches of lawn. The mortuary certainly didn't appear abandoned.

As she reached the low white building in the middle of the flowers and greenery, she was beginning to wonder whether she was doing this simply out of desperation to be doing something. Well, she was here; she'd look.

She stopped the car in the small asphalt parking area by the main entrance, then, grabbing her purse and the flashlight mounted below the dash, she walked the ten feet or so to the glass front door. It was securely locked, the interior of the building dark. No night lights? She wondered why. The deadbolt lock on the door showed no signs of having been tampered with. Nor did the front windows, and they, too, were locked.

Following a flower-lined flagstone walk, she headed for the rear of the mortuary. As she moved along the side of the building it grew darker, as this area was not lighted. She switched on her flashlight. There were no windows or doors here, no places through which entry could be gained.

She thought she heard a noise to her right. Shining her light in that direction, she saw only bushes and trees. A chipmunk or a squirrel probably. Yet something made her unzip her purse, adjust the position of her .38 so it could be reached quickly if needed.

She turned the corner at the rear of the mortuary, her flashlight beam poking into nearly total blackness now, the building blocking out any illumination from the lights in front. The lighting had apparently been done strictly to show the grounds, with no thought at all to security.

Ahead, the flagstones led through a gap between two thick bushes. Uncertain why she felt so uneasy, Janice hesitated, her hand once more checking to make sure her purse was unzipped, her .38 within easy reach. She started forward again, the beam of her flashlight fixed on the gap between the bushes.

Just as she reached the shrubs, something behind one of them moved.

Nineteen

Wondering what time it was, Lora put down her book. With no radio, TV set, or watch, she had no way to tell time, as any clocks that had been in the mortuary had been removed. And because all the windows were in the front of the building, she had no idea whether it was day or night outside, except by trying to guess the passage of time or by going up front and checking.

Standing, she stretched, then walked to the door and stepped into the hallway. Pulling the door closed behind her, she plunged the corridor into total blackness. She dared not use the lights here because the door at the end of the hallway was visible from the glass front door; the glow showing through the crack at its bottom could be spotted from outside.

Feeling her way along the wall, she reached the door and entered the carpeted reception area. Here she could see even at night because some of the illumination from the exterior lights spilled in through the windows and glass door. It was night now.

She stepped over to a window and stared for a moment at the grounds. They were her front yard in a way, and clearly, she had the largest, most elaborate front yard in town. Perhaps she would really live in a place with grounds like this some day. When she was whole.

She was just about to turn away from the window when she noticed the headlights coming up the drive. She moved back, out of sight. Who was there? Who would come here at night?

Peeking outside, she saw that the car had stopped and some-one was climbing out with a flashlight. A woman. Lora gasped, clutching the window sill.

Janice!

How? How had Janice found her? And why was she alone? Where were all the policemen she should have brought with her? No, no, she couldn't know. Not if she was alone. But why was she here?

Janice was at the door, tugging at the handle. Lora slunk back into the shadows. What would she do if Janice came in? Dropping to her hands and knees so she'd be below the window, she crawled toward the door. When she was a few feet from it, she pulled the knife from the pocket of her jeans. If Janice came in, Lora would be ready.

But Janice wasn't coming in. There were no sounds from the door now. Was she still there? If not, where had she gone? Still on her hands and knees, Lora moved back to the window, cautiously raising her head just enough to see over the sill. Janice was still there, walking away from her. And then she was out of sight, around the corner of the building. She was going around to the back; she had to be. It was dark there. Very dark. And Lora had to get there first.

She ran. Janice's showing up like this had changed every-thing. The plan would have to be forgotten now, all but the most important part. Janice had to die. If she was here, some-thing was wrong. She wasn't here for no reason. She had to die tonight. Now. She had to. It was the only way to be whole.

Near panic now, Lora ran blindly through the blackness of the hallway, one hand gripping the knife, the other extended in front of her to warn her before she ran into something. Ahead was a door. She slowed just in time, just as her fingers felt the wood. There was a room here and across it another door. She found the knob and plunged into the darkness. She was somewhere near the center of the room when her foot caught on something sticking up from the floor. Stumbling, she tried to keep her balance, and then she fell, landing on her chest, sliding on the floor tiles.

The knife. Where was the knife? She reached out with her hand, feeling the cracks where the floor tiles met. And then she touched something. The knife. Grabbing it, she scrambled to her feet, feeling for the wall. There was no time! Why hadn't she turned on a light? She found the wall, and then the door, and she was dashing down another dark corridor. She didn't need the lights now, and turning them on would only destroy her night vision. Although she couldn't see it, she ran past the room of the dead, the room where three people lay dying.

Suddenly, she wasn't sure how far she'd run, and she was certain she was about to crash into the back door. She tried to stop, but her feet lost their purchase, and she slipped, her shoulder hitting the wall, and then she was on the floor. The knife, gripped tightly this time, was still in her hand.

The door. She had to get to the door before Janice did. Crawling forward as fast as she could, she reached for it, finding nothing. Again, she reached. And again. And there it was. Her breath coming in short gasps, she eased it open, peering through the crack. It was dark. No sign of Janice's flashlight.

She was in time. A feeling of well-being, of joy, swept over her. She was in time. She could still be whole.

Blinking his eyes, Poldoski looked at the clock on the wall, trying to figure out how long he'd been asleep. It was almost eleven now, but he wasn't sure exactly when he'd dropped off.

A few desks away, Mullins, his back to Poldoski, was snoring loudly. Everyone else was gone apparently, including Janice. He hoped she'd gone to bed. These past few days had been a strain on all of them, but it had to be nothing compared to what she was going through.

In front of him was the map on which he'd been marking the spots where a young woman resembling the composite had reportedly been seen. These were mostly the sightings there had been no immediate need to check out because they were old at the time they'd been phoned in. *I saw this woman at the store yesterday, and she looked just like that picture in the paper.* Those calls.

In the southwestern section of town, he'd marked four locations: a self-service laundry, a street corner, a grocery store, and a mortuary of all places. Pushing the map away from him, he picked up his stained cup and headed for the coffee urn. If there was anything in it, it ought to be bitter goo by now, but if he could drink it, it would wake him up.

As he passed Reynolds' desk, an envelope caught his eye. It was from the highway department, DET. REYNOLDS typed on its face. Apparently having arrived after Reynolds had gone, it was unopened. Better late than never, Poldoski supposed. He picked it up and took it with him to the coffee urn, which, he found, contained exactly the oily-looking stuff he'd expected it to.

His cup full, he returned to his desk, where he opened the envelope, removing a single sheet of paper. The phone rang.

"Poldoski."

"Uh, Detective Anderson, please."

"Sorry, she's not here. Can I take a message?"

"This is Mike Simpson. She called over an hour ago and said she was on her way here. Did something come up?"

Although Poldoski remembered Mike Simpson, he saw no reason to greet him like a long lost friend. He said: "Not that I know of, Mr. Simpson."

"Could you check?"

Poldoski sighed. "Sure. Hold on." He put Simpson on hold and dialed dispatch. "This is Poldoski. Is one-thirty-three ten-eight?"

"Ten-four. Logged out at nine fifty-four."

"Do you have her present ten-twenty?"

"Negative. She's just logged as ten-eight."

"See if you can reach her, please."

"Stand by." About a minute passed before the woman in dispatch came back on the line. "One-thirty-three does not respond."

"Okay. Thanks." Where the hell was she? He pushed the

button for the line on which Simpson was holding. "She's gone somewhere, but nobody here at the moment seems to know where."

"Well, okay. Thanks anyway." He hung up.

While Poldoski tried to think of somewhere Janice might have gone, his eyes absently scanned the list from the highway department. A bakery, a cafe. Oh, crap, he thought, paying close attention to the list now. The first two places on it could have airtight compartments. The list went on: a gas station, dry cleaners, Seven-Eleven store—another possibility—two homes, a mortuary, all of them in the southwestern part of town.

A mortuary?

Heikkinen's Funeral Home, the same place one of the callers had seen someone resembling Corrine MacDougall. Well, it was close to the bakery, cafe, and Seven-Eleven store. But what about the funeral home itself? Would it have airtight compartments? He'd seen a morgue often enough, and there were certainly airtight compartments there. The slabs where they kept the stiffs pulled out of a big built-in refrigerator of some kind. The mortuary, too, would have to be checked out.

He grabbed a piece of wadded-up paper from the wastebasket and bounced it off the back of Mullins' chair. "Hey, Ed! Wake up!"

"Hey, what . . . ?" Mullins leaned forward, shaking his head. After a moment, he turned to face Poldoski. "What time is it?"

"Eleven."

Mullins grunted.

"You know where Janice is?"

"Beats me. She was here when I dozed off."

Although he was still a little concerned about Janice, he had more pressing matters to deal with now. "We've got some places to check out. You awake yet?"

"Let's get it over with. I'd like to get home before my wife and kids forget what the hell I look like." He jammed a cigar into his mouth. "Where do we have to go?"

"They're all over on Pennington." He checked his list. "Ben's Bakery, the Boulevard Cafe, a Seven-Eleven store, Heikkinen's Funeral Home. We don't have permission to enter, but we can take a look."

Mullins frowned. "A goddamned mortuary?"

"Why? They scare you?"

"There was something I was supposed to tell you about a mortuary, and I forgot."

"What?"

"I don't know. I'm trying to remember. Oh, yeah. Remember that homicide I worked a couple of days ago at Griffith Lake? The apparent mugging?"

Poldoski nodded.

"Well, it wasn't a mugging. Guy was fishing. At least that's what it looked like. Had all the gear with him. But the captain tells me there ain't no fish in that lake, and the guy was an experienced fisherman. He'd have known that. What I was supposed to tell you was that there were some similarities between this case and the merchant patrol guy who was mugged. Both were stabbed from behind. Both were old men. Both were robbed. Pretty slim if you ask me. That's probably why I forgot to mention it."

"What does that have to do with the mortuary?"

"The old guy worked there. He was a grounds keeper. At Heikkinen's."

"And the old guy was killed somewhere else besides the lake?"

"I couldn't prove it, but why else set up the phony fishing scene?"

"Oh, shit," Poldoski said.

Instantly, Janice was crouching, the .38 in her hand, the beam of her flashlight trained on the bush behind which something had moved. Then she saw something scamper away, although she couldn't tell what. It had been an animal, a raccoon possibly. Returning her revolver to her purse, she stood up, still a little shaken.

Jesus, she thought, I'm all nerves. I really do need some sleep. And yet she knew she would be unable to sleep. How could she when three members of her family were still being held prisoners by a monster? When she didn't know whether they were dead or alive?

Suddenly, she wanted to finish her inspection and get out of here. At Mike's, a strong shoulder would be waiting, one on which she could cry in privacy. She needed that at the moment. Exhausted and with the emotions of the past few days churning inside of her, she needed to let it all out in the arms of someone who cared.

Then, after doing so, maybe she could begin to deal with the likelihood that she would never see her father or sister or Mark again. Not alive.

She hurried to the back door, shining her flashlight on the lock. It did not appear to have been tampered with. There was a low cement ramp here, leading from the threshold to a small gravel parking area, apparently so gurneys could be rolled in. This was where the bodies had been delivered. Grabbing the knob, she gave it a quick twist, and to her surprise it turned. The door was unlocked. Although she had no warrant, there was nothing to prevent her from opening an unlocked door and looking inside. Going inside was questionable, depending on whether an unlocked door constituted probable cause. The rules seemed to change daily; you never really knew for sure.

Automatically reaching for her .38 with her free hand, she used the hand that held the flashlight to open the outward-swinging door. She had opened it no more than six inches when it suddenly slammed her in the face, pushing her back, knocking the revolver from her hand. Stumbling backward, trying to maintain her balance, she saw a figure in the doorway, coming toward her, and for just a moment, the flashlight in Janice's hand picked out the face, a face contorted in fear and rage, a face from Janice's past. Lora.

And then Janice lost the fight to retain her balance, and she was on the ground, and Lora was on top of her. Swinging the flashlight as hard as she could, she knocked Lora aside and scrambled away, trying to get to her feet. But then Lora was on her again, and this time Janice's wild swing with the flashlight missed. She saw the knife in Lora's hand and tried to roll out of the way, but the blade slashed across her back.

She swung again with the flashlight, striking her opponent so hard the light flew out of her hand and went out. Lora gasped.

Quickly, Janice grabbed her, struggling to immobilize the arm with the knife. Her eyes had not yet accustomed themselves to the loss of the flashlight, and she could see almost nothing. She found the arm she wanted and, standing, began to twist. Lora screamed in pain but wouldn't release the knife.

"Drop it, or I'll break your fucking arm off!" Janice shouted.

"No! I have to be whole!" Lora tried to rise, turn with the pressure to ease it.

Janice twisted harder, and Lora fell face first into the gravel, screaming at the top of her lungs. Pinning Lora's wrist to the ground with her foot, Janice wrenched the knife out of the madwoman's hand.

Tossing it away, she stepped back. "Where are they?"

Lora lay in the gravel, whimpering.

"Dammit! Where are they?"

Lora continued whimpering.

"Tell me, or you and that arm can go downtown in two different cars." When Lora didn't answer, Janice reached for the arm. It didn't matter whether she hurt Lora. Three lives were at stake, three innocent people, and the woman at her feet was a monster. But just as she was about to grip the thin wrist, the woman on the ground lashed out with her feet, catching Janice in the stomach.

The wind knocked out of her, Janice couldn't breathe. Lora was crawling away, trying to get to her feet. Janice, searching for breath that wouldn't come, could do nothing but gasp. Then Lora was standing, wobbling, and she staggered toward the mortuary. Janice, her breath slowly returning, went after her, reaching the door just as it closed and locked behind Lora.

The thing to do was run to the car and call for help. Logic said so; the manual said so. But what if she was watching one exit while Lora slipped out another? There was no point from which she could see both. And what if her family was inside . . . and Lora had gone in to kill them, to get the job done while she still had time?

Janice tried the door to be sure it was locked. It was. She ran to the spot where she and Lora had struggled, finding her purse, which had been ripped from her shoulder. Then she rushed back to the door and began looking for her .38. It was too dark to see it, so she had to feel for it with her hands. In a flower bed next to the concrete ramp, she touched something cold and metallic. Her gun.

Hurriedly fishing a credit card from her purse, she slipped it into the space between the door and the jamb. This type of lock was easily opened; the police department was constantly urging people who had them to replace them with deadbolts. This time, when she pulled the door open, she was standing well to the side, ready should Lora try the same maneuver again. She didn't.

The strap on her purse was broken. Leaving it behind, she stepped into the darkened building, the door closing automatically behind her. Her clothes were sticking to her back where the knife had caught her, indicating the wound was bleeding, though not badly, as far as she could tell.

Feeling her way along the wall, she moved slowly into the blackness. Should she try to find a light switch, or would Lora, who knew the location of the switch, be waiting for her to do just that? There was Charles Nordin's .38 to consider. She had to assume Lora still had it.

Twenty

James Heikkinen, whose home was still in Dakota Falls even though his business had moved, rolled over in his bed, groping in the darkness for the ringing phone. He finally found it.

"Mr. James Heikkinen?"

"Yes?" At least it wasn't a wrong number.

"Sorry to bother you at this hour. This is Detective Poldoski at the Dakota Falls Police Department. We need to know if your mortuary here is vacant."

"Of course it's vacant," he replied, somewhat bewildered. "The highway department condemned it."

"We'd appreciate it if you'd open it up for us so we could have a look inside."

"Now? I'm in bed."

"It's very urgent, Mr. Heikkinen. We have reason to believe that three people are being held hostage inside."

"Three people! You mean the three . . . the kidnapping that's been in all the papers?"

"Yes, sir."

"You mean the woman I saw on the grounds . . ." He trailed off.

"If you could come right away, sir, we'd appreciate it. We can't be certain they're in there, but there's a chance of it, and we need to find out as soon as possible."

"Oh, uh, all right. I'll meet you there in twenty minutes."

"Thank you, sir. Please hurry."

After hanging up the phone, he switched on the light. Beside him, his wife was sound asleep, her reddish-brown hair all that protruded from beneath the covers.

"Mildred, guess what!"

She grunted and rolled over. Well, he'd tell her later. Flinging the covers aside, he climbed out of bed and hurried to the bathroom.

Lora stumbled through the darkness, her right arm throbbing with pain. She'd heard the back door open and close. She knew Janice was behind her.

The gun. She had to get the gun. It was in the bag of groceries, in the room she'd been using as her quarters. Janice had followed her, so there was still a chance. She could still be whole.

When she reached the room she had to pass through to get to the other hallway, she slowed, began feeling her way more cautiously. She knew the building, and her pursuer didn't. Janice would not overtake her, not as long as Lora was quiet and didn't make any noises that would reveal her location.

Having worked her way through the connecting room, she entered the other corridor and headed for the door with the light showing along the bottom. When she entered the room, she was momentarily blinded by the brightness. Then her vision cleared, and she rushed to the grocery bag. The weapon was on top. She had it.

She hurried to the wall switch and turned out the light, afterimages of the brightness lingering before her eyes. Quietly opening the door, she moved back into the hallway. She was ready now, ready to find Janice.

She moved silently through the connecting room again, and into the hallway leading to the back door. Listening for any sounds of movement, she heard nothing but her own breathing. She held her breath, still hearing nothing. Where was Janice?

Then she heard the rustle of cloth, clothing brushing against something, no more than fifteen feet away. Janice was here, close. Lora aimed the gun, holding it with both hands. Her right arm was still sore, making her aim somewhat shaky. But Janice would be moving toward her; the target would be so close a little shakiness wouldn't matter.

She heard the whisper of cloth, like pants legs brushing against each other. Very close. Lora fired, the pistol flashing, jumping in her hand, the shot echoing off the tiled walls of the corridor. Something fell.

Lora waited, hearing nothing except the ringing in her ears from the explosion of the gunshot. There had been no groan, no gasp of surprise. Yet a body had fallen. Had she killed Janice instantly? Was she now whole? She had to know. Taking a cautious step forward, she hesitated. No, no, no. Janice could be playing opossum. Lora's throbbing right arm was an unpleasant reminder of what could happen in a physical confrontation with Janice. A police officer was trained in hand-to-hand combat. And this particular police officer hated her for what she'd done.

She backed away, silently, not allowing the legs of her jeans to brush against each other, putting each foot down gently, noiselessly. The light switch. It was about ten feet behind her. Her fingers lightly touching the wall, she moved backward, feeling the outlines of the green tiles she couldn't see. Then her hand touched the switch plate.

Squatting, making herself a small target, she aimed as well as she could with her injured right arm, while her left hand reached up and pushed the switch.

As Mullins drove the car out of the underground parking area, Poldoski grabbed the microphone.

"One-seventy-two, PD."

"Go ahead, one-seventy-two."

"Be advised that myself and one-ninety-six are ten-eight,

en route Heikkinen's Funeral Home on Pennington."

"Ten-four, one-seventy-two."

"PD, would you try one-thirty-three, please?" The more powerful base transmitter had a much greater range than the car radios, which sometimes could not communicate between different sections of town.

"PD, one-thirty-three," the dispatcher's voice said. After a few moments of silence, the dispatcher repeated the call. Finally, she said: "One-seventy-two, one-thirty-three does not respond."

"Ten-four, PD." Poldoski replaced the microphone. Where the hell was Janice?

When Janice heard a door open farther down the hallway, she froze, listening intently. The door closed again. Lora was in the corridor, just ahead of her. Slipping off her shoes, Janice began heading toward the sound, moving as quietly as possible, her .38 held in front of her. She paused, hearing nothing, then started forward again. She was close now, almost to the spot where the sound had come from.

Suddenly, a shot exploded out of the darkness, the muzzle flash momentarily illuminating Lora's face, the bullet passing so close to Janice's cheek she felt its wind. Although the flash had given away Lora's location, there was no time to take advantage of it. The first shot had been too close, and a second might not miss, so Janice hurled herself to the floor, raising the .38, waiting for Lora to fire again. But no second shot came, no muzzle flash to reveal Lora's face in its brief glow. Janice had done the right thing by moving quickly, but she had lost her target.

She wished now she'd kept her shoes. She could hurl one of them down the hallway, possibly causing Lora to fire at the sound and reveal herself. She thought about crawling back to where she'd left them and decided against it. The best thing to do now was to lie still, wait. Eventually, Lora would have to check, find out whether she'd been lucky with that shot.

Staring into the blackness, Janice thought she heard movement, but it was hard to judge how far away it might be. And then there was only more silence. The building made a slight pop, one of those sounds that all structures make as they adjust to temperature or humidity or stress. Usually, such noises went unnoticed, but in the silent blackness of the corridor, it seemed a cannon blast.

Janice was behaving instinctively, the things to do in such a situation having been drilled into her head by police instructors. Don't take chances, survive, get help. She hadn't done the last one, had she? It was too late now.

Instinctively? Was that the right word? She had never been in a gun battle before, had never fired her weapon off the pistol range. Still, there were things police officers knew, a logic derived from being constantly in an adversary relationship with killers and muggers and all sorts of crazy people with guns and knives.

She tried to tell herself that she had the upper hand here, that she was better prepared to deal with this situation than was Lora, that all she had to do was use her cop's instinct for survival and be cautious. Although there was a certain comforting truth in these thoughts, Janice was more frightened than she'd ever been in her life.

Suddenly, the lights came on, blinding her. She rolled, trying to get out of the way, and a shot rang out, the bullet whistling down the hallway. And Janice was aiming her own weapon now, trying to pick Lora out of the brightness. All at once Lora materialized, a faint outline in the glaring light, standing by the light switch, shielding her eyes with one hand, holding a revolver with the other. Janice's vision had cleared first.

"Drop it!" Janice commanded. "Now!" The knowledge that only Lora knew the location of the hostages had kept Janice from firing. That they were here was a reasonable assumption, but not a certainty. Her vision still clearing, she trained the .38 on Lora's legs. She had to be sure she didn't kill her.

The lights went out. Janice fired.

And then there were footsteps pounding down the hallway, away from her.

Janice's hand was shaking, the weight of the weapon it held seeming unreal somehow. She had just fired a shot at another human being. She was trembling. No amount of training, no amount of dealing with killers and muggers could prepare you for this.

Unnerved now, she felt what self-confidence she'd had crumbling. Training without experience was only an abstraction. She *had* no instinct to fall back on. She'd already violated procedure—if not common sense—by approaching Lora in a manner that had given a downed adversary the chance to lash out with her feet. She'd overreacted, hadn't thought, hadn't remembered to use the proper procedure for handling a prostrate suspect.

Janice made herself stop shaking. She had to get Lora. Later, she could fall apart, but not now, not while three lives were at stake, not while a monster was loose in the community Janice was sworn to protect. To fail now would not only be to fail her family, but to fail herself as well. It would mean she was as undeserving of her shield, as incapable of handling the responsibilities that came with it, as the sexists in the department had always believed.

Getting to her feet, she began moving cautiously forward. Think. Be careful. Get Lora.

The bullet from Janice's gun had hit Lora's jeans. A quick, violent tug at the cloth. It had taken her a moment to realize the bullet hadn't hit her leg as well.

Now, panicked by her close call, Lora had to force herself to move slowly and quietly. Somewhere in her head a voice was screaming *RUN! RUN!* but she couldn't allow herself to listen to that voice, for if she did, she would never be whole, and being whole was all that mattered. She had to think, to find a way to kill Janice.

She was in the other hallway now, near her quarters, although now there was no light coming from beneath the door to reveal the room's location.

The light. If she turned it on, Janice would see it, investigate. And when Janice opened the door, she'd be in the light, exposed, a perfect target. And across the hall was another room. A place to hide. And wait for Janice.

Or was that too obvious? Could a more clever trap be devised?

Poldoski and Mullins were driving up the private road leading to the mortuary.

"Jesus," the sergeant said, "it's sure as hell well lighted here."

Glancing out the car's rear window, Poldoski said: "Yeah,

but we're already out of sight from the street. The lights make it a better hiding place. You'd never think it was vacant."

"Looks like Heikkinen's early. That must be his car."

Poldoski looked. "Hell, that's one of ours, Ed. Christ, Janice must be here somewhere."

Mullins stopped behind the green AMC. After giving it a quick inspection, they went to the front door of the mortuary. Poldoski was worried.

Mullins pulled on the glass door. "Locked. No signs of forced entry."

"Let's try the back," Poldoski said.

As they started along the flagstone walk, they heard two muffled gunshots, fired in rapid succession. "That came from inside!" Poldoski said, turning and heading back toward the door.

Mullins was beside him. "Probable cause, wouldn't you say?"

"At the moment, I really don't give a shit. Let's do it."

"Stand back."

Mullins fired into the glass, shattering it. They hurriedly kicked away any remaining jagged pieces blocking their way, and rushed inside.

Janice had no idea where Lora was now. She'd been going from one room to the next, easing open the door, listening, then reaching in and flipping on the light as she quickly moved to the side of the doorway. She'd been leaving the doors open, the lights on. It was too easy for Lora to hide in the darkness.

At the end of the hallway, she found some light switches. When she flipped them up, the overhead lights came on at her end of the corridor.

Checking the door on her left, she found an empty room with only outlines on the floor to show where equipment or furniture had once stood. There was no telling what this or any of the other rooms she'd seen might have been used for. So far, she had not seen anything that could be an airtight compartment.

The door on her right, she discovered, led to a similar room—the same dark floor tiles bearing outlines of whatever had been here—but this one had an exit on its far side. She went to it and, switching off the light, cautiously opened the door, finding another dark hallway. There were no light switches nearby.

She turned on the lights in the room again, letting their illumination spill out into the corridor. Again, she began checking rooms, switching on the lights, leaving the doors open. Then she saw it. The next door on her right had a bright strip along its bottom; the lights in that room were already on. Was Lora in there? Would she give herself away so easily? Janice didn't think so.

She knew Lora wasn't behind her, because she'd checked those rooms. And if the lighted room ahead was a setup, only two others would serve as good spots from which to ambush her, both on the left. Tightening her grip on the .38, she flattened herself against the wall and began moving toward the two possible hiding places. As she neared the closest one, she noticed that the door was open a crack. Taking a deep breath, she reached along the wall with her hand, then pushed the door open, dropping into a crouch as she stepped in front of it, her .38 leveled. No shots came from inside, no sounds, no movement.

Suddenly, Janice noticed her shadow, and in that instant she realized there was only one source of light behind her that could be making that shadow. The door with the bright strip showing at its bottom had just been opened. Lora had outguessed her, had known what she would do. Janice dived into the room she was facing, rolling, trying to get out of the light from the doorway, just as two shots rang out, one of them slamming into the floor only inches from her face.

Lying on her stomach, Janice gripped her .38 with both hands, training it on the doorway. Come on, she thought. Come look and see if you got me. She was at an angle to the doorway and could see only a few feet of the hall. The door to the lighted room from which Lora had sprung her trap was out of sight. Janice waited. There were no sounds.

Then the silence was shattered by a gunshot in another part of the building, followed by the sound of breaking glass.

"Janice, are you in here?" Poldoski's voice.

"In here," she called. "Lora's in the building. She's armed, and she's fired four shots at me."

Janice stood and moved to the doorway. The hall was empty. Then a door at its end opened, and Poldoski and Mullins were coming toward her. Relief flooded over Janice.

"Are you all right?" Poldoski asked.

"I'm fine. Now." She wondered how they found her, how they knew, but she could find that out later. "Let's spread out and find her. She's got to still be in the building. She has a thirty-eight, so unless she's got extra ammunition with her, she's got two shots left at the most."

"Janice. . . ." Poldoski was staring at her. "What the hell happened? Your face is all scratched up. Your clothes are torn. And there's blood all over your—"

"Not now, Ron. We've got to find Lora."

"Go out to the car and call for some help, then stand by outside," Mullins ordered. "Ron and me will handle things in here."

"No way! I started this, and I'm going to finish it. It's my family she kidnapped and me she just fired four shots at. You go make your own fucking call, you son of a bitch!" She glared at him, on the verge of trembling from sheer anger.

Mullins stared at her, wide-eyed.

Poldoski grabbed his arm. "Don't be stupid, Ed. She's got a right. I'll call in, then go around back in case she tries to come out that way." He hurried off.

"There's an armed kidnapper somewhere in this building, who's taken four shots at a police officer," Janice said to Mullins. "I'm going after her. You can stay here and scratch your ass for all I care."

Mullins, looking very unsure of himself, took a reluctant step toward her. "Okay, but I sure hope you know what the hell you're doing."

"She couldn't have gone the same way you came in, so she had to go that way." She pointed down the hallway. "There's a room there that leads to another hall. That has to be where she's gone."

Mullins checked his revolver. "Let's go."

Lora ran madly down the hallway leading to the back door, desperately looking for a place to hide. They'd be in back of the building, waiting for her to attempt getting out that way. But if she hid somewhere inside, there was still a chance she could kill Janice. There was still a chance to become whole.

Suddenly, she stopped. The room of death. The drawers.

She'd just passed the room; now she hurried back to it. Inside, she began opening some of the drawers a few inches, skipping those that held her prisoners. Enough of them had to be open so the one in which she hid would not seem out of place.

She chose one on the bottom row. Lying on her back on the hard slab, she pulled the drawer into the wall until it lacked only a few inches of being closed. Then she rolled over and looked out into the room. She could see the door plainly. She would have a clear shot.

She heard movement in the hallway, and a moment later, a man stepped into the room. He was heavyset, partly bald, and had a gun in his hand.

"Christ," he muttered. "What the hell is this place?"

His eyes traveled around the room, lingering on the drawers; then he turned and walked toward the door.

Was Janice nearby? If so, she would have to come to this man's aid if he were shot. She took careful aim on the big man's back.

As they came down the hallway, Janice and Mullins had been taking turns backing each other up, one entering the room while the other stayed back, keeping an eye out, ready to assist. Mullins had just gone into a room, and Janice was in the hallway. She heard him mumble something under his breath. About her, probably.

He seemed to be taking his time, so she stepped up to the doorway to see what he was doing. Mullins was coming toward her, and behind him was a wall full of huge drawers, some of which were partially open. Oh, God. The airtight compartments.

Suddenly, only half sure of what she'd seen, she yelled: "Hit the floor!"

It was a command Mullins knew to obey instantly, and he dropped. Janice had been raising her .38 even before she'd yelled, gripping it with both hands. She fired twice, rapidly, and something slammed into her shoulder, spinning her around.

For a moment, everything was hazy, and then she realized she was on the floor, her shoulder burning with pain. His face ashen, Mullins was picking himself up off the floor. Then Poldoski was there, bending over her, asking if she was all right.

"I heard the shots," he said. "From out back."

She pointed at the drawers. "Lora. She was about to waste Mullins."

The sergeant was on his feet now, moving a little shakily. He went to one of the drawers and pulled it out. Lora lay on the slab, one arm dangling limply over the edge, still clutching the gun. Mullins turned to face them; he looked dazed.

"Twice in the head," he said. "Either one a kill shot."

Poldoski was searching Janice's face. She knew what he was looking for, but the thought that she'd just taken a human life didn't seem to register. Some day she'd have to deal with it. She might even have nightmares about it. At this moment, it only seemed that she'd done what had to be done. The implications of the act floated somewhere beyond her grasp.

Poldoski was pressing a handkerchief to the bullet wound on her shoulder. "It doesn't look too bad," he said. "But we need to get you to a hospital."

Mullins was still standing beside Lora's body. His face had regained some of its color, but he was obviously still shaken. "I just realized something," he said, looking at Janice. "You fired a fraction of a second before she did, which means she was already dead when she pulled the trigger." He shook his head. "That was as close as I ever care to come." Then he grinned crookedly. "I owe you a beer, Janice."

"A beer?"

"You saved my life. I don't suppose it's much in the way of repayment, but it's a custom in the department. Whenever one cop saves another's life, the guy has to buy him a beer." He frowned. "Or her."

"I accept." She bit her lip as a pain shot through her shoulder. "Check those compartments. See if..."

Mullins began pulling open drawers. "Oh, shit!"

"What is it?" Janice demanded.

"It's a boy. He's..."

"Is he alive? Tell me!"

"Yes, he's alive." Mullins was pulling out drawers furiously now. "Here's the woman! She's alive, too!" He yanked open three more, then exclaimed: "I found your father, too!" There was a long pause while he bent over the form on the slab. "He's alive, too, but I damn well think we better get them to a hospital in a hurry." He rushed out of the room.

"And that's where you're going, too," Poldoski said.

Janice started to say something, but the room was swimming, and the words wouldn't come. She only knew she was glad her father, sister, and nephew were alive. And she was glad Poldoski was here. The world would be a wonderful place, she decided, if only it had more Poldoskis.

Vaguely, she heard a man's voice say: "I'm James Heikkinen. What the hell happened here?"

The voice seemed to come from very far away.

Epilogue

*Her left arm in a sling, Janice drove along Pennington Boul-*evard, on her way home from work. It was about 6:15, clear and sunny, less muggy than it had been, a beautiful evening. This had been her first day back on the job after a week's paid sick leave.

Although the injured arm hampered her driving a little, particularly when she had to negotiate a sharp turn, the bullet wound only hurt occasionally now; she was mending well.

Ahead, she saw the funeral home, looking as it always had, revealing nothing of what had transpired there. Soon to be a freeway interchange, she noted. And that was all she thought about the place at that moment, because that was all she chose to think about it. People built things, tore them down, put up other things, and life went on.

No, she wasn't refusing to deal with what had happened at Heikkinen's. But it was, after all, only a building, and learning to see it as such was part of mending, which included more than just the healing of her arm. And she was mending well. In all respects.

She was again staying at her father's house, readying it for tomorrow, when he and Mark would come home from the hospital. Both were in remarkably good condition, considering what they'd been through.

Amy, however, would not be coming with them. She was in the psychiatric ward, where she spent most of her time sitting, staring off into space, unresponsive to anyone or anything. The doctors said she had withdrawn into herself to escape the horror, and that's where she was, in there with herself somewhere. They said that for now there was nothing to do but wait; in time she would probably come out of it, and once that happened, a complete recovery would be possible. Despite the doctors' cautious use of terms like "probably" and "possible," Janice found their words encouraging. Amy would get better.

Two days ago, Janice had told Mike she would not go to Seattle with him. The woman Mike needed would be a good housewife and mother, subservient, happy to be supported and protected. And for a woman who wanted that sort of life, Mike would be an ideal catch. But Janice wasn't that woman, nor could she become that woman, and that fact would constantly have eaten away at their marriage. They'd talked all this out, Mike reluctantly agreeing that in the final analysis, they probably weren't right for each other. He'd looked dejected; she'd cried. But they'd resolved it.

And now, with two days of hindsight to make things clearer, Janice had no doubt that she'd done the right thing. She and Mike had parted friends, even promising to keep in touch, and a difficult, emotional decision was behind her.

Seeing her street ahead, she slowed the Datson until it was barely moving, then, using just her good arm, struggled through the turn, wishing the car had power steering. She ended up on the wrong side of the road and, accelerating, quickly steered the car back where it belonged. Reaching her father's house, she had to fight the wheel again to get the Datsun into the driveway. It wasn't until she'd switched off the engine and climbed out that she noticed the car parked across the street, and suddenly she felt a warm glow. It was Poldoski, whom she hadn't seen all day because he'd been on a burglary stakeout. He waited for a car to pass, then hurried across the street and joined her.

"How long have you been waiting over there?" she asked.

He shrugged. "Not long. How did things go today?"

"Well," she replied, delighted that he was here to share the good news, "the captain called me in—scowling, adopting his most official manner—and said he damned well ought to reprimand me for going in alone and not calling for backup."

"Well, did he?"

She shook her head, biting her lip to suppress a grin. "No, he decided to do something else."

"What, for Christ's sake?"

"Well, once he decided I'd been sufficiently chewed out, he gave me a commendation for saving Mullins' life."

"Hey, fantastic!" He grabbed her and hugged her, gently because of her injured arm.

She gave him a one-armed hug in return, then stepped back. "You think Mrs. Fox is watching?"

"I don't really care."

"Oh, you know why I was late getting home? Mullins bought me the beer he'd promised. We went to this scroungy bar downtown. I was the only woman in the place—but that doesn't really matter. He treated me like a buddy. We went in, sat down, talked about cop stuff, and he thanked me over a beer. That's all there was to it, but it was great."

Ron grinned. Not a put-on grin. He understood.

"You done for the day?" she asked.

He nodded.

"Buy you dinner?"

"That depends."

"On what?"

"On the sort of dinner you have in mind."

She pulled her wallet from her purse and checked its contents, frowning. "Steak and lobster all right?"

"You got a date."

"Come on," she said, taking his hand. "I've got to go in and clean up first."